THEY STOOD IN THE SHADOW OF THE
STOCKADE WALL, A FEW YARDS FROM
THE MAIN GATE . . .

"We've got to run now and make our break,"
Mclafferty said, "or the whole scheme will
come unwound. If we can club those guards
without alerting the sentry up top, then our
chances are at least even."

"Run, hell, ye damned fool," Fiddlehead laughed,
"Look back behind us."

Close by a nearby wall were Fiddlehead's mule
and Mclafferty's gray horse.

McLafferty reconsidered the plan. "All right
then, you take Moon with you. She'll ride the
gray. I'll throw open the gate while you two
make tracks, and then manage on foot—slip
along the stockade wall while you've got their
attention."

"Then *you* will have to run, McLafferty," Moon
protested. "They will shoot you."

"Do what I say, you little hellcat. The only
chance we've got at Laroque without causing a
full-scale war is for you to make it up that hill
to the Indian camp. Go, now."

THE
MCLAFFERTYS

THE McLAFFERTYS

JUDE WILLIAMS

A SIGNET BOOK

NEW AMERICAN LIBRARY

PUBLISHER'S NOTE

This novel is a work of fiction. Names, characters, places, and incidents either are the product of the author's imagination or are used fictitiously, and any resemblance to actual persons, living or dead, events, or locales is entirely coincidental.

NAL BOOKS ARE AVAILABLE AT QUANTITY DISCOUNTS WHEN USED TO PROMOTE PRODUCTS OR SERVICES. FOR INFORMATION PLEASE WRITE TO PREMIUM MARKETING DIVISION, NEW AMERICAN LIBRARY, 1633 BROADWAY, NEW YORK, NEW YORK 10019.

SIGNET TRADEMARK REG. U.S. PAT. OFF. AND FOREIGN COUNTRIES
REGISTERED TRADEMARK—MARCA REGISTRADA
HECHO EN CHICAGO, U.S.A.

SIGNET, SIGNET CLASSIC, MENTOR, ONYX, PLUME, MERIDIAN AND NAL BOOKS are published by New American Library, 1633 Broadway, New York, New York 10019

First Printing, November, 1986

1 2 3 4 5 6 7 8 9

PRINTED IN THE UNITED STATES OF AMERICA

1 Michael McLafferty had been standing on the foredeck of *The Missouri Princess* for an hour or more, staring ahead at a broad, sun-glittering pathway defined by the Big River. Council Bluff's sprawling, tree-lined rim rose dead ahead and starboard as the steam-driven stern-wheeler painfully clawed its way upstream, passing by Platte River's broad, sluggish mouth and continuing toward the small frontier town of Omaha, where he would debark.

McLafferty envisioned the land sweeping away westward, a long trail up-country, one thoroughly familiar to him after ten years and more of trapping, trading, and gambling his way through the High Shining and along various rivers that fed down from the ragged, snow-hung peaks of the Rockies. But it would all be different now, to one extent or another—since tens of thousands of gold-seekers were on their way to a place he hadn't yet been—the hills of California.

The previous December President Polk had placed his official seal of approval upon countless rumors already in circulation: considerable gold-bearing deposits had indeed been discovered in California. "The accounts of the abundance of gold in that territory are of such extraordinary character as would scarcely command belief were they not corroborated by authentic reports of officers in the public service."

These words, reported in every newspaper from Maine to the Mississippi, had etched themselves upon the minds of half a nation, Big Mike McLafferty included.

He had been quits with the mountains, or so he imagined. Wild country and the frontier between had provided him with a small fortune. He had carefully hoarded his earnings from trapping and trading with the Indians as agent for American Fur, and this money he'd multiplied several times over by means of a deck of cards.

With his thirtieth birthday approaching, he decided to settle down to civilized life in the little city of St. Louis. There he had spent his early teen years as a riverfront waif, one of a number of runaways and parentless boys who managed to exist by means of odd jobs, salvage, running errands, and otherwise keeping their eyes open for any possible opportunity of earning a penny or two.

With stability and respectability in mind, McLafferty had purchased a two-story brick house complete with a big chimney at either end, and had begun to dress like a gentleman. Aloysius Benton, from whom he had learned the trapper's trade, predicted he'd never be able to stay away from the mountains—citing the examples of Jim Clyman and Jed Smith. Both had found it impossible to put danger and wildness behind them. Clyman, according to rumor, was now settled in California, having led one of the early bands of emigrants across the continent, and had become a gentleman farmer. Jed Smith? Well, he *should* have stayed down-country. One trip too many, and Indians had filled him with arrows.

McLafferty thought about insulating himself against the lure of the mountains (and one half-breed girl living among the Cheyennes in particular—he couldn't get her out of his mind, though she was married to his closest friend), and even considered running for public office. If he arranged his life so that he *couldn't* go back, then perhaps that gnawing sensation of emptiness would vanish. Why shouldn't he be a respectable member of the community? Why shouldn't he aspire to higher things?

Following a short and not very exciting courtship, Big Mike had married a proper Presbyterian woman of twenty-seven, an old maid in truth, but the daughter of a well-to-do haberdasher and land speculator—the very man from whom he had acquired his brick mansion and three hundred acres of rich bottomland.

But it hadn't worked at all. The woman tolerated his attempts to make love to her as though the whole thing were utterly distasteful, a necessary evil implicit in the condition of matrimony. And she all but insisted that he buy a Negro butler and maid, something he had absolutely refused to do. After this one great argument, his wife's bedroom door remained closed to him, and the impossible vision of Moon Morning Star began to flame even more brightly in his imagination than before.

That was when President Polk's verification of gold discoveries had been reported.

McLafferty proceeded to go on an extended drunk, and shortly after he managed to sober up, he was clapped into jail for "outrageous disturbance of the peace," the result of a free-for-all he quite consciously precipitated in the dining area of the St. Louis Hotel.

Released from his confinement, his wife refused even to speak to him. In his absence, she had bought the two slaves she wanted, with her father's blessing and assistance.

Directly thereafter McLafferty moved to a hotel room near the waterfront and began to repair his damaged fortunes by means of plying his trade in various gambling halls. One night he was called out by a local tough someone had apparently hired; Mike shot the man through the heart in a fair fight, and was clapped into jail once more—on charges of murder.

Two weeks later a jury acquitted him, and McLafferty, realizing the disaster his debut into civilized life had brought upon him, made plans to move to California, confident that he would be able to find the lode, whether by shovel or the graces of Lady Luck.

So now, at age thirty, Big Mike was on his way west once again, this time with the ultimate destination of California on his mind.

A pair of jet-black ravens swooped back and forth across the muddy current of the Missouri, dancing over the water and then alighting in a thick grove of elders on the river's east bank, directly below the bluffs. McLafferty grinned, put thumb and forefinger to his mouth, and whistled at the birds.

"Even you bastards have grown too civilized," he called out. "Why aren't you up-country, following the song dogs about?"

Three blasts from the ship's whistle, and *The Missouri Princess* edged toward the Nebraska shore to discharge twenty or so passengers—all theoretically destined for California—and to take on firewood.

He was eager to be ashore. It was time to get the hell away from the old scow, whose first mate was reported to be suffering from cholera, a disease that had been spreading like wildfire in St. Louis since the onset of warm weather. In any case, the mate hadn't been aboveboard for the past twenty-four hours, and the captain refused to speak of the matter. Well, perhaps there'd be a funeral while the *Princess* was tied up.

More than that, it was time to take to honest transportation—time for Mike McLafferty to pick up his life where he'd left off, before the ill-fated venture into propriety. He would buy a horse, a mule or two, a new Hawken rifle (maybe a cap-and-ball model this time), and saddlebags loaded with the necessaries, including a couple of jugs of rye whiskey and plenty of cigars. Mike thought about the wretched *arwerdenty* of his first years in the mountains, himself trapping beaver at the very time when the damned silk hats were putting the entire trade into desperate straits, and shook his head. Perhaps there was something to be said for Modern Times after all.

Again the steam whistle screamed three times as

The Missouri Princess sidled up to the loading docks where great piles of cordwood were heaped.

McLafferty strode to his upper-deck cabin to gather together the few things he had brought with him on this first leg of his up-country venture. He thrust an old Allen and Thurber six-shot pepperbox pistol inside his fringed and ornamented black leather jacket, strapped on a Colt-Walker .44, adjusted his short-brimmed Mexican hat, and left the room.

The gangplank was already down, and the captain and second mate stood by as would-be Californians shuffled off the stern-wheeler.

McLafferty nodded and followed the others, pushing through a throng of dockhands who were preparing to load wood onto the *Princess.*

One man caught Mike's attention, the teamsters' *booshway*, a thick-muscled Frenchman McLafferty had known for years and with whom he had more than once come to blows—several times in good-natured drunken brawls and once in dead earnest, with knives. It was Jean Laroque, a notorious bully among the rivermen, thief nonpareil, known to have killed half a dozen or more in brawls, and actually wanted for murder in Quebec.

Laroque saw him, pointed in his direction.

"McLafferty, that you in the *chapeau* of the greaser? I think I smell *pourceau*, a big swine! Come on over here, we shake hands, *mère du Christ!* After that I slit your throat."

McLafferty, pretending not to hear the Frenchman's raucous greeting, turned and, taking long strides, moved away from the dockside confusion.

*   *   *

He took a room in a two-story frame structure called the Far West Hotel and Boarding House, had a drink at the bar, and then walked about the dusty streets of Omaha's budding business district, purchasing supplies for his proposed journey westward. At the livery he paid far too much for a big gray stallion and a brass-studded saddle, but he got a fairly good bargain on a cross-eyed mule whose peculiar appearance and apparent propensity for biting any human hand that came too close had rendered the creature less than fully salable.

Supplies were short, and the town was almost literally overrun by Argonauts on their way to the California goldfields, even this late in the season. Most wagons had pushed westward a couple of months earlier, on the heels of the spring thaws. But still people came, like himself, drawn by the faint but incessant cries of ¡Oro! Nonetheless, with money to spare, McLafferty managed to put together his outfit within the space of about three hours, and with that matter settled—a pair of rifles, an old Kain-tuck flintlock and a brand-new Hawken cap-and-ball .55 caliber in sheaths on either side of the veteran brass-studded saddle—McLafferty headed back to the Far West Hotel.

Time for something to eat and a little game of monte before retiring.

The Mexican balladeer was quite good, slowly strumming his guitar and singing a series of sad Spanish songs, but the men in the barroom paid little attention. Several card games were in progress, and one or two Argonauts from *The Missouri Princess* were already drunk and somewhat belligerent. Smoke filled the room, and the "hostesses," a couple of them Indian women, served drinks and occasionally disappeared upstairs when one of the men decided he wished to avail himself of professional female companionship.

Big Mike made a point of losing his last hand at draw poker, pleaded exhaustion after a long trip upriver, put the remainder of his considerable winnings into his poke, and ordered drinks all around. Then he rose from his chair and walked over to the bar.

"Sonny, ye goin' to buy this child a drink, or ye only hold with card-thieves?"

McLafferty glanced at a grizzled individual seated beside him, a hunter down from one of the forts most likely, and nodded to the barkeep.

"Name's Fiddlehead Wilson." The old man grinned, displaying several missing teeth. "Come to pick the bones of the Californians, did ye? Trust ye know how to handle that Colt ye got strapped on. Most o' you boys keep a plaything inside your blouse, ain't that so? Ye from down South, or whar?"

"Got over the pea-green stage years ago," McLafferty answered. "Was up-country when the beaver trade played out, in fact."

Wilson wrinkled his nose, squinted, and once more displayed a gap-toothed grin. "Suppose ye know Beckwourth an' Bridger an' Meek an' Benton an' O'Bragh an' Billy Sublette an' all them lads, eh?"

"Might know one or two of 'em at that. Beckwourth, he was before my time. I met Meek once, but I don't really know him. Sublette and I have played two or three hands of cards—fact is, I worked for him as an agent, first with the Cheyennes and then with the Assiniboins. Benton? I spent the winter of '39 with that old thief, a month of it with his Crow relatives—Yellow Belly and Pine Leaf and that bunch, the Many Lodges—Big Dog and Two-Tail Skunk, and Beckwourth's kids, Iron Bull and Kit. What do you think, Fiddlehead, my friend, am I going to pass the test? Never killed a grizzly, but I've put one or two Pieds Noirs under. Didn't turn gambler until '45. Given a choice, I guess I'd still be hunting Brother Beaver."

The old-timer snorted and raised his right eyebrow.

"Ye tell a good story, anyhow, damned liar though ye be. Trapped with Aloysius Benton, did ye? What's he look like, then?"

"About as ugly as you, but he keeps his beard trimmed. Used to, at least. Haven't seen the old man since . . . '43 I guess it was."

"Ye killed buff'ler?"

"How else does a child get hump rib? Or raw liver with a dash of gall on it?"

"Wagh! Why ye all gussied up like any dude, then?"

"Wagh, yourself, you old miscreant. I suppose you've got the ha'r o' the b'ar in you?"

"Damned right, an' this child killed the monster, too."

McLafferty pushed back from the bar and laughed. "So you know Benton, do you? Where is he, then, old-timer?"

Wilson coughed, blew his nose between his fingers, and wiped them on his crusty leather breeches.

"Up ahead of ye, if ye're moseyin' west with all the other damned fools. Aloysius, he's by Gawd being a scout an' hunter for a bunch of damned fool Mormons, last I heard. Mebbe he's took to religion, I don't know. Probably went up the Platte with the first thaw."

Out there somewhere, at least.

That, McLafferty reflected, would be where Aloysius Benton would die, and not with his boots on, either. End of the fur trade, so naturally Benton would take to guiding settlers into the wilderness that he always loved and in fact always wanted entirely to himself, Indians and all. He'd taken a Crow squaw and raised her son and turned him into a trapper as well, Big Dog, a feared Crow warrior.

Benton, you old scoundrel, damned if I wouldn't like to go back to '39 myself. I got cheated and just saw the tail end of it, but it was beautiful, beautiful and fierce and impersonal as hell, didn't play favorites. Benton and Gabe Bridger have still got their hair, but that's more luck than anything else. Here I am, a man with half a dozen broken lives behind him already. . . .

"Innkeeper," McLafferty growled, "I'd deeply appreciate it if you'd bring a full bottle of your best for me and my friend here, Mr. Fiddlehead Wilson, lately of the state of Vermont."

"What the hell ye talkin' about? This old coyote's never even been in no Vermont, no sir. Born in Missouri an' never been farther east than St. Louis. Ain't never goin' to be, neither."

"Well"—McLafferty grinned—"I surely thought that accent of yours was from Vermont. I had a maiden aunt once, big busted old gal with twenty-two children, all girls, and she spoke just the way you do."

Wilson pursed his lips again. "What the hell's your name, anyhow? This child's startin' to think ye jumped out of some loony bin somewheres."

"I thought I already told you."

"Hell, no, ye didn't. Pour me a shot of that whiskey, an' tell me your name, if ye got one."

Big Mike tipped the bottle and then poured a shot for himself. "McLafferty," he said. "Michael John McLafferty."

Wilson drank. "Related to the McLafferty as used to run a tradin' post up on the Judith River?"

"Might say so. It was my post."

"Wagh! Now, this child's gettin' a fix on ye. Me, I never rode in thar, or else we would of met."

"Seems reasonable." McLafferty nodded. "So tell me, old-timer, what do you know about the girls here at the Far West Hotel and Boarding House? You got any particular favorites among them?"

"Mike McLafferty, eh? Well, I've heard of ye, an' that's a fact. Benton never mentioned my name? Hell, we was at the '26 Rendezvous together an' ended up sharin' a Shoe-shine squaw between us, for a fact. An' what about Bully O'Bragh? If ye know him, he must of told ye about me."

McLafferty grinned. "How he caught you with your head down between a Flathead gal's legs, and she put a lock on you? Old-timer, I figured that one out right away. Of course I've heard of you."

"Well, why in the name of green buff'ler dung didn't ye say so in the first place?"

"Just testing you is all."

"Ye thief! Pull this old man's leg, an' then ast him which hoor will best wring ye dry? I ought to skulp ye, that's what. Only you're buyin' the drinks, so I won't."

"What do you think, Fiddlehead? Suppose we should purchase a bit of female company? Might as well celebrate. I'll be heading for California come tomorrow—by way of Leg-in-the-Water's Cheyenne village. Going to visit White Bull, my blood brother—him and his wife and their kid. But tonight I've got a poke full of tin, and I'm of a mind to indulge a bit. Who's the Spanish girl, for instance?"

Damn my soul—that girl looks for all the world like a gussied-up version of Moon Morning Star. Older than when I last saw her, naturally, but her eyes, her mouth . . .

Wilson squinted again. "Esmeralda, Esmeralda Ramírez, at least that's how she calls herself. A fine-lookin' filly, I'll grant ye that much. Despite all the gewgaws an' such, though, she don't measure up to your wild Pawnee woman, an' mebee not even to your basic Kaw. I ain't much on fancy females, as ye might guess."

McLafferty studied the Spanish girl for a few moments, did his best to catch her attention. The resemblance was positively uncanny—or was it just his own mind playing tricks on him? One of the girl's cheeks, he realized, was badly bruised. In the barroom's smoky lamplight, he had failed to note that detail until this moment.

"She the guitar player's woman, Fiddlehead? Looks to me as though someone's been whipping on her. If a man's got a woman he cares about, he sure as hell shouldn't have her working in here with the professional ladies. This way, he's just setting a trap for himself—at least that's how I see it."

Wilson laughed. "Danny Valdez? Naw, he's got no claim to Esmeralda. She's a wild one, an' jest as 'professional' as any of 'em. Truth is, I like her best, too. Paid her price a couple of months back, then by Gawd couldn't get my danged instrument up. So we just jawed for an hour or so. Sometimes that's better than screwin'. She even done took her clothes off so's I could admire what I was missin' an' then danced for me while I sat thar an' felt sorry for myself. It were a shame, all considered. Always did have bad luck with women, jest like O'Bragh told ye, even if that particular incident never happened."

"She's got someone who likes to hit women, at least," McLafferty said, "or did she fall down the stairs?"

Wilson took off his bearskin cap, scratched at thinning white hair, and replaced the hat. "What I heard—two nights ago, a big river rat named Jean Laroque. Esmeralda wouldn't do something or other he wanted, if ye know what I mean, an' he slapped her around for a spell. Comes with the territory, I guess, just like Pieds Noirs with good beaver streams in the old days. Say, didn't I hear a story once that Mike McLafferty an' Jean Laroque spent an afternoon tryin' to cut each other up? If that ain't just one of your country tales, how'd it turn out?"

McLafferty drank another shot of whiskey and offered the bottle to Wilson. "Bastard stabbed me in the heart and left me for the vultures. After that, I started going sour."

"Sonny, a genuine mountain man's got to be able to tell a tolerable tale, when the time's right, an' ye jest ain't got the proper knack. Any case, I don't see no scars. If ye had some, why, that'd make the story worthwhile. Laroque, now, he's got a big one across his forehead an' cheek. Ye give it to him?"

"Could be—up at Fort Union. The truth of the matter is, I cut him, then pushed him over some hundred-pound bags full of flour, and he lost his knife. I jumped him and managed to knock the son of a bitch cold. I knew he was here in Omaha— saw him as I got off the steamer this morning, as it turns out."

"More or less the way this child heard it, in fact." Wilson nodded. "That were five, six years ago?"

'Yeah. Up at Union, like I said. I was working for American Fur, trading with the Assiniboins, and Laroque and his crew were with one of the company steamers. In the long run, though, we didn't do each other any really permanent damage, I guess. He's not one of my favorite people, to tell the truth, but by now he's probably mellowed a bit."

"In a pig's pizzle!" Fiddlehead snorted. "That Frenchman's the terror o' the waterfront. Ain't nothin' worse than a hawg with a genuine mean streak in 'im. You an' me both has put our share o' men under, ain't that right? But we had reasons. Laroque, he's the kind as don't need a reason. I decided right away, when I first come down hyar, it was a good notion to keep out o' his path."

At that moment, above a steady babble of human voices in the barroom, a burst of profanity exploded, French profanity.

McLafferty and Wilson turned about just as Jean

Laroque and four of his companyeros stumbled into the Far West Hotel and Boarding House.

"Speak o' the devil," Fiddlehead Wilson snorted, "an' thar the sheep-humpin' somebitch is. The skonks with 'im, that tall one's Cottonmouth Chardin, an' next to Chardin's Larue Duncan, not much to choose between either o' them an' Laroque hisself. Don't know the others, an' don't want to. Michael, me lad, from what ye've jest told me, we're subject to have some unwanted company."

McLafferty glanced at Wilson and then stared across the room at Jean Laroque. "You don't say?"

"I do say, sure as skunks get skunks. Well, word has it that old Jean Laroque's headin' west to California tomorrow mornin', come sunup. Him an' his boys been talkin about 'er for the past two weeks. That way, Omaha'll be safe for thieves an' cardsharps, anyhow."

Laroque stumbled through the barroom, jostling one of the card tables in the process and causing a momentary spate of cursing from the players. Then he caught sight of Mike McLafferty and began to weave his way toward his old antagonist.

"*Enfant de garce!*" he howled. "It is my good friend Mike. McLafferty, that was you on the dock today? *Sacre Dieu*, it does my heart good to see you, *mon ami!* This *mangeur de lard*, he hears that you are running for Congress or maybe going to become a school lady, a teacher. By God, that makes me sad, *très melancolique*. I think, Jean, now we will never be able to play with the knives anymore. . . ."

"Hello, Laroque. I see the years haven't changed you. I was hoping they might have. No fighting tonight, I'm not up for it. Have a drink, you overstuffed spaniel. It's on me."

"Ah, Monsieur Fiddlehead, you keep the bad company, *non?* You see what he did to me, this scar, eh? One day, *mon* Michael, we even the score. Is a promise I make to my dead *oncle, oui?*"

2 "Get your hands off me, offspring of the wild dog. No, I do not want your *dinero*. Let go of me, *por favor*."

Esmeralda Ramírez's words were spoken loudly, for effect, and were heard clearly even above the din in the saloon of the Far West Hotel and Boarding House. Tall Grass Tillie, the resident madame, rose from a corner table where she had been engaged in profound conversation with a balding gentleman in a gray Down East suit, and made her way across the crowded barroom to render assistance to Señorita Ramírez.

"Jean Laroque," Tillie sang out, "you behave yourself or I'll throw you out the door myself. If you're thinking to bust up the other side of Esmeralda's face, you can forget about it. You've been a good customer, but I damned well won't have my girls whipped on, you hear me? Could be there's some that likes it, but mine aren't among them. Back off now, or I'll have Eddie toss you out on your ear."

Laroque immediately turned his attention to the plump and gaudily rouged fury shaking her fin-

21

ger at him, grinned broadly, and made a placating gesture to the madame.

"*Mais oui!* The mother hen, she is thick in the tongue. My business is not with you, Momma Tillie, but only with this one, who believes herself too good to take my money. Call out Monsieur Eddie, and I will give him new lips across his throat. You are thieves, *vous tous*, you take Jean's money and give him nothing in return. Maybe I kill a few people, eh? Tomorrow, she's good day for funerals."

"*Miembro de perro*," Esmeralda hissed. "Your money, it is no good to me. Leave me alone, Señor Laroque! Go find yourself a *vache*."

The commotion had by now demanded the attention of everyone in the establishment, and a few card players made haste to gather up their money and move toward the double swinging half-doors. Those at the bar likewise began to consider possible routes of egress, for Laroque's temper was well-known, and several locals who had run afoul of the big Frenchman's displeasure subsequently disappeared, their bodies presumed to be drifting with the Missouri's silt-laden current on their way to the Gulf of Mexico. One or two others actually received Christian burials, having been gunned down in what were judged to be fair fights.

Laroque's cohorts, eager to join whatever brawl was almost certain to take place within the next minute or so, moved in behind their leader. Cottonmouth Chardin had already drawn his bowie knife in anticipation, while Duncan and the other two men were clearly contemplating close-range action with the still-holstered revolvers, newly acquired for the purpose of protecting themselves against Indians and rival Argonauts during their projected overland trek to California.

"Ed," Tall Grass Tillie yelled, "get the damned shotgun."

At that moment Esmeralda slapped Laroque across the face, hard, and pursued her initial advantage by stamping on the bridge of his foot.

Jean Laroque wiped at his mouth and laughed. Then, with an almost casual motion, he backhanded the Spanish girl into the midst of twenty or so men who were attempting to push their way toward the exit. The Frenchman proceeded to draw his revolver and began firing off rounds at the plate-glass mirrors behind Tillie's bar. Glass shattered and bottles of whiskey exploded, fragments leaping about and clattering to the floor.

That accomplished, Laroque turned, utilizing his free hand to grasp Esmeralda Ramírez by her long black hair, yanking the still-stunned girl to her feet.

"I will take *la slut* and feed her to my men," he roared. "*Non!* I will feed them to her—this night she will devour *beaucoup de viande*. After that, I myself will make her *derrière* less tight."

A shotgun roared from behind the bar, but the blast was aimed high, the first charge merely a warning.

"Out!" Tillie screeched, her painted lips forming a perfect *O*. "Damn your souls to hell and back, all of you! I had those mirrors shipped up from New Orleans."

Esmeralda scratched at Laroque's face, and the Frenchman hurled her to the floor.

"Back off, Jean," McLafferty said, his pepperbox in his left hand and his Colt Walker in his right. "You holster that damned gun or I'll drill you on the spot. Just move toward the door, slow and easy. The rest of you, get to one side. Give the man room. Don't tempt me, Laroque. When we fought before, the odds were even. This time I've got the drop on you, and you know it. Don't even think about turning this direction. I won't miss, not at this range. That's a good boy, slip it back into the holster. Cottonmouth, is that your name? Put the knife away. All of you, move on out."

"Guess ye lads be in a crossfire," a squeaky voice said from the other side of the barroom. "This hyar's Fiddlehead talkin'. Ye know me well enough, same as everyone."

Behind an overturned card table the top of a bearskin cap was visible, that and two bushy eyebrows and the octagonal barrel of a buffalo rifle.

Laroque glanced about, estimating potential danger, calculating the odds should he elect to spin and fire in McLafferty's direction. Then he shrugged and laughed, holstering his weapon as he did so.

"*Nous deux*," he said, "we will settle this later, Monsieur Michael. A tight-ass leetle greaser, she is not worth it. *Enfant de garce*, Jean, he was just being affectionate, that is all. Momma Tillie, I will see you later. *Oui*, McLafferty, you are very good with the pistol, from a man's blind side—maybe not so good otherwise. Face to face it is different, *peut-être*. Last time we fight you were *très fortuné*. But we meet again, *non*, is it not so?"

Laroque nodded, and he and Chardin and Duncan and the others somewhat grudgingly backed out through the swinging doors, into a star-filled Nebraska night.

"Ten minutes and we're closing," Tall Grass Tillie announced. "Eddie, one last drink for everyone. You girls, take your customers upstairs. The rest have to leave. We'll open again first thing in the morning, if I can get this mess cleaned up. I ought to sue that big Frenchy. It'll take two months to get new mirrors, and who's going to pay for them? I hope to God he *does* head west tomorrow, just like he's been telling everybody. That's one bunch of patrons I can well do without."

For a time McLafferty and Wilson stood together in front of the Far West, puffing cigars and exchanging anecdotes about their mutual friends, Bridger and Benton and O'Bragh. There was no moon at all. The dusty street lined by frame buildings and hitching rails was illuminated only by a yellow glow from the window of the saloon, as well as an almost identical glow from the glassed front of Platte Junction Watering Hole, on the opposite side of the thoroughfare and a half a block nearer the river. A faint sound of bagpipes issued from the Platte Junction, this establishment still doing a thriving business at eleven o'clock—inasmuch as Jean Laroque and his crew had apparently chosen not to patronize the place.

"So it's off to California, hey, sonny? Cain't see no friend of Aloysius Benton keepin' company with any of these other pitiful gold-hawgs that's been hanging around town, so I expect ye're ridin' solo? No wife nor kinfolk to slow ye down, it do make more sense that way. Mebbe I'll mosey a piece of the way with ye. Wagh! This child's been sitting his tail end too long. I'm itchy to be back in the hills. Don't know what I'm doing down hyar in civilization anyhow. Ye up for some company?"

McLafferty puffed on his cigar, admiring its orange-red tip in the darkness, and nodded.

"Figger we might as well stick to the Mormon Trail all the way to Laramie," Fiddlehead mused. "Otherwise, we'll be stopping to fix every busted wheel we come to. Give the Saints that much, they takes care o' their equipment, an' they ain't always astin' folks to haul their bacon out o' the fire. If we run up on Laroque an' his lads, I guess we can make us a detour around 'em."

McLafferty recalled earlier years, with wagon traffic struggling along the Oregon Trail to the south of the Platte, Brigham Young had elected to keep his people separated from the other emigrants westward to avoid trouble or defections. They had established a trail north of the river. Now the number of Mormons heading toward Utah country had decreased, and both trails were employed indifferently, depending only upon whether the pilgrims in question had started from Independence to the south or from Council Bluffs and Omaha.

"I'd be proud to have your company, Mr. Wilson." Mike grinned. "Shall we meet at high noon tomorrow—in front of the Jones Livery, let's say?"

"Sounds good to this old song dawg, Mr. Mike," Wilson said. "Ye done admirable in thar tonight, but it might be Laroque'll be waitin' for ye out on the trail a piece, if he finds out ye're headin' west. If so, what ye figgerin' to do about the problem?"

"Make a detour, just as you suggested. If that doesn't work out, then I guess I'll have to whip

him, just like his daddy did. Well, Jean Laroque's
not actually the worst sort in the world. I'll handle
the problem if there is one."

"That so?" Wilson mused. "Then, just who in
Gawd's green hell is the *worst*, can ye tell me that?"

"One or two Pieds Noirs I've met."

"Bug's Boys. Fiddlesticks, they weren't never the
same afer the smallpox got done with 'em. In '36,
it was. Before your time in the mountains, more
likely than not . . ."

McLafferty had just laid his pistols on the room's
bedside table and was unbuttoning his shirt when
someone knocked on the door.

It was Esmeralda Ramírez.

Without waiting for a formal invitation, she entered the room, smiled kittenishly, and glanced
quickly about, then turned to Mike.

"Señor McLafferty, I wish to thank you for what
you did tonight. That Laroque, I am very frightened of him. This is what he did to me." She
touched one tentative finger to her bruised cheek.

Not totally surprised, Mike studied the girl, taking note of the well-formed breasts that bulged
from beneath the lace fringes of her flaming red
blouse.

Damned if she doesn't remind me of Moon—
doesn't make any sense—as different as night and
day. But her eyes, her mouth. What am I thinking
of? Crazy.

"So I understand," he replied. "Well, I suppose
you should be more careful in selecting your clients,
young lady. There are many men like Jean Laroque,
though I don't suppose I have to tell you that."

"*Sí, sí*, but usually I can understand in time. I

stare into their souls, and from that I can learn much. *¿Es verdad?*"

McLafferty buttoned his shirt hastily. Bruised face or not, the girl was a stunner, and her smile, he imagined, had no doubt melted the sales resistance of many a customer. In some ways, he reflected, she had a refreshing honesty about her, a bluntness of purpose. Strong emotions and a blindness to possible dangers. Why, he wondered, hadn't Esmeralda Ramírez caught a man, gotten hitched? Well, in another place, another time, she might have been a nun or a queen. But of course, for all he actually knew, she was married. There was no moral issue involved: Esmeralda Ramírez earned her living one way, he another—and of recent date, his own was with a deck of cards and a capacity to annoy his fellow card thieves into overbetting.

Why do I keep thinking about Moon, my blood brother's wife? I had my chance with her, let it get away from me. . . .

One way or the other, Mike felt a tingling surge of desire for the Spanish girl—and that, in fact, had little to do with moral judgments. Some women enjoyed lovemaking, and some didn't. His St. Louis Presbyterian wife, for instance, toward whom he had never truly felt anything like what he was now feeling looking at Señorita Ramírez, whether it was because the dark-haired prostitute reminded him of Moon Morning Star or not.

"I wish to thank you," Esmeralda murmured, smiling and looking back at him over her shoulder. She walked daintily to his bed and lay down upon it in a pose that struck McLafferty as particularly provocative.

Wants one final customer for the night . . .

But not even the cynicism of his inner voice made any difference. Of course that's what it was, but so what? He himself had been considering precisely the same arrangement earlier, before Laroque came stumbling into the barroom and forced him to adopt the role of Good Samaritan. An hour or two of illusion, with a bit of whiskey, perhaps, to blur the edges of things . . .

"Señor Mac-Lafferty," the Spanish girl purred, "blow out the lamp and come lie with me. I will show you that I am thankful. I am always very good to my men. No, wait. First I will undress for you. You would like to look at my body? Everyone thinks I am very pretty, *muy bonita, sí?*"

She unbuttoned the red blouse, held the cloth out to either side, and turned to face him. She smiled and winked.

McLafferty took a deep breath. *"Muy bonita,"* he agreed.

He did as he was told and then sat down on the edge of the bed, suddenly and inexplicably uncertain what to do next.

Ye've been had, hawg. The lady's fixin' to milk ye dry. . . .

Fiddlehead Wilson's voice.

Esmeralda snuggled against him, biting softly at his neck and whispering Spanish words that he did not understand into his ear, then placing one hand between his legs and squeezing gently.

"O, señor," she said, her voice strangely like that of a small girl, "now I understand why you are known as Big Mike. Señor Wilson says that is your name, but how does he know? Even though I

think you are too large for me, I want you anyway. *El caballo grande.*"

A sensation of sunlight.

McLafferty turned over, shielding his eyes, and
tried to go back to sleep. Then he remembered
the girl and reached out toward her, found no
one.

He sat up, looked about, discoverd his clothing
draped over the foot of the bed.

Memory of the preceding night returned to
him—Esmeralda's faintly perfumed flesh; her eager (experienced) mouth which nibbled at him
everywhere; his own mouth on first one nipple
and then the other; him penetrating her and immediately thereafter her legs wrapped about him.
He had reached climax too quickly; then, after the
fact, she had writhed back and forth, moaning
and uttering things in Spanish, feigning, he suspected, her own climax. Well, in any case, it had
been good, it had been very good.

And now she was gone. He would directly be
gone as well, as soon as he could get his wits
together.

Had your washin' hung out to dry by a gen-u-
ine professional, by Gawd.

Wilson.

It appeared that Mike was going to have to
listen to Old Fiddlehead all the way to Fort Laramie. Such conversation wouldn't be bad. McLafferty
genuinely liked the mountain man's company. In
many ways they were all alike, he thought—Wilson,
Benton, O'Bragh, Bridger, the whole tribe of them,
a tribe that, as a youngster, he had wanted desperately to join and hence had gone to the mountains

in the first place, knowing at least a few seasons of beautiful hardship and hope and danger, fat times and starving times, before the damned Europeans and Easterners and their preference for silk hats had laid the beaver trade to rest.

McLafferty rose, stretched, stepped to the end of the bed, and began to dress. Then he thought to check his money stash, the pouch-wallet he kept in the inside pocket of the ornamented black jacket.

Missing.

"Goddamn my foolish hide . . ."

Then he saw the purse, sitting on a small table, between his two pistols. He strode across the room, picked up the stash, opened it. There was still an assortment of bills and coins inside, and for a moment he had almost decided not to count. But he realized he couldn't resist—he had to know how much Esmeralda Ramírez had taken.

"Fifty dollars," he said after a moment. "The most expensive little whore on the frontier, but half-ass honest, at least. Could have made off with the whole thing. . . ."

McLafferty grinned.

"By God, she was worth fifty. Fiddlehead, you gap-toothed old relic, you don't know what you missed that night you say you were with her."

McLafferty buttoned his shirt, put on jacket and Mexican hat, strapped on his Colt-Walker, and tucked the pepperbox into one inside coat pocket.

"First, some breakfast," he said, "and then on to Leg-in-the-Water's village. It's been a while since I've seen White Bull and Moon and young Jacques. The boy's . . . what? Four years old now. After that, maybe I'll head on to California, and maybe not. Hell, could be Moon's got an identical twin sister I don't even know about. Guess not. Leclaire's daughter, half-French and half-Indian—one of a kind."

As for the California goldfields, that remained a distinct possibility. But decisions of far-reaching import, he knew, had a way of making themselves.

He closed the hotel-room door behind him and started down the stairs.

Last bed I'll sleep in for a while. Maybe I'm trying to step back into one of my former lives. I've been told once or twice that a man simply can't do it. Well, we'll see. . . .

Fiddlehead Wilson was standing in front of the livery at the appointed hour, but now he insisted he needed another day or two to get "my gawd-damned affairs in order." McLafferty's first impulse was to ride on out, but the old trapper seemed genuine in his desire to return to the mountains, and so Mike decided to make a little money with his deck of cards until Wilson got his outfit together.

He checked into the Far West again, saw nothing further of Esmeralda Ramírez, but took in a total of two hundred and twenty-seven dollars without anyone offering to shoot him.

At length Fiddlehead determined the time was right, showing up, mules and all, outside the hotel. McLafferty collected his gear and animals, and without further ado the unlikely-looking pair, a gambler and an old salt, rode away from town.

They reached Papillon Camp just before sundown and proceeded onward for another hour, until the dusty trail ahead of them was no more than a blur, faintly discernible by starlight, the Milky Way's vast white chaos arching above them.

They camped beneath some big, twisted willows at the edge of the Platte River itself, built a small fire to brew coffee, and ate thick slices of bread wrapped about links of sausage.

McLafferty spread out his bedroll, found the ground beneath him not only familiar but even comfortable, and fell asleep immediately.

Dreamed.

Esmeralda Ramírez came to him, but she was dressed in the manner of a young Cheyenne woman, white deerskin embroidered with porcupine quills. She whispered in Spanish: "Mi alma, mi alma . . ." *Then the voice changed, and it took him a moment to recognize who it was. Not Esmeralda at all, but Moon, Moon Morning Star, White Bull's wife. And she was extraordinarily beautiful, as beautiful as the mountains themselves, as sunrise over high prairies, as the cries of coyotes at night—Moon, Cheyenne because she had lived for a number of years among those people but daughter to a Canadian trapper.*

Moon had been little more than a girl when McLafferty fell in love with her—a fatal attraction and words that he never had the nerve to speak. He and his close friend White Bull both wished to court her, but he, a young man with his future before him, realized the folly of making permanent ties and so had created for himself what turned out to be an ongoing emptiness, an ache that refused to abate. When the opportunity presented itself, he left the Cheyennes, thinking to put the problem behind him, but that didn't work either. He took a new position, went north to Assiniboin country as Sublette's agent, and remained for a time. Then the image of the half-breed girl who flitted back and forth through his dreams drew him south to Platte River country once more. By the time he returned, she was married to White Bull. That had been no surprise. In a way, it was almost a relief—seeing her happy, now a young mother.

She kneeled beside him as he lay there, sleeping, and he was unable to answer her, was unable even to move.

She kissed him on the mouth.

He tried to push her away, but his arms were lifeless, inert. . . .

McLafferty came suddenly awake, grabbed for his Colt Walker.

"Ye blamed fool, what are ye up to? The Pieds Noirs ain't got ye, not yet anyhow."

"Jesus Christ!" McLafferty wheezed. "I'm sorry, Fiddlehead. Go back to sleep, old-timer. A bad dream, I guess. Crazy, crazy . . ."

"Had my suspicions all along, Mr. Mike. Well, try good dreams for a change. A lame bull lives longer if he tries for good dreams."

Sunrise flared over the broad, shallow Platte River, orange-red fire gleaming from the big stream's surface and transforming it into a long, wavering smear of blood, vanishing away to the southeast, where it converged with the much greater Missouri.

They rode again, McLafferty on his newly acquired horse, dubbed Grayboy, and Wilson on one of his mules.

They passed Columbus, its scattering of sod and log houses, a few cattle grazing in fields of untilled prairie grasses, a single general store.

A mile or two beyond the village, they made camp, ate, talked for a time, and then slept.

Days melted one into another as the long ride continued: Loup River, Grand Island, Fort Kearney.

At the latter post they learned that Jean Laroque and his men had passed through just a few hours ahead of them, stopping only long enough to buy a few supplies.

"Two ways we can go." Fiddlehead shrugged. "Cross south of the Platte onto the Oregon Trail an' keep movin' ahead, pass 'em by. They got wagons an' cain't make the kind of progress we can on horseback. It's a pure wonder we didn't catch up yesterday or the day before that. Damned fool swamp hawgs must be pushin' their oxen half the night, two teams most likely, an' switchin' 'em. Or else mebbe we ought to ride north to the South Fork of the Loup, hunt antelopes or buff'lers, if we can find a few of the beasties."

"One other possibility," McLafferty said.

"What's that?"

"Just ride right on by. If Laroque's really got the gold fever, he's forgotten all about Omaha. Looks to me like he's determined to run his dray animals right into the prairie sod."

"He's got twenty, twenty-five men with him— let's don't go forgetting that fact, Michael. If his dander's still up, them don't make good odds. Fight when ye have to, that's what I always say. Otherwise, hang on to your mule."

McLafferty shrugged. "I detect a certain homely wisdom here, Fiddlehead. So you want to hunt pronghorns, do you? South Fork's a pretty barren drainage—you figure we'll have any luck? I'm in no hurry, if you aren't. Maybe I won't even head

for California this year. Matter of fact, I was thinking about wintering with the Cheyennes. It's been
a while since I've seen my friends—too long, in
truth. So lead on, Great Hunter."

"Ye don't have to get sar-castic. It's your hide
Laroque wants nailed to his lodgepole, if he's got
one. Me, I'm just lookin' out for ye."

They turned north and crossed Loup River, far
away from even the small outpost settlements now,
and Mike McLafferty found himself wondering
why in God's name he had ever left this sort of
existence in favor of a two-story brick house outside
St. Louis. They were into Oto and Pawnee territory now, but after a three-day venture that took
them to the headwaters of the South Fork, they
had encountered no recent sign whatsoever. Neither had they taken so much as a single antelope,
though they had come within sight of the wing-
footed creatures on several occasions. Just watching them dance away, long lines bounding and
leaping, was satisfaction enough, even if it didn't
produce any fresh meat.

They resorted to shooting fool's hens and a turkey or two, took their time, and camped early.

Moonlight now, burning the rolling prairies with
silver fire, light gleaming and shimmering from
occasional stands of elder and willow and cottonwood along stream bottoms.

"Way I figger it," Wilson said between sips of
hot coffee, "ye're about half-Irish and half-coyote,
ain't that right? Good thing ye wear that leetle
sombrero. Otherwise, your red hair'd attract every
damned Pawnee from hyar to the Sangre de Cris-
tos, for a fact. So what brought ye to the mountains in the first place? Tell me that much."

McLafferty sipped his own coffee and settled back against the bole of a young box elder, offered Fiddlehead a cigar, and lit one for himself.

"It's the truth you're after?"

"Of course, ye damned fool."

"Well, I grew up fending for myself along the Missouri River. I don't even remember my father, and my mom died of the decline when I was ten—no, just eleven. When I was fifteen, I hired on with Nathaniel Wyeth's bunch, and that's when I met Baptiste Charbonneau, just back from getting an education in Europe. You know the story— Clark sent him over there, paid the bills, and so forth. Baptiste had it in mind to go find his mother, Sacajawea, and I guess he wanted to find out if the place he came from was maybe better than the place he'd gotten to. So he was going up-country with Wyeth, and he put in a good word for me. I signed on as a kind of errand boy, and right away Aloysius Benton took me under his wing, you might say. I guess I was his apprentice, after a fashion. I learned the fur trade from him. That was 1834, and the market was still strong. Hell, I got to know some of the men whose names were already legends back in St. Louis—Carson, Bridger, Fraeb, O'Bragh, Sublette. The only really famous one I didn't get to know until just recently was Fiddlehead Wilson. I guess he never bothered to come into Rendezvous, or else he showed up late, after everybody else had moved out for the fall hunt."

"That's 'cause I was working out of Taos with Old Bill Williams, ye damned fool. How many times I got to tell ye?"

"That's right, that's right. Well, when the beaver

trade went bust, I hired on with Bill Sublette as an Indian trader, sometimes with the Crows, and sometimes with the Assiniboins or Cheyennes—and that's how I got to be friends with White Bull."

"Then ye took to gamblin' an' the like. . . ."

"Yep, that's how it happened, all right. After fourteen years or so, I realized I had more money banked away than I knew what to do with, so I went down to St. Louis and acted like the damned fool you keep telling me I am."

Wilson poured another tin cup full of coffee, got comfortable again. "Suppose ye wants to hear my story now," he said. "But first, ye got more of them cigars? A man cain't tell a tolerable tale unless he's got some good tobacco to help him along."

"I was afraid we'd get around to your biography eventually." Big Mike chuckled. "Yes. Just happen to have a cigar or two left. . . ."

In the shadows, at the edge of the light from their campfire, glimmering amber eyes were visible. McLafferty took note and amused himself with the thought that coyotes had come in to listen to the *Saga of Fiddlehead Wilson*.

"No more! *Bastante*, enough, you filthy *hijos de perros*. Maybe tonight Esmeralda walks back to Omaha, either that or I stick *un cuchillo* into someone's fat throat while you are all snoring like pigs."

Esmeralda Ramírez stood like a fury in the firelight, nostrils distended, orange reflections like sparks flashing in her eyes. But her face had grown a little haggard with the long trip up the Platte to this place a hundred miles above the parting of the North and South branches of the river, one cheek darkly bruised, and her red-velvet dress stained and torn.

"*Enfant de garce*, Mademoiselle Esmeralda, you do not look nearly so good as you once did. I am not even sure about the five hundred dollar now. I think now maybe we give you to the Pawnees and, *peut-être*, get some fat old squaw to replace you."

"Damn sight more trouble than she's worth, you ask me," Sam Kurtz growled, spitting a stream of brown juice in the direction of the Spanish woman's black boots.

"Be a good whore, Ezzie, and there might be a hunnert or so in it yet fer ya."

"Like hell! *Cabrones!* You offer me five hundred to go with you to California, now you say maybe a hundred. I say a thousand, or no more *chocha* for you."

"Show us your *tetas* now, do a leetle dance for us, and maybe we give you fifty when we reach California," Cottonmouth Chardin called out, his coarse, heavy-jowled face red with whiskey, his eyes bloodshot.

"You tell Esmeralda take three, four of you *barbosos* every night, then you wake her up at dawn. Some of you like to play rough, and I have bruises all over from your paws. You tell Esmeralda 'cook the dinner, clean the dishes, wash the clothes.' I am not your *sirvienta*. You find *una India* for that. *Mil dólares*, one thousand, and maybe I stay with you. But I want half of it now, *ahora mismo*."

"People in hell want ice-water," Smoky Joe Utti said, rising and walking to stand confronting her, thumbs hooked in belt. He was not much taller than the woman, but his body was whipcord-lean, his thin face, pale blue eyes cold. "Get down on your knees, bitch. Least your mouth ain't all wore out."

Esmeralda took an instinctive step backward, but she continued to stare defiantly at Smoky Joe.

"One thousand or you can go get sucked by your mules. And maybe I tell a few things to the *sacos azules* at Fort Kearney on the way back to Omaha, things like who it was that held up the wagonload of Santos Nuevos, those Mormons near the Forks."

"I said on your knees," Utti barked, grabbing a handful of long black hair and yanking the girl's head back.

A tremor of fear crossed the fine-featured face, and then a dagger appeared in Esmeralda's hand, drawn from somewhere beneath the folds of her velvet skirt, and she slashed a red slice along Joe's arm before a young man nicknamed Carl-the-Squint could knock the knife from her grasp.

"Shit," Utti yelled, letting go of her hair to clutch at his forearm.

Esmeralda looked at the ring of men rising up around her, real terror flashing in her eyes. She lunged for the fallen knife, had it, held the weapon out in front of her at arm's length, making feints at the air. Quick as a snake, Smoky Joe's boot flashed into the air, kicking the dagger loose and numbing Esmeralda's entire arm.

"No, *por Dios*," she breathed, and then Laroque stepped forward, backhanded her across the face so hard she fell sideways, her head snapping around. He pulled her up by her hair and held her in a kneeling position.

Laroque slit Esmeralda's dress from neck to navel, the knife leaving a thin line of blood along her flesh. He hit her again, this time on the jaw with closed fist, and when she crumpled, he turned her over and forced himself into her.

"The back door, she is still pretty tight, *c'est incroyable*," he said, laughing when he had finished. "I recommend it."

"My turn, by God," shouted Pig-Sticker Jackson, beginning to unbutton his britches.

"Back, *bâtard*," growled Chardin. "You are only *un petit chien*, here. I am the big dog. I screw her while you sit back and drool. Then maybe you get your chance."

"You son of a bitch, I'll kill you one of these nights," Jackson raged.

"No fighting, *mes amis*," Laroque said, smiling but holding a shotgun leveled at Pig-sticker. "Plenty to go around. Eh, *ma chérie*? Maybe I will have a second turn after the others are finished. You like it, *non*?" He nudged gently at her face with the toe of his boot, still showing his teeth in a smile.

They are going to kill me tonight. The thought came to her suddenly and with chilling certainty. *Madre de Dios, santísima María, ayúdame.*

Instinctively she tried to rise, to fight her way out of the circle of coarse faces, and they let her run back and forth for a time, laughing to watch her dart from one side of the fire to the other, in her panic stepping into the embers, screaming out in pain, and scattering sparks—to the great amusement of Cottonmouth Chardin in particular. When he had tired of the game, Chardin sent her reeling backward from a closed fist, then pulled her legs apart and thrust into her while Utti and Laroque held her down.

She forced herself not to scream, to keep her mind clear as, one after the other, most of the voyageurs came up to take a turn.

It is not, after all, something I have never done before, she told herself. I must keep my mind *clara, sana*. Perhaps there is a chance.... *Jesús, dulce Jesús, perdóname.* ...

Laroque was crouched over her again, his breath foul in her face, his teeth stained nearly black when he grinned at her.

"No," Esmeralda screamed, her eyes rolling wildly as she struggled with renewed strength to rise. "I beg you, *en el nombre del Padre y del Hijo y del Espíritu Santo.* ..."

"Prayin', by God." Jackson laughed. "The whore's prayin'. Ain't that rich?"

"Christ, Jean, you're not really gonna kill her, are you?" asked Duncan.

Laroque smiled, holding up the woman's own knife for her to see, and laid the tip against her throat. Then the knife plunged, bright blood pumping up over her breasts as the skin itself drained of all color.

An awed silence followed as Laroque rose, his face splattered with blood.

"Shit, Laroque," Kurtz said into the silence, "you went and wasted a perfectly good whore. Now what do we do?"

"She want to go back down the river to Omaha?" Chardin laughed. "I say we let her go."

With Jackson's help, the two lifted the body, eyes still wide, gaping throat like a second mouth, and walked her out into the shallows, heaved her toward deeper water, Laroque tilting the jug and taking a long swallow, then lifting it toward the dead girl in mock salute as her body twisted with the current, a faint white blur against darkness.

Carl-the-Squint, hand cupped above his forehead, stared at the drifting body and then turned toward Jean Laroque and began to grin.

3 It was the pain in her hand that woke her. For a short time Moon Morning Star tried to ignore the throbbing ache and return to her dream, a dream in which she and White Bull were together, a dream that in fact replicated their last hunting trip along the Platte. Half-awake now, she could still smell the odor of juniper smoke and meat juices, could still feel her husband's strong hands on her breasts as the two of them laughed and laughed, the sound ringing in clear air.

The remnants of sleep dissolved, however, the laughter fading into the yipping and wailing of a band of coyotes someplace nearby.

Moon opened her eyes, pulled herself to a position slumped against the base of a cottonwood. Coyotes, yes, and the faint trickling sound of a small stream, frogs calling and answering one another, soft noises of a horse on a long tether moving about and grazing. Stars blazed beyond the dark forms of trees along the creek, and on the western horizon she could see a pale glow where the moon, two days from full, had just set.

Her hand felt as if it were on fire, this center of

pain intensifying, resolving itself to the area of one little finger. With the return of full consciousness, her physical discomfort seemed insignificant. She leaned forward and pressed her arms against her abdomen, squeezed her eyes shut against a wave of anguish, remembering.

When they had returned to the village from the hunting trip, they had seen the wagons drawn up near Fort Laramie nearby, wagons belonging to Laroque and his men, a name that would only later come to be burned into her consciousness.

"White Bull, my husband," she whispered, "you must not trouble my dreams anymore. It is too hard for me when I awaken. It's time now for you to go to the World Beyond, where your people live after this life is over. I promise you that you will be avenged, and then perhaps I will join you. Can my people go to your Spirit World? I don't know, don't know . . . I only know I loved you, White Bull, and it hurts, hurts. Yet I will take great joy in seeing your murderers die."

Moon Morning Star, born with the name of Leclair, did not weep. After her mother died of lung fever during a terrible Michigan Territory winter when the girl was six years old, she was raised by the French fur trapper who was her father. During the next few years Leclair moved from one trapping region to another as the frontier edged westward, finally coming to live along Platte River, near the Cheyennes. Moon grew up fast and learned to take care of herself early, out of necessity, among the unforgiving realities of nature and rough men who were her father's continual associates. Jacques Leclair taught his daughter not only to read and write as best he could but also to ride like a man, to shoot straight, and to slide a shiv into the ribs of any lard-eating *merde* who tried to interfere with her. And then he had managed to get caught on the wrong side of a sow grizzly with cubs, close by the Little Sandy, and Moon had been left, at the age of thirteen, on her own.

Leg-in-the-Water's people had taken her in. Two years later she was married to White Bull. She hardly knew the handsome warrior who had brought presents to Leg-in-the-Water's lodge, but miraculously, after becoming his wife, she also fell in love with him. Together they explored a wealth of shameless and joyful sexual sensations, and they became friends as well. At times he took her off on hunting expeditions, just the two of them, a thing that no other Cheyenne male would do, and they spent days alone wandering the hills, making love, sometimes even remembering to search for game.

The trips stopped, of course, after the birth of their son, Jacques White Bull, but the love between them grew deeper. Their last journey alone together had been the first in several years, the child at last old enough to be away from his mother for a few days.

"Now," she remembered saying when she had learned of her pregnancy, "I suppose you will want to take a second wife. That is what you damned Cheyenne men do when the first wife gets fat and ugly from bearing your children. It doesn't matter, though. I will slice off my rival's nose one night, and then you won't think she's pretty. Have you picked out someone already? Tell me who it is."

"How would I dare take another wife?" he replied. "I know you, Little Warrior, and I am afraid it might not be her nose you cut off, but my manhood."

All gone, now, all that gone in one instant, one stupid, drunken white pig's impulse. My husband . . .

The moon was down, the sky completely dark and filled with stars. It was not long, then, until dawn. Moon Morning Star rose from a single buffalo robe, her body stiff from sleeping on rocky ground. She walked a few steps to the creek, splashed her face. Cold water caused her injured hand to ache fiercely, and she cradled it without thinking.

The first joint of her little finger was gone, the wound fresh. She had cut it herself, raising White Bull's war ax and bringing it down suddenly. For an instant there had been no sensation of pain whatsoever, but the finger still hung by a scrap of flesh. She struck again, completely severing the fingertip. She had not allowed herself to hesitate, for in this way Cheyenne wives made their sign of mourning for a dead husband. Then pain came, hot, like glowing steel against flesh, but still the sensation barely registered through her shock and grief.

The coyotes had gone off, their song fading into distance, and a slight predawn breeze rustled among cottonwood leaves.

It had only been one night—one night, and one day, and now most of another night. Moon tried to make sense of the moment of agonized rupture, but it seemed so long ago, a single flash when the world changed utterly.

A string of wagons had rolled into Fort Laramie in the afternoon, a train full of men heading, as so many before them had this spring and summer, to California. Such men were driven onward by fevered reports of gold, gold everywhere, big nuggets lying all over the hillsides and paving streambeds, just waiting to be picked up, if one could believe such stories. A few years earlier the white men wanted beaver plew, men like her own father, but now it was gold—yes, and often the land itself.

By evening a number of these Californians had found their way to Leg-in-the-Water's encampment, not far from the fort. Moon could see immediately that most of them were drunk. They came into the camp laughing and rowdy, calling loudly for women, making lewd gestures, and grabbing at whatever females were in sight. Sensing disaster, Moon had begged White Bull to take her and their son and ride away, but he had refused, insisting that he might be needed in case of trouble with the unruly whites.

With great dignity Leg-in-the-Water confronted the emigrants, assuring them they were welcome if they behaved themselves properly, but Cheyenne women were not for sale in his village, whatever the men might have been told by bluecoat soldiers inside the battlements of Fort Laramie.

Some whites drifted off, but several stayed. They had whiskey with them, and they began to gamble with a few of the older Cheyenne men. White Bull did not join the gambling, but along with other warriors, he remained watching, not trusting the strangers at all.

Moon refused to obey her husband's order that

she stay in the lodge. She sat by his side back away from the firelight despite his urging her to leave.

The gambling continued for hours, with no real trouble, and Moon was beginning to think her apprehensions were unfounded. She rose to slip away to the lodge, but her movement attracted the notice of one of the men, a Frenchman who swayed to his feet, drink-bleared eyes glittering, tongue running obscenely around full lips, vividly red in his grime-darkened face.

He lurched toward her, grabbed her arm, babbling as he did so.

"Pretty *tétons*, eh? You come with Jean, I show you good time. No trouble, Heap Big Chief," he added as White Bull gripped his wrist and wrenched it away from the grasp on Moon's arm. "Jean Laroque pay you good. Plenty red paint, blue beads, you like that, *non*? I give your woman back good as new, show her some tricks for you."

As he spoke, the Frenchman pulled loose of White Bull's grip and caught Moon again, twisting her about and trying to put his wet mouth on hers as she struggled to free herself. White Bull dragged her out of the man's clutches a second time and shoved him roughly away, drawing a knife from his belt as Laroque sprawled to the ground across the campfire.

The whites, who had been laughing and cheering raucously at Laroque's drunken courtship, suddenly went silent. As the Frenchman rolled out of the fire and sat up, a revolver appeared in his hand. The next instant White Bull sagged, a look of shock on his face, and simultaneously Moon heard the crash of the large-caliber pistol. Time seemed to slow down strangely as White Bull fell, crumpling by inches, and yet Moon could not move fast enough to reach him before he sprawled facedown on the bare earth.

"Now, *mes amis*, you will not move, please," Laroque called out, getting to his feet and waving his gun at the warriors who had sprung up shouting, knives and war-axes in hand. "Otherwise more of you will die. My friends and I, we leave now."

The emigrants rose, most of whom had rifles or pistols at the ready and trained on the Cheyennes. The warriors, still stunned and not completely comprehending what had happened, hesitated.

"Goddamn you, Laroque, you hotheaded son of a bitch! See what you've got us into," one of the emigrants shouted.

The whites fired several rounds and managed to make their escape. By the time the Cheyenne warriors had gotten to their ponies to give pursuit, the gold-seekers were halfway to Fort Laramie and were well within its closed gates before any of Leg-in-the-Water's men could reach them.

The next day White Bull's body was strapped to a platform for burial. He wore his bonnet of eagle feathers, and his medicine bag, ceremonial pipe, bow, and a few other prized possessions were placed around him. The women of the village tore down his lodge, and household goods were taken by various relatives, as was the custom. But Moon, her hand bound in a bloodstained bandage, insisted on keeping her husband's rifle and spotted war pony—and no one spoke openly against this breach of tradition, for many in the village had become convinced that White Bull's woman was crazy, possibly possessed by a divine or demonic spirit.

She left her four-year-old son with White Bull's

parents and rode her husband's speckled Nez Percé pony to the fort that afternoon, accompanying Leg-in-the-Water and his council of senior warriors, but the gates were closed against all Indians. When it became evident that appeals for justice would not be heard, the chief and his men withdrew. Moon, however, chose to remain near the fort.

"It is best you come, too, Moon Morning Star," Leg-in-the-Water said to her. "Revenge is not a woman's business. Your husband lies waiting for his wife to lead the mourning ceremonies. Your little son needs you. Return with us. Messengers have already left to summon warriors from other villages. Your husband's murderers will not escape."

But Moon only looked at the chief as if his words had not registered at all, and after a time he shrugged and rode away.

She prowled about the fortress walls for hours after nightfall, hoping against hope that the man who had murdered her husband might venture out. At last she took her blanket and White Bull's rifle to a cottonwood grove along the river, and after what seemed a very long time, she slept and dreamed of her husband.

Now, leaning against the bole of a tree, her blanket clutched around her shoulders against predawn chill, she waited for first light. She did not intend to leave the vicinity of Fort Laramie until she was admitted or until the man who murdered White Bull emerged.

"The Frenchman can't stay in there forever," she murmured. "Sometimes he and the others will come out. After that, my husband, you can rest. I should have heard your words, White Bull. If I had stayed in the lodge as you told me, you'd still be with me. Now all that is left me is to avenge your death. Perhaps after that I will join you. . . ."

4 Although she had no intention of doing so, Moon had dozed again. She woke with a hand gripping her shoulder, shaking her gently. She came to consciousness clawing and striking out, even before her eyes opened—opened to full daylight and the long-jawed, blue-eyed face of a man she recognized as White Bull's friend, Red Coyote McLafferty.

"Whoa, gal, whoa, Little Warrior," he said, grasping her flailing wrists. "Didn't come here to get scalped by my best friend's lady."

He held her left hand with its bloodstained bandage, stared at it more closely, then touched at the streaks of dirt and dried blood on her cheeks.

"Don't look good, hoss," muttered a grizzled, bushy-browed individual peering over McLafferty's shoulder.

"What in God's name . . . ? Jesus, Moon, what's happened?"

Suddenly, for the first time since White Bull's death, Moon Morning Star found herself weeping, tears streaming in muddy tracks down her face as McLafferty folded his long arms around her.

* * *

"White Bull was the best friend I ever had. I still can't believe it, Fiddlehead," Big Mike said that evening as they sat on the ground in front of the lodge of Bright Shield and Grass Flower, White Bull's parents.

The two men smoked cigars and talked in low voices as they listened to the sounds of the village preparing for night. Woodsmoke and cooking odors drifted from lodges into clear evening air, and from time to time a woman's voice rang out, calling a child, or a man spoke in greeting to another, passing between tepees. Westward the evening star hung against the sky, growing brighter as light deepened from silver gray to cobalt. Within the hide lodge at their backs, sounds were subdued, little Jacques whimpering briefly, Moon Morning Star hushing him with a gentle word, the grandmother beginning a lullaby.

"I wouldn't have recognized Moon. Wouldn't have known it was her at all," Mike went on. "Might not have stopped if I hadn't recognized old Ghost, White Bull's Palouse pony. It goes right through me to see her like that, all scarred up and hollow-eyed."

"Grievin' takes its toll on a woman, most 'specially a Injun, way some of 'em hack at theirselves and scarify their faces and whatnot." Wilson nodded. "Sounds like she's blamin' herself a mite heavy for what happened, too. All things considered, ye woulda done the world a favor if you'd gone ahead and kilt the swamp rat back in Omaha."

"She was the prettiest filly this side of the Mississippi. Hell, this side of the Atlantic."

"So ye've told me a time or three."

"I'm going to get that bastard, Fiddlehead," McLafferty said. "You're right. I should have killed him when I had the chance."

"One thing at a time, green'un, one thing at a time. Only way you coaxed that leetle gal to come away from the fort was by convincin' her that her man needed her an' you to give 'im a proper buryin'. I got me a feeling' that Leg-in-the-Water an' his boys will pretty well be able to handle Laroque's case, one way or the other. Mebbe the boys'll cotch him an' burn him alive—make a by-gawd county fair out of it."

Mike puffed at his cigar and shook his head. "I want to put him under myself."

"Lots o' candidates fer that job," Wilson mused. "Seems like I heered Moon-gal volunteer. I figger she's got a powerful claim."

"Like hell," Mike argued. "I'll be damned if I let her get herself shot or hung for that bastard's greasy scalp."

"Could be ye'll have your hands full keeping her from it. Lady strikes me as a mite headstrong."

McLafferty didn't respond, and the two men sat smoking in silence for a time. Mike stared into darkness. The human sounds grew quieter now, and crickets competed with frogs to fill the summer air with noise. Off in the fields horses called to one another, and the moon was rising, startlingly huge and orange behind the Cheyenne lodges.

"White Bull," Mike said into the stillness. "Hardly more than kids, the both of us, even though I was the big-time Indian trader. He saved my life more than once, and I guess I pulled his fat out of the fire a time or two. One night we got some whiskey an old man had brought up-country from a still over around Fort Kearney, and the two of us got drunker than lords. Started out telling each other our life stories, and after a while we were into hopes and dreams, women, that sort of thing. Then we got to . . . hell, I can't even remember what it was about, but we got to fighting."

Remember well enough. It was a pretty little half-breed, Iroquois and French, disposition like a badger, and only about fourteen or fifteen at the time, but we were both head over heels. . . .

"Anyway, we were too soused to do much damage, and after a while we were just gasping for breath and crying like little kids and holding on to each other's necks. Then he took out his knife, and we nicked our wrists and swapped things. I gave him my horse and my gun—that's that old Hawken Moon's got—and he gave me a couple of ponies and a buffalo robe, and we swore we'd never fight over anything again."

"An' that's how ye come to be blood brothers, eh?"

"Yep. We swore we'd always fight *for* each other after that, we'd always be there to help each other out." Mike rose, dropped the stub of his cigar, ground it out with his boot. "But I wasn't there this time, Fiddlehead. God damn it. I wasn't there."

Wilson grunted, rose also, and clapped the younger man on the shoulder. "Reckon I'll head on out and spread my roll, Big Mike. You be joinin' me, or you stayin' here with White Bull's folks?"

McLafferty shook his head, didn't trust himself to speak yet.

"S'pose you'll be movin' out about sunup? You an' the leetle gal got a long trek ahead of you, bein' she's of a mind to plant her husband up on Laramie Peak. Have a feeling his kinfolk ain't goin' to take kindly to you two making off with the body that way. . . ."

"Don't care what his kinfolk think. She wants him buried in some medicine cave, that's where we'll take him. She's got the right. . . ."

"Yep. Well. Probably won't see you in the morning. I figger to go on over to the fort, see how the stick floats thar." The old-timer hesitated, cleared his throat. "Right sorry about your friend," he said, and then Wilson turned and stalked away from the lodges.

McLafferty walked out of the village, striding rapidly, aimlessly. He climbed to the top of a low rise, stared eastward. The moon had risen higher and had lost its smoky red color. Sparse, rolling land spread away, gray and silver and black shadows in the moonlight, and off to the north the dark bulk of Laramie Peak stood against a moon-washed sky.

That's where you'll stay, my friend, in a cave up there, and I'll ride back to your village with your woman. After that, I'll kill a worthless white man, and then I probably won't be back this way again, ever. Because to tell the truth, even now I can't help thinking about Moon, about how she felt in my arms this morning, small and warm and . . . just right. Your woman, White Bull, my brother, and that's why I won't be back this way.

An owl brushed past Mike's head, wings utterly silent, and floated down into the swale, ghostly in moonlight. McLafferty shivered and walked toward the horses, untied his bedroll, and spread it out. Nearby, he could hear Fiddlehead already snoring.

*   *   *

They did, indeed, leave early the next morning. When McLafferty rose, well before sunup, Moon, dry-eyed and grim once again, had just finished rigging a travois to the Palouse. Man and woman lifted White Bull's body, still strapped to its litter, down from the burial platform and transferred it to the travois. One old woman, a few yards away, watched intently but said nothing. Grass Flower, White Bull's mother, hovered about tearfully, as did his sister, Prairie Hen, little Jacques clinging to her dress. Bright Shield, hearing the women's wails, came forth from his lodge and demanded that his daughter-in-law return the body to its platform.

"This is not right, what you are doing," he said. "Moon Morning Star, I forgive you because this terrible happening has made you not yourself, yet you must not go any further. You are dishonoring your dead husband."

"I am doing what my dead husband asked me to do," Moon replied without expression. "He came to me in a dream, and this is what he wanted. He wished to be placed in the sacred cave up on the side of Laramie Peak. I am obeying my husband, as I always have, Bright Shield."

"If you had such a dream, then you should talk to Turtle about it. His dream medicine is powerful, and he will be able to tell whether this is truly a message from him-who-is-gone or a false vision sent by some spirit who wishes us harm."

Moon turned and looked at the old warrior. She stared at him for several moments before she spoke, her face rigid and terrible, suggesting some hidden strength of will radiating from within her, a force against which no ordinary human being could prevail.

"I know my husband," she said, "and I heard his words. Now stand out of my way. I will take my son with me, because he should say good-bye to his father. If you wish to come, Bright Shield, Grass Flower, any who were his friends, you are welcome. We will go."

By now a number of Cheyennes had gathered, the women whispering among themselves and the men looking on with disapproval, but no one made a move to stop the "crazy one." Moon merely glanced about, took her son's hand, and walked straight-backed to her pony, lifting the boy in front of her. She nodded to Mike, and they rode out at a walk, White Bull's spotted pony, Ghost, dragging the travois over stones and making a clattering sound that seemed peculiarly melancholy.

It was a slow journey, and once the sun began to blaze down onto the dry, rolling country, a miserably hot one. Sweat gathered under the inner band of Mike's hat, dripped off the tip of his nose, soaked down his back. Moon rode without speaking, her eyes fixed straight ahead, and when Mike tried to engage her in conversation to relieve the tedium of the ride, she seemed not to have heard him at all.

After a few attempts, he gave up the effort, but when young Jacques, who spent the first few hours dozing against his mother's body, became fully awake and began to fuss, Mike took the child onto his own horse and talked to him.

He told Jacques White Bull stories about his father, some about heroic exploits in war and buffalo hunting, but more tales about things White

Bull and McLafferty had done together. The four-year-old listened intently for a long while, laughing at those parts he found humorous and asking remarkably penetrating questions about others. Eventually he grew tired of listening, however, and led the conversation around to his own childish doings.

"My father taught me how to shoot a bow," he said. "I'm nearly as good as he is. He even let me ride Ghost once."

"That a fact?" McLafferty smiled.

"Yes," the boy nodded. "I already shot a rabbit. And an elk. And *six* buffaloes."

"You're sure it was that many?"

"Yes . . . well, I'm not sure. This many."

The child held up both hands with fingers outspread and looked a deadpan challenge at Mike, daring him to dispute the total.

"If you say so, partner. That's more than six. Does your mama know about all those buffalo?"

Jacques glanced over at Moon, back at Mike. "No. We didn't tell her about it."

"You'll make a hell of a poker player when you grow up, Little Bull."

"Yes." Jacques nodded, not asking the question, and then was silent for a time, his head gradually drooping back against Mike's chest as he fell asleep again.

McLafferty glanced over at Moon Morning Star, saw that she was looking in his direction.

"You're good with him, Red Coyote," she said. "Thank you."

Mike shrugged, embarrassed. "He's quite a kid. I like him."

Moon merely nodded, a faint hint of a smile touching at her worn face.

During the hottest part of the afternoon they stopped beside a stream they had been following to let the horses rest. They ate some cold cooked meat Moon had brought in her saddlebags. Jacques awoke in a serious mood.

"My father won't come back after we take him to the place in the mountains," he said. "That's true, isn't it? After Frog Stalker's father had the coughing sickness, he stopped moving, and they wrapped him up and put him in a tree. He didn't ever come back."

Moon smoothed her son's hair. "No," she said, "he won't come back. But maybe sometime, many years from now, you will see him again in the Spirit Land. They say it is a fine place, with trees and lodges and many, many animals to hunt."

"That is what Grandmother Grass Flower told me. Do you think it's true?"

Moon hesitated, said, "I don't know, my love. I hope it's so. Wherever your father is, I think he is happy to have such a fine son."

"I think it's true," Jacques White Bull said in a tone of great finality. The child turned to look speculatively at Mike, chewing on a piece of meat as he did so. "When Frog Stalker's father went away, then Tall Horse became his new father. That was because Tall Horse was his father's best friend. They were blood brothers, just like you were with my father. Bright Shield told me so."

Mike glanced up from under his hat brim at Moon, waiting for Jacques to drop the other shoe. Moon studied the far horizon.

The boy's eyes were still on him, questioning, so

he cleared his throat several times, feeling the blood creeping up his cheeks.

"It doesn't always work out that way, partner," McLafferty mumbled.

Jacques White Bull took the comment in stride. "That's too bad," he said. "I like you, Red Coyote."

It was late afternoon, the light deep yellow and the shadows growing long, by the time they reached the foot of the mountains. The sun disappeared behind the peaks as they climbed a tumble of ridges and canyons on the eastern face, and nightfall found them still low on the side of the upthrust. McLafferty suggested camping, but Moon wished merely to rest for a time, until moonrise.

It came, full and round and red, before the sky turned completely dark, and they continued up a rocky draw, walking now except for the child, and leading the horses over uneven footing.

Jacques, Mike had decided, was a little trooper. The child sat upright on the pony, gripping its mane and not uttering a single whimper, his eyes glimmers of light in the shadows of his face. Moon was also silent, her body moving easily, gracefully, her head bent as she picked her way over broken ground. She led them out of the draw and onto a ridgetop strewn with lodgepole pine.

It was darker among the trees, and Mike had trouble discerning any path at all, but Moon led on, apparently quite certain of her direction.

"'You sure you know where you're going?" he asked, more to break the eerie silence than for any other reason.

"Yes," she said. "I was here once before, when we brought the bones of my husband's grandfather to the cave. That was before Jacques White Bull was born."

"Oh, well, if you've been there once five or six years ago . . ."

"I know where I'm going, Mike Red Coyote."

Silence, and the silver spell of moonlight. In a broad meadow high up the mountainside, screech owls trilled back and forth from the trees on all sides.

Mike and Moon led the horses to near timberline, the conifers growing small and twisted and sparsely scattered among stretches of bare rock. At last Moon halted, looking about her almost as one awakening from a trance. Light seemed to gather in pools in her eyes, sliding over the planes of her face. Then she nodded, left the horses, and climbed a steep tumble of boulders, disappearing beyond a stunted juniper. In a moment she reappeared.

"We will have to carry him now. The horses can't go any farther," she said.

Mike nodded, feeling slightly dazed. The whole expedition seemed too much like a dream. The woman stood above him, outlined in silver, and for a moment he was almost afraid of her.

They returned to the horses and unhitched the travois. Mike lifted Jacques from Grayboy's back, and the boy stood silent, his eyes hidden in shadow. McLafferty rigged harnesses for themselves with a coil of rope he carried on his saddle, and side by side, the man and woman made the laborious ascent, dragging the heavy travois with White Bull's body upon it over the rocks and to the mouth of a cave. Jacques followed silently on his own.

Mike and Moon stood just inside the musty darkness, gasping for breath. Mike became aware of a chilll as his sweat-soaked shirt clung to his back. Across a draw and above them he could see a patch of snow that still lingered on the heights, whiteness glimmering from its hollow in the moonlight.

A breeze had sprung up, and it whispered strangely in the chambers of the limestone cavern. Back in the depths, something else, perhaps a trickle of water, but a sound almost like the murmur of voices. Mike felt hair prickle at the back of his neck, and he reached into his pocket for flint and steel, knelt to strike a spark into a handful of dry moss and wood shavings.

"No," Moon hissed, her voice echoing back as if the syllable were whispered by a multitude within the chamber. "No fires in the Sacred Cave."

Mike dropped his fire starter and then had to feel around on the damp cave floor to find it.

In the brief flash of light as he had struck one spark he had seen . . . what?

War axes. Colored feathers and strips of fur trailing from medicine bags. Other forms. The startling gleam of skulls. Shadows that seemed to move as the brief flash disappeared.

The boy Jacques stood in the entryway, a dark figure against light filtering in from outside. At Moon's direction, they unstrapped White Bull's litter from the travois poles and carried it into the cave, Mike stumbling in utter darkness, but Moon seeming to know exactly where she was going. They placed the body on a ledge of rock and then stood for a moment in the blackness and strange whisperings and sighings of the cave.

"So long, pal," Mike said softly after a time, and the echoes sighed around him.

As they stepped back out into the moonlight, something brushed past Mike's head, something silent and large and winged. He turned for a glimpse of the thing, saw nothing. "Damned owl," he muttered.

Moon looked up at him, her expression invisible. "Yes," she said. "I felt it too."

5 A few trailing clouds drifted away eastward, remnants of the previous night's brief rainstorm, and steam rose from a stubble of ragged yellow-gray grasses now that the sun was well above the endlessly rolling rim of high prairie land. A lone heron vaulted upward from a cottonwood close to the North Platte, cutting through still air and disappearing downstream.

Leg-in-the-Water, McLafferty, Wilson, and Moon Morning Star sat their mounts and stared down from the crest of a low, bare hill toward the main gates of Fort Laramie. From the summit of the left parapet, a guidon bearer was slowly waving a banner back and forth, the flag of truce.

"Looks to this child as if Cap'n Everts has decided to invite ye in for a chat after all," Fiddlehead observed.

Leg-in-the-Water nodded, glanced momentarily at Moon and then at McLafferty.

Behind these four were the assembled warriors of several Cheyenne and Arapaho villages that lay within a day's ride of the fort.

It wasn't simply that a single highly-regarded

69

clan chieftain had been slain, bringing about this
sudden display of force, McLafferty realized, but
rather the honor of the great Cheyenne war chief
Leg-in-the-Water had been violated. He had given
permission for Laroque and his erstwhile rivermen
to enter the village. In Leg-in-the-Water's mind
the men were obliged, as guests, to conform to
Cheyenne customs in all matters, and hence were
subject to penalties if Cheyenne hospitality had
been violated. So now the fort itself was, in effect,
under siege.

The Fort Laramie commandant, however, was
clearly of the opinion that his own authority took
precedence over the will of any Cheyenne council;
hence the armed standoff.

McLafferty's thoughts momentarily drifted back
some eight years, to 1841, when the fort had been
an American Fur outpost, and he himself an em-
ployee, a trading agent under Bill Sublette. Laramie had been named for a French trapper slain by
Arapahos, as was the river that joined the Platte
close by. For a decade and more, prior to its sale
to the government, the post was something the
mountain men had depended upon during hard
times, a place to trade with Sioux, Cheyenne, and
Arapaho alike.

Now the single rash act of one man could well
bring about a bloodbath and the burning of the
government way station, because more Cheyennes
would ride in as soon as Leg-in-the-Water sent
word; after that it was merely a matter of time. In
the final analysis, a two-hundred-man federal garrison was no match for the assembled Cheyenne
nation. Even presuming that Everts could actually
manage to get a courier through to Kearney, Lar-

amie would be a clutter of charcoal and bones, before reinforcements could arrive.

McLafferty glanced at Moon. Her jaw was set and her eyes narrowed, the beautiful face now transformed into a mask of determined hatred. Given her impulsive disposition, Mike had reservations about Leg-in-the-Water's decision to allow her to accompany them into the fort. Her desire for revenge, immediate and direct, could well get in the way of any attempt by Capt. Everts to deal with the murder of an Indian by a white man. But Moon was not to be denied, and the chief had consented.

Revenge, not justice—that was what Mike wanted. He had little or no faith that white law would punish the murder of an Indian by an emigrant on his way to California. Everts had certainly not been charged with the protection of Indians—quite the reverse. And in nearly all cases, white man's law operated in one direction only. The death of his blood brother White Bull demanded individual action, not faith in a highly imperfect system. From a Down East point of view, the Cheyennes and all other Indian peoples along the trail westward were considered as armed and intelligent grizzlies, potentially dangerous animals to be manipulated or coerced into amiable behavior. When the immediate goal of westward expansion was essentially complete, whatever Indians remained would be herded onto reservations where the land lacked obvious utility to a growing United States of America.

In the present instance, McLafferty hoped the Cheyenne warriors would withdraw so that Laroque and his cohorts could continue their journey to the California goldfields. Somewhere ahead, beyond protection of upright posts and bluecoated soldiers, would come a moment of reckoning. As he saw the matter, there was simply no way for Jean Laroque to escape him. And when the confrontation came, it would have to be man-to-man. If White Bull were looking back from his place in the Spirit World, his honor could not be cleansed by the image of a Frenchman's body dangling at the end of a rope, a consequence that was highly unlikely in any case. But if Mike himself killed Laroque in a fair contest, then it was almost as if White Bull, working through his close friend, had struck back from beyond the grave.

Just what it was that would satisfy Moon Morning Star McLafferty didn't know, but he suspected strongly that she herself still wished to end the Frenchman's life. In dealing with despised prisoners, the High Plains Indians almost universally turned the victims over to the women for torture. Death by fire was not an uncommon fate in such circumstances.

Leg-in-the-Water raised his rifle and fired it into the air, McLafferty and Fiddlehead Wilson following the chief's example. The four riders then proceeded slowly toward the stockade gateway, its heavy doors now being opened to allow them to enter.

Captain Everts met the Cheyenne delegation in the midst of the parade grounds, an area partly filled by a dozen or more prairie schooners that had been brought in as a precaution against retaliation by the aroused Indians. Three adjutants stood a few paces behind their leader, while across the way, close by the Conestogas, twenty soldiers were at parade rest. A number of emigrants milled around nearby.

"I welcome the chief of the Cheyennes into the fort," Everts said in a voice that sounded rather too formal, "because I know him to be a man of goodwill."

Leg-in-the-Water nodded, his face utterly without expression, arms folded across his chest.

"I understand the situation somewhat better now," Everts continued, "thanks to Mr. Wilson here. A killing has taken place in your village, presumably by one of the emigrants to whom I am presently giving protection. Who is it that you wish to accuse? Is this woman the widow of the dead man? Perhaps she should return to your village before we discuss the matter further."

"She will stay," Leg-in-the-Water said, the tone of his voice suggesting the matter was not to be compromised.

Everts glanced from one face to another. "I've seen her before," he said. "In fact, she hardly appears Indian at all. A half-breed, perhaps?"

"You waste time with words," Leg-in-the-Water replied. "Everts, you say that your bluecoats are here to keep peace between my people and those who pass through Cheyenne lands. Now your word will be tested. That man standing over there, next to the wagon that has no canvas top, the man with the black beard, he is the one. He came into my village as a guest, and he murdered White Bull, one of my warriors."

"You saw this happen, Leg-in-the-Water?"

"Yes, I was there. Give me this man called Laroque, and I will tell my warriors to return to their lodges."

"It's not as simple as that. You follow your law, Chief, but I must follow the law of the white man. If Jean Laroque has committed a crime, then I will order that a hearing be held." Capt. Everts' gaze shifted. "You—you're Michael McLafferty, I'm told. Did you witness the murder? I understand you had a special friendship for the dead man, is that right?"

"That's correct, Captain. No, I was not in the Cheyenne village at the time. But your man Laroque, he's wanted for murder in St. Louis, if I'm not mistaken. That's a civil matter, isn't it? Look. I don't need to be speaking for Leg-in-the-Water, but if you want witnesses to what happened, there are probably twenty or so Cheyennes out there on the hill who were standing no more than a few feet away when the murder took place."

"You were formerly an agent for Mr. Sublette, I understand. You know how things are out here. In any case, you weren't present when the alleged crime was committed, and Mr. Wilson here wasn't there either. Leg-in-the-Water, you haven't even brought me a witness, let alone a corpse. How do I know there was a killing at all? Yet you've surrounded my fort, an act of war, in violation of all our treaties. I cannot and will not capitulate to blackmail. The government has charged me with protecting the emigrants and—"

"Bring the man over here," Leg-in-the-Water said. "Let him speak his words—let him tell you himself what happened."

Capt. Everts shrugged, gave the order for Jean Laroque to be called forward. One of the subordinate officers, a lieutenant named Ely Van Norden, did a brisk about-face and strode across the pa-

rade grounds to where Laroque and several of his
fellow rivermen, as well as numerous other emigrants, were standing. McLafferty recognized the
officer, remembered seeing him in St. Louis several months earlier; he recalled also that the man
was leading a troop the length of the California
Trail as a minor government effort to enforce
order along the way.

After a moment's discussion and some energetic
arm-waving and pointing by Jean Laroque, Van
Norden led the boss of the rivermen and two of
his cohorts across the grounds to the spot where
negotiations were taking place. McLafferty recognized one of Laroque's companions as Cottonmouth Chardin; the other, a younger fellow with
squinting eyes, he had not seen before, except
perhaps momentarily on the docks in Omaha.

Mike and Jean Laroque glared at each other for
a moment, and then the Frenchman grinned.

"Mr. Laroque," the captain began, "Chief Leg-
in-the-Water accuses you—"

At that moment Moon gave a cry and drew a
knife from within her bodice. She threw herself
forward, lashing out at Laroque, who leapt backward, one arm flung up to protect himself.

The squint-eyed man stepped into Moon's path
in an attempt to protect his booshway just as the
shining blade leapt forward a second time. The
steel sliced into his throat, severing the cartilage of
the voice box and dropping the young man to his
hands and knees.

McLafferty grasped Moon from behind, wrestling the knife away from her, while Everts and
Van Norden attempted to assist the stricken indi-

vidual, stanching the flow of blood with a yellow bandanna.

"*Sacre Dieu*," Laroque howled, "the bitch, she tries to kill me."

Chardin drew a revolver, backed off a few steps, and stood ready to fire should an appropriate target present itself. "*Merde alors*," he growled, "Carl-the-Squint, he's finished. Goddamn it, Jean. I tell you not to come over here."

Within moments the young riverman lay dead on the hard-packed surface of the parade grounds, and Everts ordered his troops forward to enforce the arrest of Moon Morning Star.

Leg-in-the-Water, McLafferty, and Wilson were bodily surrounded and escorted to the gates.

Leg-in-the-Water called immediately for a meeting of his council, and the mood of the group was one of black anger. A vote in favor of attacking the fort was evidently in the offing, but McLafferty demanded to be heard.

"Cheyenne warriors, listen to my words. You all know me, and you know that a sacred bond existed between White Bull and Red Coyote. We were close friends, and we mingled our blood and so became as brothers, exchanging rifles and horses. No man among you desires justice more than I do."

The members of the council nodded at the introductory remarks, but as Mike realized, they were listening merely as a formality.

"What you now propose to do will have consequences far beyond this day. It is not Everts alone against whom you will be fighting. The United States Army has many troops and many weapons.

Even if Fort Laramie is destroyed, and all the bluecoats in it, many more will come into your lands, and many of your people will be killed. Your own wives will cut off their hair and scar themselves."

Their eyes . . . What I am saying is of no consequence to them . . . they have always fought one battle at a time, and right now they know they can take the fort, at whatever cost. . . .

"You will be able to exact a terrible revenge upon the whites for the murder of White Bull, but Moon Morning Star, his widow, will be killed in the process."

"If we do nothing," Leg-in-the-Water said, "the soldiers will hang her. They will see only that she has killed one of those worthless white men. What do you say to this, Red Coyote?"

"I say you are right, Leg-in-the-Water. That will happen unless something is done, but burning the fort is not the answer."

"We continue to listen, Red Coyote," one of the old counselors said, "but we hear nothing that makes sense."

"After what has happened," McLafferty responded, "Captain Everts will make no more negotiations. You know the man better than I do, so you also know I speak the truth. But one of the officers is a man who recently led troops up from St. Louis—I know this because I saw him there last winter. His name is Ely Van Norden, and he's no stranger to these lands. He will talk to me—at least I think he will. What I propose is this: I think it's possible to rescue Moon. Van Norden knows what will happen if White Bull's widow is not released, even if Captain Everts doesn't."

"Let's say that you are able to succeed," Leg-in-the-Water objected, "yet even then, the man who killed White Bull will still not be punished. What do you say to that?"

"If I can secure the release of Moon Morning Star, then the Cheyennes and Arapahos must withdraw completely from the area of Fort Laramie. You must let it be known that you've gone off to hunt buffalo, far up the Chugwater or over to Horse Creek. The whole village must be removed."

"Red Coyote's plan will help no one but the bluecoats," Leg-in-the-Water said. "I think I must now ask my council what to do."

"Hear the rest of my words, Cheyennes. I was blood brother to White Bull, and it's through me that his spirit calls for revenge. This Jean Laroque is no stranger to me. I have fought him before, and that's how he got the scar on his face. I speak the truth. If the Cheyennes go buffalo hunting, then Laroque and the others will continue on their way to the West. I will follow him and kill him, as is just."

"Will you bring his scalp to us so that we can burn it?" one of the council members asked. "It is right for you to go on such a revenge-taking, but how can we know what has happened? If Jean Laroque is allowed to leave our lands, perhaps we will never hear any more about him."

"I too am going far to the West, but I will take Moon Morning Star with me," McLafferty said, making the decision on the spot. "That is how it should be. If I were living among your people, then Moon would become my wife, just as Jacques White Bull would become my son. I would be expected to take care of them, even as White Bull would have done, had I been killed, leaving behind me a defenseless woman and child."

Defenseless. The last word in the world one should use to describe Moon Morning Star. He pictured the knife leaping out, the young man Chardin had called Carl-the-Squint falling forward, blood jetting from several arteries . . .

But Leg-in-the-Water nodded. "We will try Red Coyote's plan," the chief said. "If he can bring White Bull's widow back to us, then maybe we will go buffalo hunting. Perhaps we will burn the fort first, perhaps not."

Guards stationed on the battlements of Fort Laramie observed what appeared to be a desperate race: two white men, one in black and mounted on a big gray, the other in buckskins and astride a mule, were fleeing from a band of Indians. The two white men turned in their saddles, firing pistols at their pursuers, while the Indians screamed and launched a hail of arrows.

By some miracle the two men were able to outrun their pursuers and were heading straight for the gates of Fort Laramie.

The soldiers opened fire at the Cheyennes, who pulled up just beyond range and milled about, brandishing rifle and lance.

Capt. Robert W. Everts was summoned immediately; he sized up the situation and surmised that some sort of ruse was under way. The fugitives, he saw, were McLafferty and Fiddlehead Wilson.

Well, it was possible that their Cheyenne brothers had turned against them, perhaps deciding to put the two whites to death inasmuch as even

Indians had better sense than to launch an assault against heavily defended battlements.

Four months had passed since Everts had taken command of the garrison, and at first he tentatively concluded that all the warnings about the treachery of the Indians were generated simply out of fear of the unknown. Indeed, he found the Cheyennes to be tractable and good-natured—at least until the present. He had believed Leg-in-the-Water to be a man of some vision with regard to the future of his own people, though suspicious by nature and, in the final analysis, a savage hardly able to comprehend the values of civilized life.

Most likely Leg-in-the-Water had turned on McLafferty and Wilson.

Everts called down to Ely Van Norden. "Lieutenant, grant those men entry and then bolt the gate again. At the first sign of an assault, a general order to open fire."

Van Norden barked out a crisp "Yes, sir!" and motioned to his corporal.

McLafferty and Wilson came charging into the enclosure, eyes wide and mounts blowing heavily.

"Gawd-cursed red divvels," Wilson howled, slipping from the saddle and adjusting his bearskin cap. "A man's a damned idjit to trust a one o' 'em!"

"A quick shift of loyalties, gentlemen?" Van Norden asked. "Those who play tag with Satan sometimes get their hands burned."

"Moralizing we don't need," McLafferty bellowed. "You bastards took your own sweet time opening up."

"The captain's a careful man," Van Norden replied, "but perhaps not careful enough. Would you like to tell me what happened out there?"

"Damned near got kilt, that's all," Fiddlehead hissed between missing teeth. "Ye got any whiskey? This child's too old to go gettin' his ha'r lifted now."

Capt. Everts walked slowly to where Van Norden, McLafferty, and Wilson were standing. "Gentlemen," he said, "welcome to my humble dwelling."

More Indians had evidently arrived, responding to Leg-in-the-Water's call for assistance, and now the total number surrounding Fort Laramie was estimated at well over a thousand. Capt. Everts, however, was still not genuinely concerned—more annoyed than anything else.

Not even with darkness did the Cheyennes withdraw, though that was what Everts had anticipated. Instead, they held their positions, and campfires glowed both from the rise and from close by the scant cover of elder and cottonwood at the edge of broad meadows on either side.

Sometimes, the commanding officer concluded, even strategy manuals were incorrect.

Fiddlehead Wilson talked with groups of Argonauts, telling them that he had just recently returned from California and that the tales of quick riches were in no way exaggerated. When one of Laroque's men protested that Wilson had been in Omaha, Wilson merely shrugged.

"Of course I were, ye dumb-ass. I come in from California two months ago, and now this child's headin' back to get some more gold. Spent 'er all on whiskey an' hoors, boys, an' had me a hell of a time all around."

McLafferty, however, was with Lt. Ely Van Norden, in the latter's quarters. The two men were smoking Mike's cigars and talking.

"I've heard of you, all right," Van Norden said. "American Fur, I believe? That, and a gambler. The word was you'd settled down in St. Louis."

"Yep," Mike replied, puffing on his cigar and tipping the ashes into an empty powder tin Van Norden had brought out, "and I've heard of you. Wounded on the Rosebud two winters back when you and your men got in the way of a band of Gros Ventres. You've been in the High Plains long enough to have some idea of the Indian mind. Am I correct?"

Van Norden nodded.

"So how long do you figure it'll be before Leg-in-the-Water loses his patience? When that happens, he won't leave off until Fort Laramie's burned to the sod, and you know it. He's got the manpower out there to take whatever casualties are necessary to get the job done. It's just a matter of having a few crazy dogs work their way in close enough. Once the tinder box starts burning, they'll find a way over the battlements, and then it's every gringo for himself."

"So you and Wilson faked a little death chase to convince Everts to let you inside? That's it, isn't it? Otherwise you'd have headed down the Platte, knowing Leg-in-the-Water wasn't going to leave his prime objective. Why come to me? It's Captain Everts you need to talk to. I gather you wish to have the half-breed woman released."

"The captain doesn't listen very well. If he has his way, he'll end up commanding a fort full of dead men."

"I hear what you're saying, McLafferty. You want me to hog-tie my superior officer and turn the bitch free? Jesus, man, she committed murder. Everts intends to hold a hearing once Leg-in-the-Water gets calmed down. She won't get strung up until after that."

"And Laroque?"

"We both know the United States Army can't turn over a white man to a bunch of angry Indians, no matter what he's done. It's just not in the cards."

"True, true," McLafferty agreed. "Van Norden, is it possible, just possible, that we could arrange for Moon Morning Star to escape? What's to be gained by hanging her? She was after the man who murdered her husband—was honor-bound to make some sort of attempt. The squint-eyed kid had the bad luck to get in the way of a sow grizzly, that's all."

Van Norden laughed bitterly and shook his head. "You want me to facilitate an escape? I'd be court-martialed and put in irons for ten years. McLafferty, you're out of your mind. I should throw you into the stockade with her."

"Desperate times require desperate solutions." Mike shrugged. "Get the woman loose, and I have Leg-in-the-Water's assurance he'll pull back. His people were all set to move south to Horse Creek for the buffalo hunt. Give him the woman, and that'll be enough for the old thief to save face. You've got to give him something, damn it, or the whole emigration route's going to get closed down, and it'll take a battalion or so to open things up again. Even that won't do dead men any good."

Van Norden puffed on his cigar, reached out to the empty powder tin.

"I would like to get my troops to California," he said at last. "There's a promotion in it for me, and the prospect of a hero's death doesn't fit into my plans just yet. I'm going to pretend that this entire conversation never took place. I'm going to tell you not to do anything foolish, even though I know damned well you'll go ahead and do it. But for God's sake, McLafferty, don't tell *me* what you're planning. If you do, I'm duty-bound to stop you. You understand that."

"Of course," Mike nodded. "Well, I had to give it a try. Everything's a matter of strategy, when a man gets right down to it. So Leg-in-the-Water and his boys wipe out Fort Laramie and burn the place to the ground, what the hell? Fiddlehead and I ride off to California in the morning and won't even hear about it until we're down the road a piece. You feel up to a few hands of poker later this evening, Ely? Might as well let me steal your tin. It's not going to do a dead man any good."

"You put the matter in the most charming way." Van Norden smiled.

She hated being locked inside the small room with barred windows, but even more she hated being helpless. If only the knife had struck true, then her purpose would have been fulfilled, and it would not matter what the whites might do to her.

But that wasn't correct either. In acting upon her desperate need for revenge against White Bull's murderer, she had forgotten about her own son, little Jacques. Would he be all right without her? This new loss would come so directly upon the death of his father that in years to come he would scarcely remember what had happened at all. Such were the minds of children, as she herself well knew, their capacity to blunt pain, to hold grief inside them for years at a time, throughout the long succession of seasons that growing to adulthood required. Jacques was four years old, barely of an age for memory to retain events in their proper sequence. Then came some spark, some sudden awareness that one thing happened after another and could be held in memory in a fashion that represented reality. Moon herself had recollections back to her third year, but several of her friends could recall nothing in particular until after a fourth or even fifth winter had passed.

Would Leg-in-the-Water adopt her son, or would White Bull's parents? The latter seemed most likely, but in either case, then Jacques would be as well served as any child without parents possibly could be.

Moon recalled the death of her own mother and then, long after that tragedy, the death of her father. But she was older—Jacques was still so small, just changing from infanthood to boyhood!

She stared out through the barred window, saw groups of emigrants moving about. Some of them pointed in her direction.

Then White Bull's murderer came to the window and stared in at her, grinning and looking quite pleased with himself.

She spit at him and turned away, walked to the far wall, and refused to look at him again.

"*C'est la pudeur*," he said. "If only Jean had time, he would have taken you with him after he kills your buck. You spit at me, but I could make love to you so that you would wish not to spit anymore. Your lips, they have other uses, *non?* It is bad luck, *ma chérie*, now they will hang you, and we will both miss out on something good. I will bribe the guard, *peut-être*, and he will let Jean come in to visit with you. I show you what a big white man's toy looks like. You hear stories, ehh?"

She turned, glared hatred at him. "Jean Laroque," she said, her voice little more than a hiss, "I killed your young friend, but it's your blood I want. Leg-in-the-Water and McLafferty will capture you and turn you over to the Cheyenne women for torture. If they are able to rescue me, I'll cut off your white man's toy and force you to eat it before we burn you. But maybe not. Maybe I would like to see for myself what it's like. You have money? Go bribe the guard, then. There's a bed in here, and no one will think to disturb us. I'll be waiting for you, darling. . . ."

Laroque studied her face, ran the tip of his tongue back and forth between his lips. He nodded, turned, and was gone.

Moon approached the barred window, looked out in either direction. She could see the guard, but Jean Laroque had vanished.

Had she encouraged him sufficiently? If he somehow gained access to her, she still had the small, sharp-bladed knife White Bull had given her, a weapon she kept beneath her dress, in a pocket sheath under her breasts. After all, the soldiers could hang her only once. One thrust to the throat, and White Bull would be avenged, his memory honored.

*   *   *

Just before sundown the guard opened the safety window momentarily and pushed a plateful of food and a container of water inside. She waited a long while before touching anything.

It grew quiet in the enclosed area outside the cell, and Moon tried to sleep—but sleep would not come. Was Jacques all right? What had they told him? Was he old enough to comprehend the truth?

Hours passed, and she presumed the darkness had run half its course. Jean Laroque did not return—and Moon was uncertain whether she felt relief or disappointment. But if there was a way . . .

A few more hours and dawn would come. What would her captors do with her? She thought of the possibility of insisting that she was white, not Indian at all. With skin lighter than a Cheyenne's and a good command of English, she would be able to make a fairly good case for herself. In all likelihood, she could force Everts to give her the benefit of his vaunted white man's law. There were certain extenuating circumstances, after all, and even a prison sentence would not blunt her purpose but only postpone it.

Of course, it was possible that the soldiers would simply have her shot tomorrow, and then it would be over. Laroque was on his way westward, could be out of Cheyenne lands within a few days. If that happened, Leg-in-the-Water would in all likelihood take his revenge against some other whites. But Red Coyote McLafferty was also on his way west and had taken a vow for revenge. The thought gave her some solace, but the issue lacked certainty. McLafferty, after all, was a white man, and whites often allowed matters of honor to fall by the side of the trail.

At last she dozed, then awakened suddenly, trembling. A voice. Had White Bull spoken to her from the land of the dead?

"Moon, damn it, where are you? Wake up—we've got about two minutes to get you out of here."

Red Coyote.

He grabbed her hand and pulled her forward, out onto the parade grounds and past the shadowed figure of a guard recumbent upon the ground, apparently unconscious.

Close by the stockade wall, in the shadows a few yards from the big gates, Fiddlehead Wilson joined them.

"What took ye so long?" the old trapper muttered. "An' where in hell's Van Norden? Thought he was goin' to spring the gate for us."

"Old Ely kind of got tied up, I guess you might say. I let him win a few hands of poker, and that was probably a mistake. In short, he began thinking the soldiers could hold off the entire Cheyenne Nation if need be, and so I had to club him over the skull and filch his key to the jailhouse door. Everts doesn't trust his own gendarmes, I guess. Anyhow, I cut up one of his blankets to bind the good lieutenant with. Gagged and everything, Van Norden's as pretty as a picture. Now, what we've got to do is get by those two sentries, then run like hell before the boys on topside start taking target practice on us."

"Shouldn't be no great problem." Wilson snorted. "Jest strike up a bit o' conversation and then clump 'em."

"You take the short one, and I'll take the tall one," McLafferty whispered. "Just don't split the poor devil's head open beyond repair. And remember, once we're out of the gate, we're still not in the clear. Everts has set double watch tonight. The bluecoats have Whitney .44s up on the battlements, and they know how to use them."

"Guess we'll do us a bit o' mule dancin' then. Well, this child's a mite old, but I guess I'm up for it."

"The lieutenant," Moon whispered, "he's tied up? I don't understand . . ."

"He wouldn't listen to reason," McLafferty said quickly, "so I had no choice. Damn it, Moon, now you do what I tell you. Stay right with me and Fiddlehead, and don't go tearing off on your own. If we get hit, either of us, don't stop. Keep running straight for the hill, but weave back and forth so as not to make an easy target. There's enough moonlight coming through the clouds for a good marksman to draw aim, but that can't be helped. We've got to make our break now, or the whole scheme may come unwound, if you'll pardon the jest. Now, then—we've got to club those guards without them making a fuss and alerting the lads topside, then our chances are at least even."

Fiddlehead laughed. "Run, hell, ye damned fool. Look back behind us."

Close by the wall were Wilson's mule and McLafferty's gray.

"I'll be damned," Mike said. "I'm not even going to ask how you managed that little miracle. But how are we going to get the animals through the gate without alerting the watch? Did you think it through?"

"O' course I did. Ye figger this old hawg's some pure greenhorn? After we do the job on the sentries, I'll bring the varmints up, real quiet like. Then we open the gate, and away we be."

McLafferty considered the plan. "All right, then. Take Moon with you. She rides the gray. I'll throw open the gate and you two make tracks. I'll manage on foot—slip along the stockade wall while you've got their attention."

"Red Coyote, then you will have to run," she protested. "They will shoot you."

"Do what I say, you little hellcat. The only chance we've got at Laroque without causing a full-scale war is for you to make it up that hill to Leg-in-the-Water. Move now."

6 Lt. Ely Van Norden, his head bandaged due to a scalp wound he had received during the escape of the Cheyenne woman, stood on a parapet with Capt. Everts, the two officers taking turns with a field glass, scanning the hill and lowland groves of elder and cottonwood along the Laramie River to one side of the fort and the North Platte to the other.

"They seem to have withdrawn, sir," the lieutenant remarked, not for the first time. "The watch says there's been no sign of them since last night."

"It's my fault twice over," Everts admitted. "First for agreeing to talk with that damnable squaw present, and again in falling for a simple ploy—allowing wolves back into the sheepfold. I want them brought in, Van Norden. I don't care if it means taking on the whole Cheyenne Nation. I want that woman and I want Wilson and McLafferty—God in heaven! I want McLafferty! How could I have been so stupid?"

Van Norden shook his head gently. "You really had little choice, other than that of holding what would have amounted to a civil trial. Even then, if the woman hadn't been allowed in right off to make her accusation, she would almost certainly have made some kind of attempt on Laroque's life at the hearing, presuming you'd held one. Beyond that, what if the chase had been real? We'd have had the rare treat of watching the savages kill two of our own."

"It was a difficult situation all around, but that doesn't excuse anything," Everts said. "In the first place, Indians aren't allowed to testify in either criminal or civil proceedings. But damn it, I needed at least some kind of witness. Hell, Van Norden, I saw it coming—I saw it in the woman's eyes. And yet, savage or not, one doesn't expect such a thing. My intuition said one thing, my civilized intellect another."

"Captain, your actions were completely prudent and befitting a commanding officer. You're blameless in the matter."

"Will that, in effect, be what your report says, Lieutenant? I'm beginning to feel that you'd prefer to see the matter dropped. I won't have it, Van Norden."

"Of course, sir. I do think it would be advisable to wait, however. McLafferty and Wilson, at least, aren't going to remain with Leg-in-the-Water's people forever. Things will go much more smoothly if we take them once they've left the Cheyennes. We could send out scouts—"

"Bloody hell! If your men can't handle the task, by God, I'll put a price on their damned heads. All the cutthroat scum of the East Coast is on its way to California. There's hardly a man in ten of them who would hesitate to kill a fugitive for a thousand dollars."

Everts turned away from the parapet, took two rapid steps along the walkway, turned back, hitting the palm of his hand with a closed fist. "I hate having been outwitted. Why in hell didn't I realize something was up?"

"None of us had any inkling. Why on earth would two white men risk their lives to rescue a widowed squaw? She's a beauty, to be sure, but that doesn't account for it."

"These mountain men"—Everts scowled—"they're no more than savages themselves. I'd have supposed better of Michael McLafferty, however. Sublette thought highly of the man."

"That was before McLafferty turned professional gambler, and blood brother to the dead Indian. What do you make of that, Captain?"

Everts shook his head. "By this time tomorrow, if there's no report of indigenes in the vicinity, I'll grant the emigrants leave to pursue their journey—and glad to be rid of that ugly Frenchman and his band of degenerates, the others as well. More wagons camped on the far side of the river already, waiting permission to cross. You haven't been here, haven't seen it. Thousands of them, thousands, all of them hell-bent for sudden riches. Well, I'll expect you and your troops to bring in the fugitives. Ely, I tell you I've had nothing but trouble with these bands of gold-seekers ever since I took command of Fort Laramie. Some are good, upstanding men, but others represent a criminal element, the dregs of society. God knows what brands of mischief they've left behind them— deserted families, warrants for their arrest, debts. . . . It's America's destiny to possess the continent, and I believe that, but we're allowing it to occur at the hands of the worst of men. With luck, I'll be relieved of this wretched command by the end of the year. I'm hoping for transfer back to West Point and, of course, for a promotion. Another few incidents like this one, and I'm likely to end my career in the military as a private."

Everts scowled, cleared his throat, and continued. "Bring in McLafferty and the girl—the oldtimer as well. He's as guilty as the other two. After you've done that, you're free to police the trail as you see fit, in accordance with your command from Washington."

Van Norden touched one hand casually to the brim of his hat. "As you wish, Captain," he said. "But for God's sake, sir, don't turn the damned voyageurs loose with a thousand-dollar reward in mind. You'll be asking for mayhem from here to the Pacific. For that kind of money, they'll be shooting one another. You'll have a wagonload of white scalps before it's over."

"That's entirely up to you, Lieutenant. Bring them in, and there'll be no need for such measures. I'm proud of my record, Van Norden. I will not have such a blot as this botched job upon it, whatever the cost. Do you understand me?"

"Quite clearly, sir," Van Norden replied, repeating his salute before turning to descend to the parade grounds.

Lt. Van Norden, accompanied by his own thirty troops and an additional thirty from Fort Laramie, drew up at the edge of Leg-in-the-Water's encampment the following afternoon near sundown, having experienced no great difficulty in following the traces of a village of several hundred people moving across the plains toward Chugwater. The women were still at work erecting lodges for the night, and the chief himself strode out to meet the soldiers, standing with his arms crossed before the occupied area as if to prevent entry by the bluecoats.

"Moon Morning Star and Red Coyote McLafferty are no longer with us," Leg-in-the-Water said in response to Van Norden's inquiry. "We have not seen them since we left Fort Laramie. Red Coyote told us he was going to the great water to the west. Moon Morning Star and her son went with him, for he has taken his brother's family as his own. I cannot tell you more than that."

"No doubt the old fox is lying, sir," muttered Van Norden's aide, a burly, black-mustached sergeant by the name of Wells. "We'll turn them up when we search the camp, likely."

"Would you care to call him a liar, Wells?" the lieutenant hissed, and then said aloud, "May I assume we have your permission to search for them here, Chief Leg-in-the-Water?"

The chief seemed to swell at these words, the lines around his eyes deepening into a granitic scowl.

"You doubt the word of the war leader of the Cheyenne people, Bluecoat Chief?"

A number of tribal elders had gathered behind the chief, each with arms crossed and appearing as immovable and hard-faced as a block of stone. And behind these was a casual grouping of younger warriors, some mounted, others on foot, all armed, although the rifles, lances, and bows were not at the moment lifted.

"I certainly had no intention of insulting Chief

Leg-in-the-Water," Van Norden said, his gaze touching the warriors and beyond them the village. "I thought perhaps someone in your village may—"

"If you do not wish to call me a liar, then you have no need to enter our camp," the chief said. "There is nothing here for your men, and it may be that my young men will take offense. If that happens, then lives may be lost needlessly. I cannot always control the young warriors."

"I personally believe every word you speak. Leg-in-the-Water is well-known for his straight tongue," Van Norden replied. "But the Great White Father in Washington—"

"If the Great White Father does not believe my words, then let him come here and tell me so. You have let the murderer of White Bull go free, and yet you bring soldiers among my people to look for one who has done an honorable thing. Tell your White Father that Leg-in-the-Water has no more ears for his words. You may leave us in peace, but if the bluecoats come to our village again, there will be blood. That is not what I want, and I think you do not wish this to happen either. I have no more to say to you." The chief abruptly drew his buffalo robe closer about himself and turned back to the village.

"Chief Leg-in-the-Water," Van Norden called out.

The Cheyenne leader stopped, faced the troops again, but did not speak.

"If you *should* happen to see McLafferty and the girl," the lieutenant continued, "you'd better let them know that Everts will probably post a reward on their heads—and Laroque and some of the others aren't likely to be particular how they collect a thousand dollars. You tell them that."

Leg-in-the-Water did not reply. He merely turned away again, not looking at the lieutenant or his men as he strode back toward the encampment. The elders turned also when their leader did, but the younger warriors remained in place, staring at the troop, a wind lifting locks of long black hair, brushing at feathers on heads and lances.

Van Norden watched them for a long moment, then turned in his saddle to signal his own men to move out. "Shit!" he muttered.

"Sir, you know they have the fugitives in there," Sgt. Wells said. "May I ask why we don't simply go in after them?"

"You heard the chief, Sergeant. McLafferty and the girl struck west for Laramie. So we're returning to Laramie for further instruction."

"But, sir . . ."

"Frankly and confidentially, Sergeant, the fugitives are not worth the lives of a dozen or more good men. Perhaps Captain Everts feels differently. I'm proceeding, as ordered, using my best judgment. That's why I'm an officer, as I understand it. Any more questions, Wells?"

Van Norden snapped the last words with an impatient glance at his subordinate, who shook his head and pressed his lips firmly together and did not venture to question the lieutenant further.

"Moon Morning Star," Leg-in-the-Water said after Van Norden's troops had vanished into the distance, "it is no longer safe for you here among the Cheyenne people, even though you have been one of us for much of your life. I have told you the bluecoat leader's words. The captain at the fort will not give up so easily. He will have you arrested—he will try, at least. And that will cause war between us and the bluecoats. Perhaps he will even attempt to arrest me, I do not know. Yet I believe you will be better off, safer, someplace away from these lands, at least for a time. You have promised before all that you will take revenge upon Jean Laroque."

Moon could see what was coming. "I will not leave without my son," she said. "You must not ask that of me."

"I would never do such a thing, even though Bright Shield would like it to be that way. No, we have always respected the wishes of the children in such matters, and Jacques White Bull clearly wishes to remain with his mother. But my counselors will not allow me to send a young mother and her child off alone—such a thing would be banishment, and you have done nothing except what the honor of your husband required. . . ."

"When a warrior dies," Bright Shield said, "then his family must take in his wives and children. Often a brother is obliged to become a new husband, though he must court the woman and receive permission to marry his sister. I have no other son, however, and yet my son had a brother— and that is Red Coyote. Daughter-in-law, you must take this man as your husband, and he must agree to care for you and for little Jacques. If this can be so, then I will feel better about allowing the child to leave us. Red Coyote, will you agree to my request?"

McLafferty glanced at Moon, then had difficulty in swallowing. "I have also taken a vow for revenge," he said. "Someone must avenge the honor of the one-who-is-dead. It would not be sufficient for the warriors to take scalps from the Crows— and that would only renew war between the two nations, in any case. The man who committed the murder is the man who must die. If what Van Norden said about a price on our heads comes true, then I may not have to search for Laroque at all. He will not be foolish enough to come after me among your people, but once we are away from Cheyenne lands, perhaps he will be trying to find me. I will make it easy for him—when the time is right. I will follow him clear to California if I must, and then I will bring the man's scalp back to Bright Shield, so that he may hang it from his lodgepole. I will take Moon Morning Star and Jacques White Bull with me, if they are willing to go. When we have accomplished our task, then we will return to Leg-in-the-Water's village."

"If ye wants my opinion, Mr. Mike," Fiddlehead Wilson snorted, "ye're a damned fool if ye show your face around here until after the gov'mint's sent Everts to fight the British, or some such. Sure the boys'll be havin' another war before too long. Until then, ye're inviting trouble to your table. Wagh! That's what this child thinks."

"Moon," Bright Shield asked, "will you accept our judgment? Your husband would have wished it, I think, and that is why he and Red Coyote—"

"I belonged to one-who-is-dead, but now I belong to no man. If Red Coyote wishes to go with me and so help to avenge the man who was his brother, then I will accept that. My father-in-law knows I am in mourning. He knows I have no wish to think of another husband—not now, and probably not ever. I loved the man who was father to my son, and my thoughts are only upon avenging his death."

Moon glanced at Bright Shield, saw deep pain in his features—the same pain that possessed her. She stepped toward the older man and put her head against his chest. He embraced her, clumsily patted at her hair.

"You were a good wife to my son," Bright Shield said. "Grass Flower and I will miss you very much. We are losing a son and a daughter as well, and also a grandson. Perhaps one day you will return to us, just as Red Coyote says. He is a good man, Moon Morning Star. Together you will accomplish this thing for one who was dear to all of us."

Capt. Everts was, of course, furious. The response was no more than Lt. Van Norden had anticipated.

"You mean to tell me that you allowed that old fraud to bluff you out of searching for the fugitives? Has it occurred to you, Lieutenant, that even two hundred or so Cheyenne warriors are no match for sixty United States troops armed with government-issue carbines?"

"In my judgment, sir, the natives would have resisted. The matter, to my mind, did not warrant starting an Indian war. My orders from Washington are to protect emigrants along the California Trail. Stirring up hostility among the indigenes would seem to work at cross purpose to that objective, sir."

Everts spat on the ground, paced rapidly back and forth on the parade grounds. After a while the captain, struck temporarily dumb by the extremity of his disgust, turned his back and strode away to his quarters.

Within the hour he returned, hammer in one hand and several sheets of paper in the other, and began tacking up notices in various locations inside the stockade. When he finished, he dispatched a corporal with the remaining hand-printed signs to be posted outside.

When the captain had returned to his quarters, Lt. Ely Van Norden strolled over to the front of the headquarters building to read the parchment Everts had nailed there. Carefully inked in very large block letters, it read:

Reward
$500 APIECE
for the return of the fugitives Moon Morning Star, a half-breed woman wanted for murder, and Michael McLafferty, gambler, late of St. Louis, wanted for aiding in said woman's escape from custody of the United States government.

Van Norden took off his hat, rubbed one hand hard down across his face.

"Good Christ, Everts," he mumbled, "this is the last thing we need. But I guess I saw it coming."

Van Norden returned to his quarters. He could see in what direction his next orders from the captain lay.

The Cheyennes continued their move south to the Chugwater, the entire exodus like a strange parade, first through a deserted land of scrub cedar and sage barrens, alternating with meadows and stands of pine and fir. For twenty miles they continued beside Laramie River, Leg-in-the-Water and a few of his warriors riding ahead, another band of riders trailing the group. Boys drove the great herd of horses, while women, children, and old people walked along casually. The atmosphere was almost that of celebration, despite the grim events of the past few days, people happily talking with one another as they led travois-harnessed horses. Even a number of the omnipresent camp dogs had small bundles strapped to their backs, while others dragged miniature travois rigs.

On the second day they reached the mouth of the Chugwater, which the women decided would be an excellent site for the village. Word of the decision came to Leg-in-the-Water, the warrior chief nodding his agreement.

Within the hour skeletons of tepees began to rise, bundles of poles were unwrapped and set into place and fastened with leather thongs, the women and children working together.

Words of farewell had already been spoken, and McLafferty, Moon (with Jacques clinging to her from behind), and Wilson continued upstream along the Laramie.

The stream ran rapidly, cascading along through stretches of rapids. Forested ridges swelled up on either side of this seldom-used trail, which would ultimately bring them once more to the North Platte River at the mouth of the Medicine Bow.

McLafferty's plan included a possible interception of Laroque and his men, somewhere near Independence Rock and Devil's Gate, where the California Trail turned up the Sweetwater on its way toward South Pass and Fort Bridger.

Moon talked little during their four-day ride to the Platte, responding briefly if at all to attempts at conversation by either McLafferty or Wilson. Jacques, however, was not so taciturn, seeming to prefer riding with one or another of the two men, whom he bullied into telling stories as they moved along.

By afternoon of the third day, coming down Muddy Creek toward the Medicine Bow, Mike ran out of tales, much to the disappointment of Jacques White Bull, who thereupon demanded that he be allowed to ride with "Uncle Fiddlehead." The latter, he insisted, would never run out of stories to tell.

Moon cooked their meals, fresh venison that McLafferty had managed to take, but she herself ate little. Wilson's peculiar mixture of coffee beans, dried willow bark, and sage buds produced what Mike considered a vile-tasting brew, but it was sufficient for Moon, and McLafferty began to badger her, as he might a child, to get her to eat.

"You are not my husband, Mike McLafferty," she shot back, "and you are not my father, either. I will eat when I feel like it, and not before. There's only one reason why I came with you at all."

"You don't have to get pettish, Moon. We've both got a job we've set in front of us, and we'll be able to do it a great deal easier if you don't turn yourself into a skeleton."

"Damn you," she said, her dark eyes blazing. "I'm not your wife, whatever Bright Shield and Leg-in-the-Water said. Keep your distance and leave me alone."

"Come along now, Moon child," Wilson put in. "Mr. Mike, he's just tryin' to be helpful. O' course you're mournin' for White Bull, but ye cain't do him no good this way."

Jacques swallowed the mouthful of meat he'd been chewing, glanced from one adult to another. "They're right, Mother," he said. "You always tell me to eat so that I'll grow to be as big as my father."

Moon stood up, was about to throw her coffee, tin cup and all, into the campfire when she caught herself. "Now even my own son turns against me. If I'm not hungry, then why should I have to eat? Not because two *gringos* say I should."

"So's ye don't starve, that's why." Fiddlehead laughed, his gap-toothed grin gleaming in firelight. "Wagh! This child never seen such a cantankerous filly. Other than your big *tétons*, ma'am, ye don't weigh much more'n a stick right now, if ye'll pardon my observation."

Moon laughed softly in spite of herself, inwardly reflecting on the fact that men, basically, were all more or less alike. Seldom did they ever see a woman as more than her simple physical being—and that flaw of vision, she had long since concluded, applied to virtually everything. Men dealt with the surface of reality. Foolish children, that's what, and she hoped her own son would grow to manhood with greater powers of discrimination.

"Here, Mother," Jacques said, handing her a portion of roast flesh. "You must eat because—"

"All three of you against me? All right, then, I'll eat, if it pleases you so much." She pressed the morsel into her mouth, gagged momentarily, and then began to chew. She swallowed. "Are you satisfied now?"

"We're all growing edgy," Mike said. "Hell, Moon,

go ahead and starve yourself if you're of a mind to. I don't suppose I'll need any help in attending to our mutual friend. A female just gets in the way when a showdown comes. Isn't that so, Fiddle-head?"

"Ain't getting' into this one, if ye don't mind, Sonny."

Moon glared at McLafferty, part of her wanting to cry and part of her wanting to laugh. "I missed once," she replied. "I won't miss again. I will take Laroque's scalp when the time comes."

"With a little luck"—McLafferty shrugged—"he'll turn out to be twins. Then we can both do what pleases us."

Fiddlehead Wilson thought things over that night.

What he saw: a man and a woman who were basically attracted to each other but who, owing to circumstances, were in no position to admit to their feelings. Moon was mourning deeply for her dead husband. The lopped-off finger didn't mean much. That was to be expected. What was highly unusual with Moon was the degree to which grief had been converted to hatred, and hatred to abso-lute determination to secure revenge with her own hands.

As for Michael McLafferty? For whatever crazy reason, the man had gotten stuck on Moon years since—in fact, that was how he'd ended up being White Bull's blood brother. It had all started over this one particular female, sometimes bad-natured and maybe the prettiest thing in the mountains. Made a man growl just to look at her, by Gawd.

Whatever the case, Fiddlehead concluded, it would be best all around if he himself found some reason for leaving the two of them alone for a spell. Bright Shield and Leg-in-the-Water had given Moon to Big Mike, and right now that giving was creating a problem.

A more immediate problem than even revenge against Laroque lay in keeping clear of the brass-button boys. Everts wasn't likely to forget he'd had a prisoner scuttled out of his own jailhouse and out through his own bolted gate. If he took the trouble to send Van Norden after Leg-in-the-Water's band, he damned well wanted Moon for hanging—and McLafferty and Old Fiddlehead as well, for pulling it off. Good idea to stay clear of them boys . . .

Back to the matter at hand: here was a man that was stuck on a woman, only she was hitched to his best friend. Then Gawd's ax came down, and he found the lady given to him by her own people, only she's got something else on her mind, and it's going to take a long while to get over it. But still, it made sense. There was a kid to raise, and what man wouldn't want to bring up his own best friend's whelp? The woman would come around, Fiddlehead was certain of it. . . .

Well before sunup, while Mike and Moon and little Jacques were still sleeping—McLafferty twenty feet from the campfire on one side, Moon twenty feet on the other, almost like admitting that they really wanted to be sleeping together—Fiddlehead Wilson quietly untethered his mules and rode away.

When McLafferty awoke, he found this note scrawled in charcoal on a flap of tanned deerhide:

> Gone to visit with Bridger.
> I'll be waitin fer ye.
>
> —FW

Man, woman, and child made good progress the next several days, hitting the North Platte and following it north through a deep gorge, then barren sagebrush hills, past evil-smelling alkali lakes, eventually coming to the Sweetwater's mouth and the strange granite dome of Independence Rock, a big gray mound heaped up from the surrounding plain, like the tip of a great gray egg.

At young Jacques' insistence, they took the time to climb to the top of the promontory.

"Might be a good idea at that," Mike agreed. "You can see for miles from up there. Could be we'll catch sight of some smoke or something— some sign of our friends on ahead."

It was near sunset when they reached the top, Jacques having made much of the climb clinging to Mike's back. They drank from a pool of clear rainwater in one of several catch-basins in the granite, rested, gazed out at a wide stretch and tumble of country around them. Southeast they could see the alkali flats they had passed, and to the north the shining loops of the Sweetwater as it meandered across its broad valley, water brassy gold in late-afternoon light. They saw no sign, however, of either Laroque's party or of bluecoats—no human presence whatsoever, in fact, as far as they could determine. A herd of antelope raced across the gray-green plains eastward, apparently set to flight by something, and above them a trio of ravens drifted in circles, one swooping low and shrieking at the human invasion of avian territory.

Jacques screamed back at the big birds, waving his arms and then stumbling and falling down in a heap of laughter. Mike and Moon glanced at each other and smiled, wind blowing a strand of black hair across the woman's face. Then suddenly, miraculously, she was laughing too, in tones of sheer delight, sheer pleasure in being alive, as the ravens, all three of them now, made another threatening turn, squawking indignantly.

On impulse, perhaps the same impulse that had prompted the woman's laughter, Mike scooped up Jacques on one arm and threw the other around Moon's waist, bear-hugging her against his side. For a moment she was pliant, leaning on him and grinning up into his face, but then she caught herself, stiffened, and shrugged out of the embrace.

Still, Mike thought, her temper had improved in the days since Fiddlehead's departure. They had both been sorry to discover the old mountaineer's note, Moon reacting at first almost as if she had been deserted.

"You can go too, if you want," she had told Mike. "There's no need for either of you men to be stuck with a woman and a baby. I can take care of Jacques and myself, no matter what Leg-in-the-Water or Bright Shield may have said."

"No doubt, no doubt," he teased. "But then who'll take care of me?"

Nonetheless, in spite of Moon's initial response, without Fiddlehead's presence as a sort of buffer between them, she and Mike almost of necessity came to rely more on each other's company.

They camped near Independence Rock that night, proceeding up the Sweetwater in the morning. During the next few days, they passed between the Green Mountains to the south, several snow-capped peaks visible from time to time, and a lower range to the north, the drainage itself rising

gradually to a gentle, sloping summit at South
Pass. They were well over seven thousand feet in
elevation, but the Continental Divide appeared
here as nothing more than a swell in a sagebrush
plain as they crossed on toward Green River, known
to many as Seedskeedee.

Near the pass they were overtaken by a thunderstorm, but finding no shelter on the broad,
sage-dotted expanse, they rode on, wrapping buffalo robes over heads and shoulders and plodding
through the downpour of rain mixed with sleet
and some wet snow, becoming thoroughly soaked
and miserable before they managed to find slight
protection beneath a stone outcropping. They
spread saddle blankets for a makeshift windbreak,
but the wind and wetness blew in anyway.

Just before sundown the storm ended, light
from the west pouring in deep golden for a brief
time, and then the breaking clouds shining in-
tense crimson, which gradually faded and deepened to maroon and then to night. The period of
sunlight was not long enough to be of any use in
drying things out, however, and even with the aid
of gunpowder from Mike's canister, they were
unable to produce more than a smoky, slow smol-
der that gradually reduced their collection of damp
sagebrush to ash without putting forth any discernible heat.

With nightfall, the sky cleared and the temperature dropped to near freezing, not uncommon at
this altitude in late May. Before long both Moon
and Mike, in their still-wet clothes, were shivering
uncontrollably, and Jacques, although Moon had
managed to keep him relatively dry in the shelter
of her body, was whimpering with the cold. Mike

sprinkled more powder on the smoldering brush and was rewarded by a quick fizzle of sparks and a rotten-egg odor of smoke.

"Best we can do is hang on to each other, I guess." He shrugged. "For warmth, damn it, Moon," he added as she shot a quick, mistrustful glance at him. "What the hell else would I want with you? You should see yourself right now. You look like a damned wet cat, and you're just about as friendly."

She glared at him for a moment and then began to giggle. She nodded, still shivering, and they wrapped their damp blankets around the three of them together, leaned back against a big boulder, Jacques comfortably sprawled across both laps. The two adults slept little that night, for they were still miserably cold. At first Moon stayed stiff, trying unconsciously to minimize contact, but toward morning she dozed, her head resting against McLafferty's chest, and in her sleep she curled tight against him. She woke with the achingly familiar sensation of good, male warmth next to her, and she was painfully aware of how much she missed such a presence.

They saddled up at daybreak, letting the sun dry their clothing. The warmth grew quickly as morning progressed, and by the time they had been on the trail for a couple of hours, they were more or less comfortable again. Moon, for her part, was almost cheerful. She tried to reestablish the distance between herself and Mike, feeling somehow obscurely unfaithful to White Bull, but she found herself more and more often forgetting to remain aloof. As they rode, she began to talk, and it was almost as if the first few words released a whole flood of pent-up communication. To the utter surprise of both, she seemed intent on telling him her whole life story, even things she had never told White Bull—how at times she felt very much an outsider in Leg-in-the-Water's village; how she never really learned to get along with the other women, having been raised among men; how she always loved riding and hunting better than cooking and sewing, and the distance that preference seemed to create between herself and others among the Cheyenne.

"I guess I never really learned how to get along with anyone. I think I was always lonely, maybe ever since my mother died, when I was just a little bigger than Jacques. Then, when I was with White Bull, I wasn't lonely at those times. Well . . ." She finished helplessly, tears beginning to glitter in her eyes.

"Tell you what," Mike said. "Let's cut our wrists and swap horses."

"What? What does that mean?"

"Never mind. I don't want to have to fight you first."

She looked at him, puzzled for a moment, and then grinned, wiping at her eyes with a fist as a child would.

The next day, near a crossing of the Green River, McLafferty's big gray suddenly seemed to explode, screaming in fright and rearing up onto its hind legs, eyes rolling. Then it lunged sideways, scrambling partway up a rocky slope and skidding, tipping back. Mike managed somehow to launch himself out of the saddle as the horse fell.

It seemed to him that he hung in the air for a

very long time. He tried to twist as he saw a pile of
rocks coming at him. Felt impact, saw an immense
flare of red, fading to utter black. Heard a woman
screaming from a great distance away. Then there
was nothing, nothing at all.

7 Chaos, utter chaos for a space of several heartbeats, and the world was coming apart yet again.

Moon fought to control Ghost, the Palouse also shying, skipping sideways, and twisting its neck around so that she could see the whites of its eyes, the flared nostrils. The pack mule pulled its lead rope loose and fled, bellowing. And as she struggled with her own panicky animal, she watched McLafferty's gray fall, the man flying out of his saddle and landing heavily in a pile of rocks.

Then it was over. Ghost stopped fighting and stood trembling, while Grayboy scrambled to its feet, unhurt. In the sudden stillness Moon became aware of another sound, a thin buzzing, and she saw a rattler coiled defensively, trapped between Mike's inert form and a shelf of stone.

For a moment she felt paralyzed, waiting in cold horror for the snake to strike.

He may be dead already, she thought. Please, no . . .

"Cool head, *ma chère*. Fear shuts off the mind, and that is all we have over the other *bêtes*."

113

Her father's voice. She drew one deep breath. The snake continued to rattle, head up, tongue darting, but it still hadn't struck.

Must not move quickly. Mustn't frighten it.

She turned cautiously to Jacques, the boy clinging to her back and as yet utterly silent, perhaps also paralyzed with fear. She pressed a finger to his lips in sign for silence, saw understanding in wide, frightened eyes.

Slide down from the saddle, slowly, slowly. My child—lift him off, safe place. Now the rifle—ease it out. Nothing sudden . . .

As soon as she let go of the reins, the Palouse bolted, hooves clattering on stones as it ran back up the trail to join Grayboy and the mule. Moon froze, her eyes fixed on the snake. The buzzing tail vibrated faster, black tongue flickering rapidly as the wedge-shaped head moved from side to side. Moon glanced at Jacques, saw that he stood motionless where she had placed him, his gaze fixed on her and his small face white.

She lifted the rifle, checked the powder in the firing pan.

The first shot has to count—the only one I've got. Anyplace other than the head, and it will strike instantly. Can't get too close, though—might strike anyway.

Cautiously, Moon moved a few steps nearer, saw the tongue movements speed up again as the big timber rattler studied her. She knelt, one knee raised, placed an elbow on the knee, the barrel balanced on that hand. She leaned her cheek against the smooth wood of the stock, pressed the butt firmly against her shoulder, squinted.

Drops of perspiration slid down from her forehead toward her eyes, and she withdrew her hand from the trigger to wipe her face. She sighted again, set the triggers, heard the buzzing intensify again at the metallic click. The snake's head still wove back and forth, and she fixed the sights at the center of the motion, waited for it to pause for a moment, just a moment. Willed her own hands to absolute steadiness, squeezed.

The crash echoed along the canyon walls, and the thick, gray-green body of the rattler flew back against the rocks, slipped down beside McLafferty, tail still vibrating, the writhing form still trying to coil even though the head was completely gone, nothing but a few splinters of bloody bone.

Moon lowered the rifle, caught her breath in one convulsive sob. The last drop of strength seemed to have drained from her body. She let her eyes close for an instant, then felt a small hand on her arm, looked up into Jacques' anxious face.

"It's still alive," he whispered. "Look. We've got to do something. Mike—"

"No, darling, it can't hurt Mike now."

"Are you sure?"

She brushed the hair back from the child's tense face, kissed him, and then rose and went to McLafferty, who still had not moved. She was almost afraid to touch him, afraid to find out for certain.

He lay sprawled partly on his side, partly on his stomach, his face turned toward her. His eyes were nearly closed, slits of white showing under the lids. She couldn't tell whether he breathed or not. She passed a hand in front of his nose, thought she detected a slight stir of air.

Please . . .

The prayer was addressed to no one, anyone, any entity that might hear.

She slipped her fingers under Mike's neck, slid them slowly along the base of the muscular throat.

Yes, there was a pulse. She held her fingers pressed against the spot for several seconds longer to make sure the throbbing she felt was actually in the man's throat and not in her own fingertips. She turned to nod at Jacques, who stood anxiously behind her.

"Mike's all right?" he whispered.

She sucked in a quick breath. "He's alive, Little Bull. That's all I know."

"But he'll be all right," the child insisted, his eyes fixed on hers and begging her not to disagree.

She hugged him against her for a moment and then rose wearily, picked up the body of the rattler, and flung it far out and down the river. She felt a quick stab of pity as she watched the long form, still twisting helplessly, ride the current for a time and then disappear beneath swirling water.

She turned her attention back to the man. Another wave of hopeless fear swept over her.

Can't lift him. He must weigh two hundred. . . . Even if I could, it might not be safe. His neck, his back . . . ? Michael Red Coyote, why won't you wake up? You can't leave me too. . . .

The horses and the mule had stopped a few hundred feet back up the trail and stood watching, eyes still rolling. Moon approached them slowly, speaking soothing words. Ghost let her approach and take the reins, followed reluctantly as she led down to the river, the other animals trailing at a cautious distance. She unfastened her roll of blankets from behind the saddle and rigged one on sticks of driftwood to shade the unconscious man from the blazing afternoon sun. Then, not knowing what else to do, she carried water from the river and bathed his face, speaking to him as she did so.

"You come back to us, Michael McLafferty. I'm not going to let you get away this easily. Damn you, you come back."

She continued putting water on his face, let some trickle down the nape of his neck. She kept talking to him, sometimes pleading, sometimes badgering him to show some sign of life. Her vision grew blurry, and she wiped at her eyes, found that she was crying.

Something about that big, strong, beautiful male body—yes, beautiful, now utterly helpless, inert. The arms, lying careless, flung out to the sides—those arms holding her warm and close all that night after the thunderstorm . . .

She shook her head, bit down on her lips.

Jacques stepped forward, touched hesitantly at Mike's cheek. "Wake up now, Red Coyote," he said. "It's morning, and Mother is cooking something very good for breakfast."

McLafferty stirred, pushed feebly at the ground with his arms, groaned. "Son of a bitch," he mumbled, rolling onto his side and opening his eyes. "Moon?"

"Yes, Red Coyote, I'm here. You must try to get up, Michael McLafferty. I can't lift you, and we can't stay here."

"Can't," he said after a long pause, rolling onto his back, eyes closing again.

"No! You're not going away on me again," Moon

shouted, growing angry, but Big Mike only muttered a few indecipherable syllables and lapsed back into unconsciousness.

"Damn you," she yelled, tears again streaming down her cheeks.

She checked her emotion, ran her hands over his arms and legs, looking for broken bones. Lying as he was now, she could see a gash and a huge, purple swelling on his left temple. She bandaged it with a wet cloth, and he muttered and flailed one arm vaguely in her direction.

It was time, she knew, to set about getting the semiconscious man away from the crossing. The trail was frequently traveled, particularly in this year of gold-seekers. They had avoided the emigrant routes as much as possible, but there were only so many fords on the Green, with its steep canyons and its powerful current. Setting Jacques to keep watch on Mike, with instructions to call her if anything happened, she began to gather materials for a travois.

She found two sufficiently long pieces of driftwood, cedar saplings washed down sometime during flood, lashed them together with shorter cross members, using rawhide thongs, then stretched her buffalo robe over the frame, also lashing that into place with thongs. The project took more time than she would have liked, but there was no help for it.

She dragged the makeshift litter to where Mike lay, and managed with great effort to roll him onto it, covering him with another blanket and fastening him to the frame with wide strips of deerhide. She had to use another long pole as a lever to raise the end of her makeshift travois into position so she could hitch it to her pony.

She judged that they had been at the crossing for well over an hour, and she kept watch on the trail anxiously as she worked. Even when they were moving once more, progress was extremely slow. McLafferty now stirred and groaned whenever the motion of the travois over ground jarred him, every pained outcry seeming to stab through her own body.

She rode Mike's gray, with Jacques behind, and led her spotted horse, the travois scraping along behind. They climbed back up above the bank of the river onto relatively level ground over the rim, where she turned off the trail immediately, heading upslope through a stand of scrubby juniper. The going was rougher, and she had to set her teeth against the jolts and Mike's frequent moans.

She found a small stream in a draw that led them well out of sight of the emigrant path, and a short distance up the ravine opened out into a meadow ringed with cedars and pines. There was evidence of previous human habitation—bits of charred wood from cookfires, and a couple of brush huts such as the Shoshone people built, these in a state of collapse—as far as Moon could determine, several seasons had passed since anyone had been there.

She quickly set about making them a shelter. She considered rehabilitating one of the huts, but decided, instead, that they would be safer from casual detection among the trees. It was not difficult to construct a creditable lean-to of saplings and cedar boughs, Jacques watching solemnly and trying to help, bringing twigs and sticking them here and there, but darkness overtook her before the work was finished.

She cut more branches to make a bed for the injured man and managed to transfer him to the shelter. McLafferty seemed to be coming closer to consciousness, moving restlessly and mumbling words, occasionally opening his eyes and appearing to recognize Moon and Jacques White Bull. As Moon quickly built a fire and dropped pieces of jerked venison, dried salmonberries, and rice into a pan of water to make a stew, the boy sat beside the man, staring intently into his face and talking to him, trying, in his childish way, to encourage Red Coyote to come back among the living.

Moon turned away abruptly, feeling tears burning behind her eyelids again. "I'm going down to the creek, Little Bull," she said. "I think I saw some watercress down there, and some wild onions in the meadow. They'll be good with our dinner."

"I don't like watercress or onions, Mother."

"I do," she snapped, and then regretted her abruptness. "I'll be right back, son," she added softly.

"Shall I come help you?"

"No, I think you should stay with Red Coyote. You're helping him a great deal."

She almost ran away from the shelter among the trees, stopped when she reached the open meadow. There was no moon, and the sky was crowded with stars. She could hear the horses nearby, soft grinding sounds as their jaws moved, could make out their forms vaguely in the faint light, White Bull's Palouse a pale blur, the gray and the mule darker ones. The spotted pony moved away from the others, came up to her, and nudged at her shoulder with his nose. Moon rubbed the long forehead, scratched at the coarse hair between the ears.

"What is wrong with me, Ghost?" she said to the horse, cradling its head. "I have always been the strong one, and now I find myself ready to weep all the time like a silly woman."

The horse blew air out in a soft snort and nuzzled her hand hopefully, the stiff hairs on its muzzle tickling.

"No," she said. "I am sorry, I didn't bring you any treat this time. You should listen to me now, because I need your advice. There is no one else I can talk to."

Ghost nickered softly, then dropped its head and plucked a mouthful of the lush meadow grass.

"It is that red-haired one back there. All along I have been telling myself that we are only together because we have a common goal, that we can help each other to reach that goal. But now . . ."

Her voice trailed off.

Yet now I am terrified that he will die. I don't want my life to be separate from him now. . . . White Bull, my husband, I am being disloyal to you. You have only been gone a short while, and already . . . But I will be strong for you, I promise. I can't help what I am feeling, but I won't . . .

A soft, purring, trilling sound from the trees, another answering.

Screech owls.

A sudden wave of coldness in her midsection. She remembered the last time she had heard the gentle, falling cascade of notes. It had been when she and Mike and Jacques were taking White Bull's body up to the sacred cave on Laramie Peak.

"An omen?" she whispered into the darkness. "Does this mean that I must bury Mike McLafferty, the Red Coyote, that he will die also, my husband? I have promised you that I will remain faithful, even though . . ."

It is their mating call, Moon Morning Star. You know that.

The voice startled her, speaking so distinctly in her ear, no, from inside her own head. Whose voice?

White Bull's.

"My husband, what does this mean?"

But no answer came back from the darkness, only the soft trilling of the birds hidden in their trees.

She returned to the lean-to more confused and troubled than when she had left.

Jacques ran out to meet her. "He's awake, Mother. Red Coyote was just talking to me."

Moon ran a few steps to the shelter, knelt to look inside. In the light from the cooking fire, she could see that McLafferty was sitting bolt upright, looking around himself questioningly.

He saw her, grinned. "Esmeralda, you pretty bitch," he said. "Give me back my money."

Moon bit back a quick stab of something that felt very much like jealousy. "You must lie down again, Michael Red Coyote," she said. "You've hurt your head and you don't know where you are."

"Likely story," he muttered, but he lay back. "Come kiss me, then. What the hell, you were worth the fifty."

"Who is this Esmeralda?" she asked, annoyance

creeping into her voice. "I am Moon Morning Star."

"That's what they all say. I think I'll sleep a little while."

"No you won't," she snapped, shaking his shoulder. "You will wake up and eat some of this food I've cooked."

"Civilization," he grumbled. "Like hell." Then his eyes opened again and he squinted at her, suddenly sat up once more.

"Moon. It's you. What the hell are you doing? Why are we sitting here? We've got to go after Laroque. He's right over there. I just saw the son of a bitch."

"No, Mike," she said, wrapping her arms around his neck and struggling with him to keep him from rising. "That was a dream. Listen to me, you *tête-chou*. Listen to me, and I will tell you what has happened."

He relaxed suddenly, flopped back down, groaning. "God, my head . . .

"I know," she murmured as one would to soothe a child, taking his head into her lap and smoothing gently at the hair that had fallen over his forehead. "I know. Now you must sit up and try to drink a little broth. Then you can sleep again."

She managed to get some of the liquid from the stew into him and felt better for it. Jacques ate hungrily and then crawled into the shelter and went to sleep, curled against McLafferty's side. Mike moved about fitfully, occasionally moaning in his sleep, and Moon rummaged through the saddlebags until she found some willow bark, which she brewed into a tea, wishing intensely that she had paid more attention to the herbal remedies the older Cheyenne women had concocted for various injuries and illnesses. Willow bark, she knew, was good for pain. Blackroot was good for stomach disorders. Something else was supposed to help brain fever, but she could not remember what it was, had no idea whether it would be useful for concussion, anyway.

She woke him enough to make him drink some of the willow-bark tea, and he seemed to sleep more quietly after that. She sat at the edge of the shelter and looked out at the stars, listened to night sounds. The owls had stopped calling. Did that mean they had found each other?

It is their mating call.

Had she only imagined White Bull's voice, trying to justify her unruly feelings?

After a time it seemed to her that McLafferty was sleeping too soundly, and she shook him until he groaned and turned onto his side.

Then she lay down in the opening of the lean-to and drifted into sleep. When she awoke, there was thin gray light filtering in through the trees, and she found she was lying with Red Coyote McLafferty in her arms, Jacques on the other side, sitting up and watching her with a little smile.

McLafferty continued for the next several days to drift between periods of consciousness and long intervals of heavy sleep, but Moon was sure that he was now showing definite signs of improvement. Further, he had been eating a little of the food she prepared, and on the fourth day he awoke ravenous.

Moon managed to snare a rabbit and a pair of quail, and she could catch as many trout as she might wish from the stream, but she shared the belief common to both Plains Indians and mountain men that such small game imparted no real strength. Large animals, however, did not seem to come to the meadow to graze or to the stream nearby to drink, perhaps because of this new human presence or perhaps because of previous occasional use of the spot as a campsite by the Shoshones. Whatever the cause, when McLafferty showed signs of genuine appetite, Moon made up her mind to go hunting for real game, deer or elk or antelope.

It was midmorning when she left, giving Jacques minute instructions on what to do in her absence. She had some misgivings about leaving the young child and the injured man alone, but she assured herself that there had been no sign of any danger, either human or otherwise, in all the days that they had been there, and she did not intend to be gone more than a few hours. In Moon's mind, it was vital to obtain meat that had strength in it, to restore power to the man.

She rode up out of the draw and over a ridgetop into the next drainage, following game trails but finding no sign of recent passage by deer or elk. She gradually made her way to higher country, at midday stopping to rest her pony near a spring that seeped out from the base of a bluff and into a swampy meadow area, the ground thick with wild iris and glacier lilies blooming at the edge of a patch of snow. She turned Ghost loose to graze, and then she drank from the little trickle of water, rested with her back against a fir tree at the edge of the clearing.

The sun was warm on her face, and she leaned

her head against the rough bark and let her eyes drop closed, her mind drifting as she half-dozed.

Everything had been strange since the terrible juncture, White Bull's death. That one moment, and all of life had changed, could never be the way it was again.

Now she found herself bound in various ways to McLafferty, a man whom she had known before only as her husband's friend. And since Mike's accident, she had come to realize he was very precious to her, not only as a partner in this undertaking of revenge, but as a man, as one she cared about deeply.

She remembered Jacques' face when he had discovered her sleeping with her arms around Mike, the small smile, the hopeful eyes.

Our son needs a father, Moon Morning Star.

Perhaps. There would be a time to think about these matters, but only after Jean Laroque was dead. And that could come only after Mike McLafferty had recovered.

Time to get going, then, time to find game and bring it back to help the man regain his strength. It pleased her that she was the hunter, she was the one to bring game to the lodge where the man waited, depending on her for sustenance.

She opened her eyes, looked about for Ghost. It was not far away, grazing. When she rose, the head came up, a lily dangling absurdly from the mouth.

Then the animal's nostrils flared, and its eyes rolled to one side, it blew out a sudden breath and went galloping off downslope.

"Ghost," Moon called sharply. "What . . ."

A snorting bellow, sudden impression of ungainly motion, and a grizzly broke out of the trees across the meadow, head up and charging at her.

For a moment she was frozen with fear, and then she was moving, her rifle clenched in her hands as the enraged bear shambled toward her.

Le coeur, you must hit him right in the heart, nowhere else. Monsieur Ours, he can keep going with fifty bullets in him.

She raised the rifle, willed her hands to be steady, fired.

The hump-backed grizzly kept coming, didn't seem in the least affected by the .55-caliber lead ball.

Missed. My baby. Mike Red Coyote . . .

It was upon her. And then it stumbled, its front legs collapsing. The beast bellowed, tried to rise, small eyes reflecting shock, puzzlement. It turned, rolled slowly onto its side, the big claws twitching feebly. The bear let out a long, shuddering sigh and then ceased moving, the outstretched head nearly at Moon's feet.

She remained for a long moment rooted to the spot, unable to move even though her senses told her that the danger was past. Then she knelt, touched the coarse, thick fur. The eyes were open, beginning to glaze, lips drawn back in a convulsive snarl. The massive form, the dished face peculiarly pathetic in the immobility of death. She stroked the great head.

"Go well into the Spirit World, my brother."

The words White Bull had taught her to say, the prayer, half-apology, expression of regret to the animals that one needed to kill in order to live.

The creature seemed far too large for her to

skin by herself. It was almost sacrilege to butcher it in any way, but the Cheyennes believed there was immense strength, even magical power, in bear flesh, and so she cut as much of the meat as she thought the pony could carry and left the rest of the great mutilated form for the coyotes.

"Your little brothers may feast, Old Man Coyote. If you exist, I thank you for this bear."

She found Ghost in an aspen grove downslope, still rolling its eyes and trembling, and led it back with some difficulty. She had even greater difficulty in convincing it to carry the bear flesh rolled in a portion of its hide, but eventually, with soothing words and a great deal of stroking, the Palouse allowed itself to be comforted, and Moon loaded it and led it back toward the camp.

It was late afternoon when she walked down the draw, leading the horse and its burden of strength-imparting bear meat. She felt like singing and whooping in the manner of Cheyenne warriors when they returned to the village after some great exploit. But as she came into sight of the meadow, she stopped and then drew Ghost back into cover.

Two additional mules were grazing not far from the lean-to.

Someone here. I should never have left them . . .

She tethered Ghost short, out of sight behind a copse of firs, and then cautiously approached the lean-to, rifle at ready. From her angle of approach, she could not see inside the shelter, but in front, a tall, disreputable-looking individual dressed in filthy buckskins leaned on the barrel of a Hawken.

She stepped from cover, raising her own rifle barrel and pointing it dead-center at the man.

"Don't move," she sang out, the words loud in

the afternoon quiet. "You're dead if you so much as move."

The stranger turned slowly, not letting go of his own weapon, she noted. He squinted at her, and then the skin at the corners of sharp blue eyes wrinkled with an amused smile.

"You must be the one we been waitin' fer, the lady of the house, so to speak." He nodded, and at the same instant another man stepped out of the shelter, Jacques behind him and grinning happily.

"Dang it, Moon, if ye ain't the most inhospitable female critter Gawd ever saw fit to drag out o' the muck. Ain't ol' Red Coyote taught you no manners yet?"

Moon stared in disbelief. It was, of course, Fiddlehead Wilson.

"Moon Morning Star, lately of the Cheyennes," Fiddlehead continued, "I want ye to meet Aloysius Benton of jest about everywhere west o' the Big Muddy. Don't take it personal about lookin' down the snoot o' that buff'ler-plugger, Aloysius. This purty little piece here just might be the orneriest thing around, next to old Eph. She's naturally loaded fer b'ar."

Moon nodded to the stranger, and then she began laughing, laughing irresistibly, the sound ringing among the trees as the two old mountaineers shook their heads in puzzlement.

8 Moon found Mike wide awake, sitting upright inside the shelter and sipping from a flask his friends had evidently provided. She scolded him for drinking whiskey, insisting it would make his head worse, but was more than a little pleased when he laughed at her and ignored the instructions. She returned across the meadow to fetch Ghost, brought him in, and dumped the meat in its hide wrappings in front of the lean-to, without comment.

Aloysius Benton was the first to realize the nature of Moon's kill. "By the great blue balls of Jaysus," he exclaimed, then ducked his head and touched the brim of his greasy felt hat. "Beggin' pardon, ma'am, but that looks to be griz fur."

"Grizzly bear, yes." She nodded.

"You went out and shot a damned grizzly while I was asleep?" Mike asked.

She nodded again, not allowing her expression to change at all. "Leg-in-the-Water's people say there's more strength in this meat than in any other. I thought it might be good for you."

"Mother killed a bear," Jacques breathed, his eyes large.

Fiddlehead let out a guffaw. "Mr. Mike, I reckon she's got ye out mountain-manned. Didn't ye mention once how ye never kilt Old Ephraim?"

Moon eventually allowed herself to be prevailed upon to tell the story of the grizzly, and then she set about building a fire and preparing dinner. All in all, she thought, it had been a most satisfactory reception.

"I know a lot o' the Injuns swears by it, how it's strong medicine an' all, but myself, I never could much stomach the taste o' bear, so beggin' yer pardon, ma'am, ol' Fiddlehead'll jest chaw on this bit o' buff'ler jerky I got here."

"Can I have some of your 'buff'ler jerky,' Uncle Fiddlehead?" Jacques begged. "I don't stomach the taste of this, either."

Secretly, Moon had to agree with her son and the mountain man, but because she had decided it was imperative for Mike to eat the meat, she chewed on her portion of stringy, strong-tasting flesh and said nothing.

Darkness had fallen, and the group of companions were scattered around the cooking fire outside the lean-to. McLafferty sat propped against a bedroll, his face pale in flickering yellow light, an ugly contusion on his forehead still prominent, but he was alert and fully coherent, looking far better than he had at any time since his fall. He ate the food Moon passed to him with apparent relish, as did Aloysius Benton, either not bothered by the taste or not wishing to offend the cook.

"Turn-around." Benton chuckled. "Last winter a griz was eatin' me. Kilt the beast, though. Fair's fair."

"You should try it, Little Bull. Look how much good it has done for Red Coyote already." Moon smiled.

"I think Red Coyote is better because Uncle Fiddlehead is here, and Mr. Benton, too," Jacques said.

"Cain't hurt that child, droppin' 'im on his head." Benton laughed. "This hawg remembers a time up on Milk River when Michael hyar fell off a bluff an' landed feet up. Hundred foot or more, as I recall."

Mike grinned, held up his chunk of roast bear in salute.

"Perhaps. Still, it is very powerful meat," Moon insisted.

"Cain't disagree with ye there," Wilson said, straight-faced.

Moon laughed, too happy with the day's developments to be insulted. "You're lucky you didn't join the bear in the Spirit World, Fiddlehead Wilson. Tell me why you weren't riding your own mule."

"Like I tol' Mike an' the younker hyar, he come up lame with a rock in his hoof a few miles this side o' Bridger's Fort, so when I got to stewin' about what was takin' the three of ye so long, I borried a critter from old Gabe, and me an' Aloysius come lookin' for ye. Took us some fancy huntin', it did, too, an' then what do we get fer it but danged near a .55-caliber ball in our hides? I tell ye, Big Mike, this be a dangerous leetle catamount ye got, for sure. Beware o' Cheyennes givin' presents hereafter."

"I haven't shot any friends yet," Moon protested.

*   *   *

Moon cleaned the tin plates from dinner as the men prepared to turn in, the two old-timers carrying their bedrolls a few feet back under the trees, away from the shelter. Mike finished his third cigar and crawled into the lean-to, Jacques already inside. Moon spread her own blankets outside, beyond the fire.

In a few seconds Jacques' head popped up, peering over Mike's shoulder.

"Aren't you going to sleep with Mike and me, like you've been doing?" he asked in his penetrating little voice.

"Red Coyote is feeling well enough tonight, so I don't think I'll have to do that," she said in a firm, sweet tone, feeling the blood creeping up into her cheeks.

Benton left the following day, explaining that he had unfinished business at Bridger's Fort—some matter of a young Mormon woman whom he'd rescued from a band of Pawnees and who now insisted she intended to marry his adopted Crow son, Big Dog. The girl's betrothed had paid Benton a price for rescuing her and then decided he didn't want her after all. Chances were good that Aloysius, Big Dog, Big Dog's wives—the Mormon girl and Two-Tail Skunk—were going to set out for the California goldfields, with Benton primarily interested in seeing the Pacific Ocean before he turned in his traps, as he put it.

McLafferty still had fierce headaches and periods of dizziness, and both Moon and Fiddlehead were determined to keep him where he was for another day or so. For his part, Mike was restless, with a sense of time lost from the hunt for Laroque, and his friends did not have an easy job convincing him to wait longer before being on his way.

"Hawg-tie ye if we gotta," Fiddlehead threatened. "An' don't think me an' the b'ar-killer hyar cain't do 'er, nuther. Personal, I figger if ye don't never come face to face with the Frenchie, that's okay too. He'll fetch it, one way or t'other, and that's an end to the problem. Truth is, Mike, Laroque's still behind us—ain't been to Bridger's post, anyhow. So jest easy down."

"The hell with both of you. I'm no kid. Don't need a mother, or a Dutch uncle either," McLafferty said. "You can dither around here for a week if you want, but I've got me a Frenchman to kill."

With a gesture of impatience, he rose and started away from the fire. At the second step a sword of fire seemed to pierce his skull, and then a wave of purple washed up over his vision. When it cleared, he found himself lying full-length on the ground, Moon and Wilson standing anxiously over him. He returned to his cedar-bough bed, feeling a little foolish and decidedly angry with his body for letting him down.

Fiddlehead went off to hunt something "a might less powerful than b'ar, iffen ye don't mind, ma'am." Mike spent his time dozing and watching Moon as she moved about, pretending to be very busy, although Mike could not figure out what could possibly occupy so much time in such a camp as theirs. Eventually he came to the conclusion she was avoiding talking to him.

At length the answer dawned.

"It's what Jacques let out of the bag last night, isn't it?" he asked when the child was some distance off, playing with a collection of pebbles.

"I don't know what you're talking about," she returned quickly.

"Why, you're pretending you don't even know me. What Jacques said about you sleeping in the lean-to—"

"You were very sick, Red Coyote. I didn't think I should leave you alone, that's all."

"Yeah. I just wanted to say, um, I understand. What you were doing, how it didn't mean anything, and I won't throw it up to you. So maybe you don't have to work so hard at making believe I'm not here."

"That's very kind of you, Mr. McLafferty," she snapped, her cheeks deep red. "All I did was save your life."

"Try to be decent, Moon. I'm saying . . . well, thank you."

She nodded, walked over to Jacques. McLafferty watched her hips moving in the soft deerskin dress. Couldn't seem to help watching.

Yes, and sometimes I would come up out of the blackness a little bit. Remember dreams, remember other things, maybe dreams, maybe not. Waking up once, perhaps more than once, and her lying against me, soft body pressed up tight to me . . .

Forty-eight hours after Benton's departure, McLafferty was up early and seemed to be his former self, grooming Grayboy before breakfast and whistling and singing as he tended the horse.

Fiddlehead glanced at Moon, and she nodded.

While Mike was eating, Wilson cleared his throat.

"Guess it's time to move out," he said. "Looks like the sickling's back among the living. The river rats is still behind us somewhere—at least they ain't passed us by. I been keepin' a close watch on the trail. Could be they cut over to the Sublette route, o' course, an' might be halfway to Salt Lake by now, but I don't figger it. No sign o' Van Norden an' his troops, nuther. Well, that's peculiar, considering. Ye feel up to a pony ride, Michael?"

"Is it wise?" Moon asked. "I hoped we might delay for another day."

McLafferty nodded. "Let's go kill a few men," he said. "I was thinking about an ambush. Hell, I'm still having headaches from time to time, but gambling men don't die of that. Lead poisoning, maybe, or the jolt of a hemp line, but not a little tap on the head. Let's pack up that delicious bear meat and mosey ahead. Sublette's Cutoff might be a good place to wait, now that you mention it. If Laroque's behind us, and that's likely, he'll have to make a decision when he reaches the fork in the trail—and that might be the perfect moment to take care of our unfinished business."

"Ain't sure you're quite up to it yet." Fiddlehead shrugged, half-seeming to change his mind. "But the plan has merit, that's what this child says. Mebbe the b'ar-killer an' me can scheme a way o' putting a round of lead into Laroque's hide."

"Like hell," McLafferty said, getting to his feet and beginning to pick up his things.

By midafternoon they drew abreast of a wagon occupied by two young men and two young women—Bud and Bessie Johnson and Sam Harrington and his kid sister Elizabeth, the latter a thin and pretty red-haired girl of sixteen.

The four were not gold-seekers but instead were

on their way to Oregon's Willamette Valley, thinking to acquire land and to create a new life for themselves; Kentucky was getting too crowded. They'd sold the farms they'd inherited, pulled up stakes, and headed west toward what they saw as a new land of immense opportunity.

But right now the tongue of their wagon had come unbolted, and the two men were having difficulties making a proper repair.

"Babes in the woods," Fiddlehead snorted as he dismounted and slipped under the wagon to assess the extent of damage.

Johnson and Harrington deferred to the crusty old man—realizing, perhaps, they had no other choice.

"Michael," Wilson sang out. "Get my peen hammer out o' the saddlebag—an' that little leather pouch full of nuts an' bolts an' whatnot. It's part o' my fate—havin' to pull the fat out o' the fire for green'uns."

Mike dismounted, blinked his eyes as vision blurred for a moment, and then brought Fiddlehead the things he needed.

After a few minutes of alternate cursing and pounding, Wilson called for a wrench. "Thar," he said, sliding out from underneath and brushing the dust from his greasy leathers. "Good as the day she was built. Gents, I figger them repairs ought to be worth an evening's company, to say the least."

"Bess and Elizabeth'll be happy to fix supper for all of us." Bud Johnson grinned, shaking hands first with Wilson and then with McLafferty. "We haven't got much in the way of meat—just some bacon. But Bessie makes real good dumplings with it."

"We'd welcome your company, Mr.—Wilson, was it?"

"We have meat," Moon said, nodding to Mrs. Johnson and wondering at the same time if the woman might be pregnant. She wasn't showing as yet, certainly, but something about her complexion . . .

"Is it deer meat?" Elizabeth asked, her voice soft and nonassertive, almost timid.

Fiddlehead laughed. "You folks is in for a treat—by Gawd, give ye real strength for your journey. Bear, that's what, old griz hisself. Moon hyar, she done kilt the beast. Well, what we palaverin' for? Two, three hours o' good runnin' time left. Let's move out."

The group camped early, Wilson directing them to a spot protected by a grove of cottonwood and aspen, no more than a few yards to one side of the main wagon road. A clear stream gurgled down from the mountain, and to either side wheatgrass was plentiful—somehow having been missed by the endless sequence of emigrants that season of gold madness.

Bud Johnson got a fire going, and red-haired Elizabeth Harrington fetched water from the stream—in a kettle, for tea, the usual morning and evening beverage consumed by the young adventurers.

Fiddlehead called Sam Harrington aside as though he were going to explain something about the wagon repair made earlier. The mountain man knelt next to the rig, pointed.

"Take my advice, sonny, and sorta do what ye can to postpone dinner a spell. Unless ye got leather stomachs, ye ain't goin' to be overly fond o' griz meat, no matter how much medicine it's got. I'll jest slip away easy like an' see if I cain't scare up some venison or three-four jackass rabbits. No point in the lot o' ye riling yore innards."

Harrington glanced back at the others, shrugged, nodded. Wilson then pointed aimlessly at some indeterminate portion of the rigging, rose, mounted his mule, and rode off in an easterly direction toward a growth of pinyon and juniper.

Within half an hour he was back, riding full-tilt, the hind quarter of a pronghorn in tow. But all realized the agitated expression on Wilson's grizzled face had nothing to do with dinner.

"What is it, Fiddlehead?" Mike demanded. "What's afoot?"

"Trouble, Michael. Laroque an' his gang o' cut-throats ain't half a mile back down the trail. Damned near rode right into their midst, I did. Must be gettin' old—losin' my caution or summat. Could be they'll ride on by, could be they won't. Any case, we ain't exactly ready for no showdown. I got me a scheme—see what ye think."

"Let's hear it," Moon said. "Ambush them?"

The young emigrants glanced from Wilson to Moon and Mike, appeared somewhat horrified.

"These men are dangerous," Mike explained. "They killed Moon's husband at Fort Laramie. I've known the leader off and on for years. The women aren't safe here and—"

"You're serious, then?" Bud Johnson asked. "No one we've met along the trail has been anything but friendly toward us, all the way from Independence. Even that one bunch of Kaw Indians just drank tea with us and then rode off—"

"Kaws ain't Jean Laroque an' his river scum," Fiddlehead cut in. "Hyar's what we do. Bessie an' Elizabeth thar, they come with me an' Moon an' Mike an' the kid. We move our varmints up behind that leetle rise yonder an' wait. Laroque'll see your campsmoke, mebbe mosey in for a look-see, mebbe jest keep goin'. You boys cut some steaks an' get 'em cookin'. Act natural, whatever that is. Me an' Big Mike'll keep ye covered in case o' difficulty."

"Killed Moon's husband?" Bessie Johnson asked. "Are you after them, or what?"

"No time for talking," Moon said. "Let's do what Fiddlehead says. Now we know where they are—we'll find a better time for . . . The women have clothes in the wagon? We must hide them."

"Wilson, is this some kind of a joke?" Sam Harrington demanded. "We're not total greenhorns, you know."

"Trust the old hawg what fixed yore wagon, sonny. You're by yorselves, ain't seen no one or nuthin'. Let's get movin' hyar. Ain't no time for discussions."

They watched from the rim, weapons ready, as two men on horseback approached the Johnson and Harrington camp—not Laroque but Cottonmouth Chardin and a second individual whom neither Mike nor Fiddlehead recognized.

The two did not dismount. Chardin asked a few questions as his accomplice rode over to the wagon, glanced around, and returned to the campfire.

Then the voices grew louder, still not clearly

discernible from the hillside above, and Bud John-son stood up, placed his right hand on the butt of the pistol he wore. Harrington also got to his feet, gestured with a closed fist.

"This could get ugly," Mike whispered, grasp-ing hold of Bessie Johnson's arm for fear she was going to bolt and run off down the slope in a misguided attempt to assist her husband.

"Start yellin' an' ye'll get the both o' them kilt," Fiddlehead hissed. "Them two ain't the real prob-lem. They's twenty-some more of 'em jest down the road. Look—ye kin see their prairie skow over the tops o' the trees."

"If we shoot now," Moon said, "there are two less. The others will come—most are on the big wagon—they'll be afoot. This is a good place to target-practice."

"Too many of 'em for us right now," Mike said. "Hang on to your temper, Moon-gal. It's just one man we're after—not Laroque's whole damned army."

Triggers at the ready, they watched as Chardin raised one hand and then turned his horse about, riding off, his friend trailing along behind him.

When the ox-drawn wagon and men on horses had passed out of vision along the road to Bridger's Fort, McLafferty stood up, nodded. He turned to fetch the animals.

"Was the tall man the one who killed my fa-ther?" Jacques White Bull asked. "Why didn't you shoot him, Mother?"

"No," Moon replied, "it wasn't him. Just one of his company. But now we know where Jean Laroque is, we'll follow, wait until the time is right, just as Mike says. White Bull's death will be honored."

"Quit flappin' yore lips an' get on down an' eat," Wilson said. "Bud an' Sam have probably burnt the steaks to cinders by this time. This child's goin' to ride along the road a piece—jest to make sure the Frenchie's bedded down proper. Moon, make me some coffee—the way I like it, now, damn ye! This toothless catamount ain't about to turn tea-drinker in his old age, no sir."

As darkness swept in over the high basin and range country, Fiddlehead made his way back to the Johnson and Harrington camp, dismounted, slapped his mule on the rump, and left it to forage.

"Three miles or so on up ahead," he growled. "Lost interest in ye, I reckon. Whar's my coffee, Moon Morning Star?"

They remained in their camp for two more days, observed from a distance as four separate small caravans of wagons rolled on past toward either Bridger's Fort or Sublette's Cutoff.

The Johnsons and Harringtons mended harness, greased the bearing pins of the wagon, and around the dinner fire listened appreciatively as Fiddlehead told elaborate lies about his many adventures and Moon talked about her father and her girlhood on the frontier, as well as giving a full account of the recent events in the Cheyenne village and at Fort Laramie. Elizabeth in particular listened in enraptured awe, remarking several times that it all sounded like something from one novel or another that she had read.

On the third day Wilson came in from his morning's hunt with news that soldiers were on the trail. "Ely Van Norden an' his lads, Mr. Mike. Once they've passed by, we've got all our problems ahead o' us, by Gawd."

McLafferty turned to Johnson and Harrington, rubbing at his temple and grimacing in momentary pain before he spoke. "You folks had best tie in with the soldiers," he said. "That way you've got safe passage. The bluecoats are on their way to California, so you can stay with them as far as Raft River, where the Oregon Trail swings north. Nothing like a government escort, when you get right down to it—four aces, and another up your sleeve, just in case."

"Damned good idee," Wilson agreed. "By Gawd, we'd appreciate it if ye'd sort of forget to mention ye ever saw us, though. Turns out Van Norden, the lieutenant, he's after our hides. The doings at Fort Laramie, ye understand."

Sam Harrington glanced at the others, then at little Jacques, and nodded agreement.

"You mean we won't see you again?" Elizabeth asked, turning to Moon. "I—"

"Probably not," Moon replied. "Perhaps we'll come to visit this . . . Oregon. I hope it's everything you want it to be. I think you'll meet a handsome young man there, Elizabeth. I think you'll be very happy. Be patient, little sister, and be careful as well. You too, Bessie."

Without thinking, Moon allowed her gaze to drop to the attractive young Mrs. Johnson's abdomen. Bessie, as if understanding the significance of Moon's glance, blushed and smiled at the same time.

Moon had a distinct impression Bessie Johnson had not as yet chosen to share a particular bit of news with her husband—probably because Johnson would be extremely hesitant about setting out on so long a journey if he had known.

"Ain't no time to get all female-sentimental," Fiddlehead muttered. "Out hyar folks jest sort of run into each other. It happens. Take me an' Mr. Mike, for instance. Turns out we had a drink together in Omaha, an' damned if we didn't find out we was both friends with the same scraggly old coyote. So naturally we hitched up."

"Yes." McLafferty laughed. "And you can see the trouble it's gotten us both into. But Fiddlehead's right, folks. First, the safe thing to do is let the soldiers give you safe escort. Second, I've got a feeling we'll be seeing one another again before too long. Maybe at Bridger's Fort, unless you leave with the bluecoats. As it turns out, we can't very well arrive until Lieutenant Van Norden and his troops have left, though."

Wilson began to laugh.

"Jest thinkin' about how Laroque an' Gabe Bridger are goin' to hit it off." He grinned, pulling his whiskers at the same moment. "With a leetle luck, old Jim'll have Laroque's skulp nailed to a hitching post when we get thar. Jean's bound to start throwin' his weight around, an' with Bridger, that's a sure-fire shortcut to the happy huntin' grounds, as more than one brush wolf has found out. Him an' leetle Kit Carson between 'em, I tell ye, it were a joy to watch. Take the time Carson kilt Chounard, for instance—"

"If you wait for Fiddlehead to finish this story,"

McLafferty cut in, "the soldiers will be halfway to Raft River. Folks, I think we'd best get our farewells said. You've got one path to follow, and we've got another."

9 With the Johnsons and Harringtons gone, Moon, Mike, Fiddlehead, and Jacques moved ahead at a leisurely pace, riding away from the main trail and into the drainage of Little Muddy Creek, a tributary stream to Black's Fork of the Green, the small river that ran past Bridger's outpost. There they intended to gain information from the Shoshones in Washakie's village as to the whereabouts of both Laroque's bunch and the bluecoats. The Shoshone encampment was generally close by the fort, except during those times when they moved south into the Uintas or north to the Wind River Range for hunting purposes. The bond of friendship between Jim Bridger and Washakie, in fact, was well-known throughout the mountains.

By late afternoon they came down into the pretty little valley up on Black's Fork where Jim Bridger's trading post was situated, a ragtag collection of buildings partly surrounded by a low stone wall, as Fiddlehead described it, hardly a fort at all.

They stopped five miles or so short of the post itself, not wishing to run afoul of either the river rats or Van Norden and company, and Fiddlehead rode alone into Washakie's village for the purpose of gaining information.

Within an hour he was back, grinning.

"The coast be clear," he said. "Empty as your basic peavine at Christmas. Gabe run the Frenchman off, an' the troops has all moved out, Van Norden an' his crew an' some others as well. So let's head on in. Seems we're expected for dinner."

"What happened?" Moon asked.

"Van Norden and his bluecoats have headed west?" Mike added. "The Harringtons and Johnsons with them?"

"Yep. The soldier boys are sticking to Laroque real close, figurin' to keep him from stirrin' up too much trouble, I guess. First night Laroque and his buddies pulled in to the port, they headed straight for Washakie's camp an' got the Injuns drunk. Then your old friend Jean took a fancy to a married lady. Would of been all right, too, 'cuz her husband was happy enough to loan 'er out, but he didn't want 'er bruised up, it seems, an' then Laroque wouldn't throw in any extra tobacco to pay fer the damage. Would of been a knife fight, likely, but the outraged husband was too drunk to do much good, an' Laroque an' his friends hightailed it back to Bridger's with half of Washakie's boys on their tails, such as could still stand up."

"What is Uncle Fiddlehead saying, Mother?" Jacques asked when the trapper paused for a moment. "I don't understand the part about someone loaning out his wife."

"Shh," Moon said. "Just listen, son. I'll explain it all to you when you are older."

"I'm old enough . . ."

"What did Gabe do about that?" Mike asked,

leaning forward to scratch Grayboy behind the ears.

"Wal, Gabe was able to get things calmed down, more or less. He paid off the woman's husband himself, plannin' to take it out in trade with the Frenchie, no doubt. But then when Van Norden an' his soldiers showed up, Washakie's bunch figured they was there to back up Laroque, what with Lieutenant Edgeworth an' his bluecoats already at the fort, so the Injuns damn near started a new Injun war. Gabe an' Vásquez got Washakie's warriors cooled off again, but it cost 'em a sight o' blue beads an' cook pots an' such, and Bridger sent the whole lot, Frenchies an' bluecoats both, packin'."

Fiddlehead squinted and pursed his lips.

"They headin' for Raft River, I take it?" Mike asked.

"Ain't but a fool would try the Hastings in dead summer, Michael. Ye know that."

"How are Gabe and Louie?" Mike asked, lighting a cigar that he had managed to find. "Utah Sue's in a family way? Heard a rumor about that, actually."

"Yep. Mizz Bridger's about ready to pop any day now, I reckon. She's bigger'n a buffler cow, but she ain't looking too healthy. I reckon things'll be okay once she has the younker," Wilson nodded. "She's a right sweet leetle lady, Mizz Sue is. Ol' Gabe's a lucky man to have her, an' he knows it, too. He don't let on much, but I guess he's a sight worried about her."

"What's wrong with her?" Moon asked.

"Reckon you'd prob'ly know more about it than me," Fiddlehead shrugged. "Some kinda female complications, is all I know. Sue's a Injun, but she don't strike me as bein' all that strong, to tell the truth."

Moon nodded and fell quiet, thinking over what she had learned, while Wilson continued talking, reminiscing for no particular reason about times he and Bridger and Benton had spent in the mountains during the glory days of trapping.

As they rode on toward the post, Fiddlehead and McLafferty entered into a competition, each trying to top the other's tall tales and egged on by Jacques White Bull, who was an enthusiastic and wide-eyed listener until he fell asleep, leaning against Fiddlehead's arm.

"Wal, Mike, looks like we done wore out our audience." Wilson chuckled, motioning toward the sleeping child. "Guess leetle Bull's got the right notion. We come a far piece today, and I'll be ready to get some shuteye once we reach the fort."

The patron of the establishment, known as Gabe to his friends, along with his partner Louis Vásquez, greeted Mike McLafferty with bear hugs and enthusiastic avowals of satisfaction at seeing Big Mike still wearing his "ha'r." Inside the trading post that was also Bridger's house, a small, pretty woman whose belly was swollen with obvious pregnancy also embraced McLafferty and nodded shyly when introduced to Moon.

Aloysius Benton and his irregular family were indeed gone, Mormon girl and all, presumably on their way to the goldfields, according to Bridger and Vásquez. Brigham Young himself had come up from Salt Lake City, and Gabe had presided over a kind of "premarriage divorce hearing," complete with the presence of a gen-u-ine Washington, D.C., Injun agent and an army lieutenant, all parties now departed. It was quite a story, and Bridger told them all of it.

"Yep," he said, "I had some doin' to convince the ol' Saint what she was supposed to get hitched to that he really didn't want the girl anyhow, on account of her bein' dead set against him and also on account of him havin' a pretty full complement of wives as it was. Besides that, the leetle lady had been matin' with Benton's Crow son, an' that alone sort of put cold water on things. Hell, we managed to get 'er smoothed over pretty good, an' the Saints is gone back to Salt Lake, an' Big Dog's off to make his fortune, Aloysius with him. Things seem to be on the quiet side, now that all them's gone and yer ol' companyero Laroque too, Big Mike."

Bridger sat on a wobbly kitchen chair tipped back on its hind legs, his feet up on a plank table in front of him. His long face, with its leathery skin and two deep furrows running up the sides of the cheeks, seemed both kind and mournful, but his voice was humorous. Moon took an instant liking to the man and to his partner, Vásquez, as well, a smaller, dark-haired man who treated women with a certain courtliness and spoke in a broken mixture of Spanish and English. Utah Sue, smiling, sat near Moon and watched Bridger as he talked.

She loves Bridger very much, Moon thought. But she is not quite sure he loves her, even though it is easy enough to see that she is everything to him, also.

"You have a beautiful child," the young Ute

woman said softly to Moon when Bridger stopped talking for a moment.

"Thank you. I see you will also have a little one before very long. Will it be your first?"

"The first, yes."

"Then you are hoping for a boy." Moon stated her conclusion rather than asking a question, for she had never yet known a woman from any tribe who did not fervently want her firstborn to be male.

Utah Sue nodded, glancing up at her husband. "Yes. For Brid-ger."

The men had by now resumed their own conversation, and Sue continued talking to Moon, softly, confiding in her as Moon realized with some surprise. She was not accustomed to other women confiding in her.

"I have prayed to the black robes' Jesus and to Coyote Man also, and once I went off by myself and fasted for many days so the spirit people would help me to have a man-child. Brid-ger doesn't like it, though. He says he 'don't hold much by priests and mumbo-jumbo of any flavor.'"

Moon chuckled at the girl's wickedly accurate mimicry of the trader's drawl. She decided she liked Utah Sue, liked her very much.

"I hope that some of them will take pity on me, though," the girl went on, her face growing unaccountably sad. "I have tried to look ahead, but I can't see my baby. I can't see anything. I don't know what will happen. Sometimes I am afraid, not for me but for Brid-ger. He should have a strong wife to bear him many sons, and I am not strong enough. Perhaps this baby will die. Perhaps—"

"That's foolish talk," Moon said firmly. "All women are afraid before they have their first child, and then the baby comes and they laugh at themselves. I know because I felt that way before Jacques White Bull was born."

"Yes, that is what the Shoshone women tell me, and the women of my own tribe as well," Sue said, but her tone of voice suggested that she was not convinced.

"That's because it's true," Moon said. "Yet you must not do any more fasting," she added. "Didn't you hear that little one inside you saying, 'Mama, I'm hungry'?"

The pregnant girl laughed, but despite her own words, Moon felt a shiver at the back of her neck, a premonition she silently scolded herself for, even as she had scolded the Ute woman for having fears.

At Bridger's insistence, McLafferty and his party agreed to rest at the fort for a day or two. Mike was not yet fully recovered from his blow to the head, the trip to the fort bringing on a recurrence of the fierce headaches. There was a further consideration as well, for Bridger's Ute wife had grown extremely attached to Moon and begged her to stay until the baby was born, an event those at the post expected daily.

The labor began on the next night, just after supper. Despite admonishments from her husband and Moon as well, the Ute woman only picked at her evening meal, her face seeming drawn and tense. With a gasp she suddenly rose from the table and walked unsteadily into the bedroom. Moon got up to follow, glancing at Bridger, Gabe shooting a worried appeal at her.

"You stay," she told him. "It is probably nothing, a false alarm."

She found the girl in the next room, curled on the bed with her hands clenched against the swollen abdomen, her face twisted and slick with perspiration. Sue's eyes were closed and her jaw muscles were flexed hard to keep her from crying out.

Moon sat down beside her and took her hand. The girl gripped Moon's fingers and looked up at her, eyes huge and frightened. When the spasm passed and Sue relaxed again, Moon stroked her hair and smiled at her, speaking in what she hoped was a reassuring tone.

"It's started, little one," she said. "Now it won't be very long before you hold your son in your arms. This was not the first pain, was it?"

Sue shook her head, still trembling, but her expression a bit less terrified.

"You should have told someone, your husband or me."

"I wasn't sure," she whispered. "I have had pain before."

"Well, I'm here now," Moon said. "I will go tell your husband that he will be a father very soon, and then I'll come back and stay with you."

Sue nodded but clutched at Moon's hand again.

"I will just be a minute," Moon reassured the frightened girl, then stepped out of the room.

When she made her announcement, Vásquez, Fiddlehead, and McLafferty let out a whoop and pounded the expectant father on the back. Bridger grinned, and then his face twisted into a frown of worry. He stood up abruptly and headed for the bedroom.

Moon placed herself in front of the door. "When

women are giving birth, the father goes off to another place with his men friends. Men do not have the strength to attend birth-giving," she said firmly.

Bridger glanced at her and then shouldered past as if she didn't exist. Moon took a step to follow him, and then, seeing Jacques watching the proceedings wide-eyed, his small face tense and puzzled, she went to him and hugged him, kissing him on top of the head.

"This should not trouble you, my small man. In a few hours, Utah Sue will have a new little one, and perhaps she will let you see it and touch it if you are very good. But for right now, Uncle Fiddlehead and Michael Red Coyote and Mr. Vásquez will take you to visit Wild Plum and her little boy in the Shoshone village. Perhaps Mr. Vásquez will give you a piece of sugar candy and let you ride his red pony, I don't know."

"*Seguro*," Louis Vásquez said, rising. "We will go right away to catch the *caballo rojo* for this small *caballero*."

Jacques glanced from his mother to the Mexican trader. "*Caballero* means horse rider, doesn't it?"

"Means more than that, means the very best horse rider, *sí*. There are not many real *caballeros* these days."

Jacques nodded. "Do they eat sugar candy?" he hinted.

"Ai, much candy, *amigo*."

Satisfied, Jacques put his hand into Vásquez' rough paw and went out with him, Fiddlehead and McLafferty following.

When Moon returned to the bedroom, Bridger

was kneeling beside the bed, holding both Utah Sue's hands in his own and staring into her face.

The girl looked up when Moon came in. "I have told him that this is not a man's place," Sue said, smiling a little. "But Brid-ger is stubborn. He has never done anything I have told him, not even once."

"That ain't true, and you know it, Sue. Orders me around like a tame raccoon. Hell, I cain't even take a leak 'less she okays it."

"The things you say . . ."

Sue's face suddenly contorted again as another pain gripped her. Bridger went ashen, and he held on to his wife's hand as if to keep from drowning. The girl drew her knees up and let out an involuntary, gurgling moan. Gabe clutched at her hand even harder.

"Is it s'posed to be this bad?" he whispered to Moon, who shrugged, forcing her face not to betray her own concern.

"It's never easy on a woman to give birth. You men should remember that ahead of time," she said lightly.

Gabe looked back at his wife, his expression so profoundly stricken that Moon regretted her light tone.

"Is there a woman in the Shoshone village who is skilled in midwifery?" she asked. "If so, perhaps it would be good for you to go and fetch her. I have only the experience of my own labor, that and watching a few other births."

Bridger nodded, and smoothing his wife's hair and kissing her on the forehead as the second pain eased, he went out, his expression dazed.

Moon talked to Utah Sue, speaking of whatever

came to mind to distract the girl, growing quiet when a birth pang came and merely holding Sue's hand until her face relaxed again. The pains were coming extremely close together for a point so early in labor, and she reported this to the expectant mother as a good sign.

"Often a first baby comes very quickly," she said. "Sometimes the mother doesn't even know it's coming before it's here. I think your son will be in your arms very soon."

Sue smiled, her face wan and gray, and the shiver passed up Moon's spine again.

She shouldn't look this way, I know she shouldn't. . . .

Moon went on talking, forcing her voice to be cheerful, unconcerned. She told Sue the story of the bear, having to halt in the middle of the recitation as the girl squeezed her hand and cried aloud at another spasm, apparently even more severe.

Pipe Woman, the Shoshone midwife, arrived soon after, with Bridger hovering at her shoulder. She ordered the man to leave, and for a time Gabe seemed ready to do battle with the big, rawboned Indian woman. But when Sue's next pain gripped her and she writhed on the bed, panting and unable to suppress a loud moan, the color drained from Gabe's face and he fled, appearing on the verge of tears.

Moon was relieved to have the older Shoshone woman presiding, was happy to carry out her orders, still sitting beside Utah Sue and talking to her between pains while the midwife sat on the floor and stitched at a piece of beadwork on a moccasin. The pains continued coming at intervals of perhaps five minutes, but nothing else happened. The midwife examined Utah Sue several times, shaking her head.

"Baby not ready come yet," she would mutter, and go back to her beading.

Pipe Woman was decidedly uncommunicative, and yet, as the pains continued and Utah Sue began to show signs of exhaustion, even the Shoshone's broad, unresponsive face began to demonstrate concern. As hours passed, Bridger would appear in the doorway from time to time, looking an anxious question, and each time Moon had to shake her head, he would withdraw, appearing more haggard and worried than before.

Toward morning Utah Sue lapsed into periods of exhausted sleep between pangs, her breathing becoming shallow and ragged. Pipe Woman was grim and demanding, acting as if she were angry with the mother and shouting at her to "Poosh!" as the pains commenced. But by this time the girl seemed too weak to comply, so dazed that Moon wasn't even sure she heard the commands.

Thin gray light was filtering through the small, parchment-paned window when the pains began coming faster and harder, Sue now seeming to awaken fully as each one commenced. She gasped for breath and tried to bear down as the midwife ordered her to do, giving great, heart-wrenching groans of agony as she did so.

At last the baby's head emerged, and with another agonizing, supreme effort by the exhausted mother, the child was born.

Moon sat down by her friend when it was over, gently wiped perspiration and tears from the small face as Pipe Woman severed the umbilical cord and wrapped first the baby and then the after-birth in soft deerskin blankets. She handed the infant to Moon without speaking and left the room, carrying the afterbirth with her. Moon understood, for the Cheyennes as well were careful to bury the placenta, performing a special ceremony some-where away from the lodge, where an evil spirit could not find it and so cause harm to the newborn.

Sue lifted her arms weakly for the child, and Moon placed it against her breast. The new mother fumbled at the wrappings, not having strength even for that small effort.

"It's perfect, Little Mother." Moon smiled. "You should be proud."

"Girl or boy?" Sue whispered.

Moon hesitated, then said truthfully. "A girl, but don't worry. Your next one will be a boy."

Utah Sue stroked a finger across the tiny head, an expression of concern on her face.

"No," she said. "Brid-ger will have to love this one for both of us. There will not be another."

"Don't be silly. You're exhausted, that's all. Of course you feel weak. You will be fine after you've slept."

Sue shook her head, her voice growing weaker and her eyes dropping closed.

"Take care of Brid-ger," she whispered. "It will be very hard for him. I would ask you to stay, but I see that your heart is with Red Coyote."

"Hush, Little Mother," Moon said, stroking the damp hair back from her forehead. "You need to sleep now."

She heard a faint noise and looked up, saw Gabe standing in the doorway, his eyes fixed on the bed and his face ghastly. Moon smiled, picked up the baby, and held it out toward him.

He brushed past her, knelt beside the bed, buried his face against his wife's neck.

"Sue, damn it, don't leave me now," he said in a broken, choked voice.

"Brid-ger," she whispered, lifting one hand a little way from her chest and then letting it fall again.

Then Moon saw the stain, dark red against the brown blanket, already soaked through the wrappings Pipe Woman had put in place. She looked up, stared at the small face, lips parted slightly so that a gleam of white teeth showed, the big man still lying halfway across her, his wide back shaking with sobs.

Moon put a hand on Bridger's shoulder, no words forming themselves in her mind. Then she left the room.

She found Mike and Fiddlehead at Vásquez' cabin with Jacques, told them her sad news, and then, exhausted, lay down to rest on a cot in the cabin, hugging Jacques tightly against her. She did not expect to be able to sleep, but several hours later she awoke, alone in the building.

She stepped outside, saw the others in a silent group near the trading post. With them was a Shoshone woman, Utah Sue's baby in her arms. And walking away slowly, head down and shoulders hunched in his buckskins, Jim Bridger carried his wife toward his bay horse. In a few moments he rode out of the fort and toward the white-topped, shining range of the Wind River Mountains, Utah Sue still cradled in one arm on the saddle in front of him.

10 "Don't let them diggers get your ha'r, nor the tom-fool Saints, nuther," Jim Bridger advised them as they saddled their animals and otherwise prepared to continue their venture westward. "Truth is, ye got one Gawd A'mighty desert out to the far side of the big Salt Lake. A wise man might be of a mind to go the other direction, considering the time of year. Way I see 'er, that Hastings Cutoff ain't much better'n a damned death trap. Ye wait for cloud cover, or ye travel by moonlight, or ye end up as dried-out as any fish on a riverbank in the middle of summer, which is just what ye're goin' to have to deal with. Get across 'er quick, though, an' that should put ye ahead of yore old friend Benton, as well as Laroque and leetle Lieutenant Ely What's-His-Name. Me, I wouldn't take that child too serious, but the Frenchie's another breed o' cat altogether. You take care that he don't get your skulp 'fore you collect his. Got dollar signs in his eyes, he do, an' pure wolf pizen in his veins. You look out for Miss Moon an' the little 'un, you hear me?"

"Me an' Mr. Mike," Wilson replied, wrinkling

his nose and squinting, "we'll get whar we're goin', all right. Don't be frettin', Gabe. Coyote, he keeps an eye open for Injuns an' damned-fool white men, just like always."

"Shore he does." Bridger grinned. "Jest remember not to pet no rattlesnakes, that's what this hawg says. Ain't none of us gettin' any younger, so keep your damned powder dry an' your tongue wet. Good luck to ye, an' if ye do cotch up with Aloysius, tell him I done sold his skulp to Washakie, an' I expects him to deliver it on time, too."

McLafferty, straight-faced, adjusted his black Mexican hat. "Benton'll be pleased to hear that, I'm sure. So long, Gabe. Give my best wishes to Louis when the old thief sobers up."

"Miss Moon," Bridger continued, making a self-conscious bow, "they ain't no way I can thank ye for helpin' Utah Sue along the way ye did. Yes, an' this old hawg-hunter too. We ain't never ready for a visit from Death Hisself, ain't never ready. But the leetle one's doin' well now, thanks to you. Ma'am, I ain't such a one as to get overly sentimental, but you are a genuine angel of mercy. I don't know how I'd of got through it if ye hadn't of—"

"Sue was a good woman," Moon replied. "She loved you, and she would not have gone on into the Spirit World if there had been any choice. You will remain in my thoughts, Jim Bridger. Perhaps we'll be back before winter, I don't know. If all whites were like you, there could be peace between the Nations and the Americans. Yes, we will be back if that is possible."

She kissed the mountain man on the cheek, nodded, and then mounted Ghost.

For a moment Bridger actually appeared to be embarrassed. He stepped back, nudged at a prickly poppy bush with the side of his moccasin. "Another thing to think upon," he said, "though it ain't truly none of my business. Revenge. Chances are it don't solve nothin'. Got to play the cards ye're dealt, like Mike says. Me, I'd ruther see ye keep plumb away from the guldanged swamp rats. Well, you know what ye got to do. If they bought what I told 'em, ye shouldn't be meetin' up with Laroque or the looie either this side of the Humboldt, an' by then ye'll have the jump on 'em."

Bridger lifted little Jacques up behind his mother, the child laughing as Jim tickled his ribs.

"I don't believe any of your stories," the boy said, "but they are good to listen to."

"Not even the true ones, ye weasel? What about them?"

Jacques laughed and pulled at Moon's hair. "Not even those!" he exclaimed, glancing at Mike for the expected expression of approval.

"Go with the Great Coyote, folks," Bridger said. "Ye'll always be welcome here to the post."

A breeze carried twin scents of running water and bitterbrush upslope from Black's Fork, and a silver smear of sun rose above the mountains to the east as McLafferty, Moon, and Fiddlehead Wilson urged their mounts ahead, up the trail toward Salt Lake.

Mike hunched his shoulders forward and moved his head from side to side. The road west had been a long one already, and a good deal more had happened than he could ever have guessed when he left behind that two-story brick mansion in St. Louis. Little enough in life, he surmised, was even generally predictable. He had started west to get away from what had become intolerable to him, his conscious purpose being simply that of reaching California and making a second fortune for himself, whether with his deck of cards or possibly by means of striking it rich in the goldfields. During the interval since leaving St. Louis, old Zach Taylor had been sworn in as new President of the United States, and the former president, Polk, was apparently in failing health, already dead for all anyone knew. Half of St. Louis had burned down, according to word brought by the most recent courier to Fort Bridger, and he himself was a wanted man, under federal warrant. A five-hundred-dollar reward had been offered for the apprehension of Moon Morning Star, "a half-breed female," another equal amount for "the gambler McLafferty," and he and she and an unlikely mountain-salt by the name of Fiddlehead were in full pursuit of a French outlaw who had killed—or else they were being pursued by this same outlaw, who had a lust for the gold their scalps would bring. . . .

None of it made a hell of a lot of sense.

He, Mike McLafferty, was hopelessly in love with a woman who apparently cared for him, yes, as if he were a member of her family—which of course, in a very real way, he was.

Somewhere ahead lay a showdown that could bring about the deaths of all three of them—not three, four, the boy as well, who had already lost both his father and his people. Jacques—"leetle weasel" as Bridger called him—could end up being the ultimate victim of the insanity that was afoot and was bound to be carried to its conclusion.

"Wake up, Red Coyote," Moon called to him. "I do not want you to fall down and bump your head again. Your skull is not as hard as you like to pretend."

The skim of ice on the waterbuckets that morning, midsummer or not, was a subtle reminder the warm season was not fated to last forever and that success in reaching California lay in crossing the final barrier of the Sierra Nevada before autumn blizzards closed the passes. A tale of the ill-fated Donners, resorting to cannibalism and freezing and starving to death, was well-known by anyone attempting the overland trek.

Ahead lay Salt Lake Desert, the Hastings Cutoff, one that would save them precious time. Two hundred miles shorter, the route would allow them to make up much ground, providing they survived. Since they were mounted rather than driving wagons along, their chances on this score were relatively good. Once ahead of Laroque, perhaps somewhere over on the Humboldt River, an ambush or night attack would be possible.

Wagon ruts ran clear before them, the road relatively level for a time, next upward across a plateau, then down to Muddy Fork. They rode on until darkness made further travel too dangerous, reaching Red Sand Spring.

On the seventh day after their departure from Bridger's Fort, they were finally able to look down upon the floor of Salt Lake Valley with its numerous small Mormon settlements. Salt Lake City itself was visible, a patchwork of streets and houses, sporting half a dozen larger buildings constructed of adobe bricks. Crops were growing in green rectangles, flush to the desert's edge.

Beyond the settlement lay Salt Lake, blue gray under billowing summer stormclouds, islands rising dreamlike from its surface, water stretching away northward.

"It is . . . beautiful," Moon said. "The only city I was ever in was St. Louis, when I was just five years old, on our way west from Michigan. I remember some large buildings, not much else."

"Salt Lake's a pup, as these things go," McLafferty replied, admiring in spite of himself what the Mormons had wrought out of the desert. "St. Louis is much larger now. Lots of big places—Memphis, New Orleans. Back East there's Philadelphia, Chicago, New York, Boston."

"So I've heard." Fiddlehead chuckled. "But this child ain't never seen 'em. Ye been to them places, Mr. Mike?"

"Memphis and New Orleans, not the others."

"Then how do ye know they even exist, tell me that. All my life I been hearin' about Washington, D.C., but I don't figure they *is* such a place. She's jest a dream that everybody's been havin', that's all. If somethin' bad happens, it's because of what some infernal fool is supposed to have said in Washington. No, by Gawd, I ain't goin' to believe in stuff I cain't see with my own eyes, an' that's sure as buff'ler dung."

McLafferty laughed, shrugged. "I suppose you don't believe the world's round, either."

"She look *round* to you?"

"My father told me that," Moon said, "how it spins like a ball in the sky. But out on the prairies, along Platte River, it looks nearly flat. In the mountains it's jagged. Here, half of it is filled with water. Perhaps we can never see enough of it at one time to know."

"Hear what this child's sayin'?" Fiddlehead demanded. "Now what ye got to say for yourself, McLafferty?"

There was a good deal less traffic along the trail now. The route to California had branched several times. Sublette's Cutoff had left the main trail at Pacific Creek, even before reaching the Big Sandy, to the east of Bridger's Fort. Another alternate route went north, close by Gabe's post, joining the Sublette Trail at Bear River. Yet another ran off to the north from Salt Lake City, tying in with Hudspeth's Cutoff at Raft River—the latter being the route, almost certainly, that Laroque and his companions had taken, as well as Van Norden and the Johnsons and Harringtons.

McLafferty turned south, avoiding the Mormon capital, and the group passed through an area sparsely settled with farmhouses. Cattle grazed and crops were growing, wheat and corn among them.

Fiddlehead Wilson nodded appreciatively. "The old swamp looks almost civilized, now, don't it?" he asked no one in particular. "Brigham the Good, he knew best. Bridger was wrong, but whoever would have thunk it? Industrious as a bunch of damned ants, these folks be."

"If a man's got more than one wife," McLafferty remarked, "it keeps him extra busy out in the fields. The usual problem with whites west of the Sandhills is not enough womenfolk. The Saints, though, they've got too many, and that's how they've solved the problem. For all the talk about evil Mormons, it's the ladies who seem to find it most attractive. I went to one of their missionary meetings in St. Louis, just to see what the pitch was. Perhaps women don't mind sharing a man as much as we've been led to believe. That way in the Nations, too."

Moon glanced at Mike. "True," she said, "but it doesn't mean the women like it."

"Wagh!" Fiddlehead snorted. "I've seen many a lodge with more'n one wife, an' damned few of 'em was unhappy."

"I would not wish to share my man," Moon persisted, "I mean, if . . ."

"It's a peculiar business, all right. Smoke ahead— look thar! Ain't just grass burnin', nuther. She's the remains of a house, by Gawd."

They turned from the trail, thinking to investigate what had happened, and found the remains of cattle, hastily butchered out in the fields, the house a heap of embers, still burning in places.

McLafferty dismounted and walked to the edge of a gutted log building, kicking the toe of his boot against a charred timber end.

"Riders comin' this way," Wilson called out, "an' the hawgs don't look friendly."

McLafferty returned to Grayboy, yanked his Hawken from its sheath, and sat waiting.

Moon studied Mike's face. The expression appeared serious. "What do you think they want?" she asked.

Mike recognized Brigham Young, and with him Wilford Woodruff, a thin-lipped man with insane pale-blue eyes. There were a dozen others, younger men, followers, not leaders. McLafferty had seen Young and Woodruff before, three years earlier, at Mount Pisgah.

"You are under arrest, all of you," Young called out. "Throw down your weapons immediately."

The entire posse was armed, and now numerous rifle and pistol barrels were leveled at Mike, Fiddlehead, Moon, and little Jacques—the latter clinging to his mother as if attempting to appear smaller and younger than he was.

"Don't reckon we will at that," Wilson drawled. "This hyar ain't no way to welcome citizens of the by-Gawd United States of America."

McLafferty slowly directed his Hawken at Woodruff, whose general demeanor, at some irrational level or another, he found that he simply did not like.

"Commence shooting, boys," Mike called out. "Must be quite a challenge to gun down strangers passing through, a woman and a child among them. I figure we'll send one or two of you along to see your Maker in the process. This Hawken of mine will drop a buffalo at two hundred yards, if a man can aim right. At close range, it'll put a monstrous big hole in a man. Be a shame, though, a bloodbath over nothing at all. We're just passing through."

"Lay down your weapons," Young insisted, becoming slightly red in the face—a man, apparently, used to having his orders followed.

"Guess not," Mike said, "at least not until you boys put yours away. I don't like having pistols pointed my direction. Moon-gal, you plug the leader here. If this is how the world ends, we might as well do it right."

Young studied the situation, glanced sideways

at the Indian woman, and noted that she did indeed have a pistol pointed straight at him.

"You're charged with wanton destruction of cattle, arson, and murder. Don't force us to kill you without giving you a trial first. By the laws of Zion and Deseret, you're entitled to a fair trial, and that's a great deal more than you gave the wretches you burned to death, God-fearing people."

"Ain't never been here before," Wilson said. "You fellows has been readin' the Good Book upside down, that's what. Jest come over from Bridger's Fort."

McLafferty smiled, winked at Brigham Young, causing the church leader to purse his lips into a scowl.

"You're the bossman, am I right? Gabe told us about that bet he made with you—about the bushel of corn. Look, gents, I believe you've apprehended the wrong people. Would two men and a woman and a child be likely to go around burning houses? Be glad to help you chase down the ones responsible, though."

Young didn't move for several heartbeats, staring into McLafferty's eyes. Then he nodded, turned. "Put away the firearms, brothers," he snapped at his own men. "I choose to believe these people. They are pilgrims, just as we were."

Woodruff frowned but nodded his approval of the leader's words.

McLafferty sheathed his rifle, and Fiddlehead and Moon lowered their weapons also.

"You're on your way to cross the desert, then?" Woodruff asked. "It's no place to take a child, Indian or not. Hastings' description of the crossing has lured more than one soul to death by dehydration and heatstroke. If you're wise, you'll turn back, ride north to Raft River."

"Good advice, without question," Wilson agreed. "We got us our reasons, though. Figurin' to catch up to a murderer of our own, as she turns out. Took the cutoff to get ahead o' the skunk. Ye got any idee who done this hyar? Someone burned up inside the house, was they?"

"A man and his wife," Young replied. "Their Ute hired hand got away, came into town to alert us. We buried the remains two days ago, then rode ahead to the edge of the desert in hopes of apprehending the criminals."

"We conclude they must have doubled back," Woodruff added. "Then we find you people here at the sight of the butchery and— "

"I get the picture." McLafferty frowned.

"You're a family, I gather," Young said, smiling for the first time. "Man and wife and child and . . . older brother?"

"Exactly." Mike nodded. "Yes, this is my wife, the former Moon Leclair—our son, Jacques—and my brother, Frederick. McLafferty's our name. We're on our way to California to homestead, but we're also after the man who murdered a close friend of mine."

"This individual was heading westward?" Woodruff asked. "Was he alone, as far as you know, or in the company of others?"

"About twenty or so of them—Missouri River boatmen, a few French Canadians, mostly American. The leader, a man named Jean Laroque, is the one we're after."

Young and Woodruff exchanged glances.

"French," the Mormon leader said. "That at

least matches the description Tom Crying Owl gave us. Perhaps we should have brought him along with us, after all."

"Might of been a good idea," Fiddlehead concurred, "if he's the only one as would recognize 'em."

"Laroque," a rangy, sun-browned individual behind Woodruff said musingly. "I've heard that name before. Now I recollect—it was the young people who mentioned it, a single wagon, a man and wife, another pair who were sister and brother, all on their way to Oregon and alone. They'd been traveling with soldiers but had lost a draft animal and been left behind. They came to my place looking to buy an ox."

"Do you recall their names?" Mike asked. "Johnsons and Harringtons, by any chance?"

"Those were the names, all right. Nice folks. I tried to warn them against the Hastings route, but they were determined to go that way. Wanted to make up lost time, I suppose, and it seems they also wished to avoid this person you've named, this Laroque. I invited them to stay with me until another train of emigrants came along, but they were eager to be gone. Foolhardy, just the four of them that way, and two young women at that."

Young said, "Apparently this Laroque and his fellow savages have somehow given us all the slip, cut down from the north to this route. It seems likely they've gotten out onto the desert, where I am unable to pursue them. Now Brother Desmond tells us there's a small party of young people out there. They may be in great danger. And if you pursue them, you're putting yourselves in great jeopardy as well. Two men alone with a woman and a small child—such a venture is foolhardy in the extreme. You must understand that."

"Yes sir, we do," Mike agreed. "We do indeed. But perhaps there's a way of cutting the odds a bit. We'll see when the time comes."

"Mr. McLafferty," Young continued, "I'm a man of peace, the leader of my people. We have come to this land of Deseret to avoid persecution such as we suffered at Nauvoo. Indeed, we've come here to found a new country where we may live in harmony and according to the precepts of the Almighty. We've caused the desert to flower, and we've found a way of living in peace with the natives of this country, our friends the Utes. But now we discover ourselves overrun by emigrants— wild, unprincipled men who cross our lands in the hope of finding their fortunes in California, sometimes wreaking havoc, as in the present instance, as they go. What are we to do? If we block the migration route, then federal troops will be sent. No, I cannot do that. This man, Laroque you say, is not the first to have committed an outrage this year, and in all likelihood he will not be the last. I believe in justice, sir. I do not always turn the other cheek. And for this reason I'm prepared to offer you a thousand dollars should you and your brother succeed in bringing me proof of the man's guilt and of his death. I will keep my word, for that is sacred to me. Furthermore, you and your family will be welcomed as settlers in this nation of Deseret, should you choose to remain upon your return."

McLafferty urged his gray closer to the Mormon patriarch and extended a hand.

Young grinned slightly, caught himself, clasped Mike's half-closed fist. "Your brother, Frederick, he's a veteran trapper, I take it? He sounds like a trapper friend of mine, Aloysius Benton."

"That he is. He knows your friend Benton—in fact, we both do. We heard he was heading for California. That's what he told Bridger, anyhow."

Young nodded, gestured to his men to ride on toward Salt Lake City. He himself, however, lingered for a moment.

"I should have known it," he said. "It's the devil's lure of gold in California. Gentlemen, I pray that same gold doesn't rob you of your good wits. As I said, return to me with proof that this Jean Laroque is the man responsible for what has happened here, and I will reward you—money or land, your choice. Perhaps I spoke hastily, however, and my conscience now directs me to suggest that it would be preferable for you to bring the man with you rather than simply evidence of his demise. I see the gleam in Frederick's eye, but I assure you I have no use for scalps. God Jehovah would not wish to have so obscene a trophy nailed to his lodgepole, if you understand my meaning. Well, good luck to all of you. Personally, I'm of the opinion that the murderers have gone off across the desert. It's possible you may find them out there, quite dead."

"It's a strange kind of justice they work around here," Mike reflected. "We were tried and found guilty, then tried again and acquitted. Now we've been deputized, so to speak. Tell you the truth, though, the old fox knew exactly who we were— knew there were warrants out for both of us,

Moon. I think he knew about Laroque and his crew as well. Not sure why, but I've got that feeling. Must have picked up the scuttlebutt at Bridger's Fort."

"Ain't nothin' surprises this child," Fiddlehead growled. "But she's a damned cinch certainty that if the river rats burned those folks out, Jean didn't head back in the direction o' Salt Lake City. No sir. An' that means they're up ahead of us, and not very far, nuther. That how you see it, sonny?"

"Right, Brother Frederick. Old Jean must have figured out that Bridger gave him a bum steer and cut back south to this route looking for us."

"Red Coyote, if Laroque's ahead of us on this trail . . ." Moon began, her eyes fixed on his in concern.

"Know what you're thinking. The Harringtons and the Johnsons. If Laroque and his men catch up with them alone out there . . . Bessie and that pretty little red-haired Elizabeth—only the two men to protect them, one a kid and the other barely more. I don't like the sound of it. All we can do is hope we catch up to them first, I guess."

"That bein' the case, maybe we'd better quit with the jawin' and get to humpin'," Fiddlehead put in.

They rode in silence for a long time, and then Fiddlehead turned in Mike's direction, his leathery face twisted into a scowl.

"Whar the hell'd ye come up with that name, anyhow? Ye did a good job o' yarnin', I admit, but why 'Frederick'?"

"Fiddlehead, old friend, you never got around to telling me your Christian name."

"Ain't got one no more. Seem to have lost it somewhere along the trail."

"So," Moon broke in, "now my son and I are *your* family?"

"Well, Leg-in-the-Water gave you to me, didn't he? I probably could have claimed you, in any case."

"Only helpless women are claimed. You hear my words, Red Coyote. I have death on my mind, not life. I cannot think beyond what must still be done. You were my husband's brother, and that means you're my brother as well."

"Have it your way, then," Mike said. "One way or the other, we're still family."

11 They found several sets of wagon tracks and followed them across Salt lake Basin into ever more arid lands, then up over the Stansbury Mountains and partway down the westward slope of that range, halting just at dusk. Great towers of cumulus had been forming through the afternoon, and rain began to fall shortly after sundown. McLafferty and Moon strung up a storm blanket, tying off two corners to a gnarled, outreaching arm of juniper and anchoring the opposite corners with fractured sections of sandstone.

Fiddlehead hummed softly to himself as he built a good fire under overhanging rock, feeding the blaze with handfuls of dead juniper fronds and pieces of twig, then, as the flames gained, with larger segments of pitchy wood, hewn from a downfall by means of his hand ax. Smoke swirled up, sometimes blowing in under the stretched blanket at moments when the gusty wind changed directions.

"Wagh!" he cried out. "We're in for a dinger, folks. Rain on the desert can be a gen-u-ine experience!"

"Bad spirits going to get us?" McLafferty asked.

"Ye'll think bad spirits, sonny. Why'd ye suppose I chose this leetle hilltop for a campsite? If the storm swings this way so's we get more'n a few drops, like now, that ravine down below is subject to be runnin' six, seven feet deep in mud before morning. Salt Lake itself wasn't even thar until one night back in '09 when me 'an old Pierre Charbonneau was camped north of hyar, on Bear River it was. So much rain fell that the whole damned valley jest filled up with water, an' she's been that way ever since. Gawd's own truth."

Jacques looked up at Moon, knowing that he could tell by the expression on his mother's face whether Fiddlehead was lying or telling the truth. This time he saw "utter nonsense" in her eyes.

"It's not the remains of an old ocean, then?" McLafferty asked as he opened a saddlebag and took out an oilcloth bundle that contained meat. He sniffed at the contents, shrugged, and strode over to the fire.

"Where'd ye ever get such a fool notion? For a hawg that knows how to read an' write as good as any schoolmarm, ye sure ain't got an ounce o' common sense."

As they cooked dinner, sipping coffee as the meat sizzled on a spit over dancing yellow flames, initial sporadic drops of rain increased in intensity. The nearly full moon vanished in the east as thunderheads swept over them, and lightning strikes scratched darkness over the now-invisible length of the Cedar Mountains across Skull Valley, to the west. Night boomed with noise, and the rainfall became regular, spattering on the stretched blanket and causing the campfire to hiss as droplets touched hot-burning juniper.

"You and Charbonneau, hey? What were you doing down this direction in '09? I always heard that Bridger discovered the lake in '25."

Fiddlehead grinned, firelight gleaming from his incomplete mouthful of teeth. "Problem is, ye've made the mistake o' thinkin' that Gabe tells the truth. Hell, that sore-nosed badger tells lies for a livin'. Reason Lewis and Clark never made no mention o' Salt Lake is because it just weren't thar at the time. Like I said, she filled up one night in '15."

"Took six years to fill up?"

"What ye talkin' about, ye damned fool? If ye'd listen careful, ye might get one or two things straight."

"The lake is what remains from the time before Old Man Coyote made the world over again," Moon said, smiling, allowing Jacques to sip from her coffeecup, "when Beaver went down into the water and brought up some mud. That's Bright Shield's version, at least."

"I miss Grandfather and Grandmother," Jacques complained. "Will we be able to go back to visit them soon?"

"Not for a time, Jacques. Do you think our supper is ready yet?"

"Maybe," the child replied.

"Injuns explain everything they don't understand by sayin' Old Man Coyote done it," Fiddlehead grumbled. "Mr. Mike, ye got any o' them cigars left?"

"I managed to acquire a new supply at Bridger's Fort." Mike nodded. "Part of my winnings from Louis Vásquez. I take it you'd like one?"

"Am I allowed to smoke also," Moon asked, "or is this ritual only for the men?"

McLafferty chuckled. "I don't suppose Leg-in-the-Water's council is going to find out about it. Moon, you're likely to pick up all the white man's vices before you're done."

"I have to smell them anyway. I think they must taste better than they smell, or no one would smoke."

"Being around Fiddlehead has a bad effect on everyone. Here, I'll light one for you. Don't breathe in, though. Just puff at it."

She puffed, began to cough.

"What do you think, Moon?" Mike asked as he rose to inspect the chunks of hissing meat.

"I think cigar smoke smells better than it tastes," she replied.

Again the rain increased in intensity, and night became very dark except in moments when lightning flashed. Thunder roared, echoing from sandstone bluffs and reverberating off across the darkness of Skull Valley.

"Suppose there'll be a lake out ahead of us in the morning, *Frederick?*"

"Not from no little mist like this one. Cigars an' coffee is all right, but Old Fiddlehead's near to starvin'. Come on, folks, let's eat."

The wind-driven rain had become a virtual downpour, and not even the overhang of sandstone sufficed to protect their campfire. They huddled together beneath a sopping-wet storm blanket that whipped in the wind, threatening to fly loose. Water puddled and dripped through while rain splashed in from whichever side the gusts happened to be coming from.

Moon lay between Mike and Jacques, with Fiddlehead beyond the child. A pair of wool blankets and two shaggy buffalo robes covered them. Lightning flashed close by, illuminating broken rock formations around them, and the world was filled with an almost deafening noise.

As she lay in the drenched darkness, Moon thought of the wagon tracks stretching across Salt Lake Basin and beyond. Neither Mike nor Fiddlehead had spoken of the matter; she had to admit to herself that it seemed likely Laroque's men were, in fact, following tracks laid down by the wagons belonging to the Johnsons and Harringtons. She tried to convince herself the former rivermen had been delayed sufficiently by the wild-goose chase Jim Bridger had sent them on to prevent their catching up to the others before Mike and Fiddlehead and herself had overtaken the wagons.

Jacques burrowed sleepily against his mother's side, and Moon found herself resisting the temptation to snuggle against Mike McLafferty, breathing quietly but, she thought, not asleep. On the other side of her, Fiddlehead also snored, his grunts and rumblings all but rivaling the ravings of thunder.

At last she slept, and dreamed.

She was perhaps ten years old, and she was following her father through a forest unfamiliar to her. It was difficult to keep up with his long strides, but when she called out to him, her voice was so frail that he could not hear her. Within moments Leclair vanished over a boulder-strewn crest and was gone.

She was alone, and so she climbed to the summit of a dome of rocks, thinking to look far away in order to find the village where her father had gone.

The pinnacle turned into a basin-shaped valley, a small one, and she found herself surrounded by men. They all had guns, and the weapons were pointed at her. She stared at the threatening faces and realized they were all the same—each one identical to the others.

"If only Jean had time," the faces said, all speaking at once, "he would have taken you with him. You spit at me, but I could make love to you so that you would wish not to spit anymore. . . ."

A knife appeared in her hand, and the men began to laugh, became distorted, demon-creatures of some sort or another, painted red and white and ocher and wrought with intricate designs that seemed to mean something.

She sprang forward, screaming as she did so, screaming wordlessly, and struck with the knife.

Blood. Blood ran in thick streams about her feet, she could feel the warmth of it. And a man lay stricken before her, a faceless man in the dirty rags of the rivermen. . . .

Rifle fire, repeated shots, dimly heard . . .

Moon awoke, struggled to free herself from the heavy covering of robes. The rifle shots? Only the storm blanket snapping up and down, one of its corners come loose. Nonetheless, she reached out instinctively to assure herself that Red Coyote was still beside her. He stirred, mumbled something incoherent, and then he too awoke. She felt his arm come up, and she knew the Colt pistol was in his hand.

"Moon, what is it? What . . . ?"

"It is nothing," she whispered. "My spirit went wandering in a dream, that is all. I didn't mean to awaken you, Mike McLafferty. Go back to sleep now. I am fine."

"Well, our shelter isn't. Another five minutes and we'd all have been sleeping in the rain."

Mike slipped from under the covers, braced himself against rain-filled gusts of wind, struggled out of the shelter, and Moon heard the soft thuds of rock being set into place. The edge of the storm blanket ceased to whip about, and in a moment McLafferty, wiping water from his hair and face, climbed back under the robes.

"This hyar ain't no night to start matin'," a voice growled. "Gawd curse ye, go back to sleep."

The storm abated shortly before dawn, the absence of noise awakening Mike. He rose and hacked with his knife at a section of dead juniper until he had a double handful of dry slivers. These he lit, nursing the fire carefully until it was burning well and putting the remains of the previous night's roast in close to the flames.

He led the horses and mules to a clear spring close by the campsite, watered the animals, and filled the canteens and ten-gallon oak barrel. This water, he imagined, might be the last they'd find before entering the desert itself.

After a quick meal, the little band resumed its relentless westward march. Morning sun glittered from every rock and bush, and thorny succulents had magically burst into flower—petaled waxen cups of bright gold and scarlet. The featureless, salt and alkaline floor of Skull Valley gleamed with a thousand pools of strangely blue-green water, each of them only a few inches deep. Hawks and vultures and eagles drifted in a clear sky, hovering on wind currents, apparently not interested in hunting at all, but merely playing on the air.

By noon they had reached the edge of Salt Lake Desert itself, an almost featureless expanse of alkali flats stretching westward toward mountains called the Silver Islands and the Goshutes, these dimly visible as irregular gray-purple shadows along the horizon.

Already the pools of rainwater that had lain all about a few hours earlier were gone, and heat waves rose from the floor of the desert, giving everything a dreamlike quality.

"One last leetle bunch o' junipers up among the rocks over thar," Wilson noted. "Best we take what shade they're willin' to give us an' wait for sundown or damned near. Ye don't see no wagons out ahead, do ye, sonny?"

Mike shook his head. "If they're out there right now, and they must be, the boys aren't going to be in very good shape, come nightfall. Maybe the vultures'll beat me to Laroque after all."

"Don't say such things, Red Coyote. Elizabeth, Sam, the Johnsons—they're out there too."

Jacques' small face rumpled up as if he were about to burst into tears. "Is Liz-beth going to die? I like Liz-beth."

"Right ye are, Moon-gal." Fiddlehead nodded. "Don't you worry yerself, Little Partner. We ain't gonna let nothin' bad happen to Liz-beth, not if

we can help it. They're travelin' lighter than
Laroque's gang. Hell, they'll be all right. Lots o'
wagons has managed to get across there somehow
or another. As fer the Frenchie, that somebitch be
too mean to die o' thirst. Let's get on up to the
scrub cedars. Ain't a damned thing around hyar
for the varmints to graze on, they'll have to content themselves with sagebrush, I guess. All three
o' us have another cigar. Might be our last, ye
know."

A full, white moon rose in a clear sky spangled
with stars. Light shattered in planes of gray-silver
brilliance, the hard salt and alkali surface over
which they rode being turned into something
that was itself almost alive.

Fiddlehead's mule smelled water and attempted
to turn toward it, but Wilson cursed softly and
jerked back on the reins.

"Saltbrine, ye dunghead idjit. How could it be
anything else? Jest keep goin', and we'll find ye
some grass an' a runnin' stream up ahead some-
whars."

Even by moonlight the wheel tracks of the wagons were distinct.

"Shag them overgrown cows along, ye dumb-
fool kids," Wilson muttered, speaking what all three
adults were thinking. "Trouble is, they likely ain't
got no idea in the world the river rats is on their
tail."

"We will catch Laroque first," Moon insisted,
her face set. "He is not expecting us to be behind
him, either. Perhaps we will find him this night,
and then he will not be able to hurt anybody. It
will be that way because it *must* be, that is all."

Mike rode beside her, his eyes turning to her again and again.

She sits straight in the saddle, the child in front of her now, asleep against her breast. Her hair burns silver, its jet blackness transformed in moonlight. Even the faint odor of her is driving me crazy. Got to get hold of myself, I'm not thinking right. She's been there, in the back of my mind for, what? Six years, six years. A little pocket of madness, and I've never been able to build a wall around it. Moon-child, Moon Morning Star. Whatever it was that drew me to the High Shining in the first place, even though I had no idea at the time, it's all contained in this woman, my brother's wife, my dead brother. What is it you wish me to do, White Bull? Even if I knew, it wouldn't change the way I feel, it never did change anything. I ran from it, but she was always there, is still there, demon-haunted now, just as she was when we took you up the mountain, my brother, and left you in the medicine cave. Moonlight splashed all over her face and hair, moonlight . . . her proper element. Crazy. This goddamned desert is so flat it blurs everything, and a man can't think clearly. All right, she's my sister, then, but I'm going to stick close and see to it the kid grows up, I'm bound to do it, even if she decides to take another husband one day. Beautiful, like the songs of coyotes at night, like moonlight in water. . . .

"Look," Mike said, shaking himself out of his reverie, "there's water up ahead—a lake, for God's sake."

"On yore map, hawg," Fiddlehead muttered. "Salt ponds—must be a dozen or so, from what Gabe told me."

The skeleton of a wagon, a burned-out shell, as if growing from the featureless salt plain.

Moon whispered, stared, stricken, at McLafferty. "Red Coyote . . . ?"

Her voice had a plaintive quality now, the tone almost that of a child asking a parent to deny some terrible reality, to make it vanish in the omnipotent control adults are supposed to have over events.

Instinctively, wordlessly, Mike took her into his arms, pressed her head against his chest. "Could be it's not theirs," he said, knowing with a terrible certainty that he lied. "Maybe another party that left Bridger's about the same time decided to go the Hastings road. No sense jumping to conclusions."

"Mr. Mike's right this time, Moon," Fiddlehead agreed. "Let's get on, see what we find up ahead. At least there ain't any bodies."

Then, a few miles farther along, they came to evidence of a campsite, fresh.

Moon handed Jacques to Mike and dismounted quickly, looked about, kneeling, staring intently at something.

"What is it, Moon?" Fiddlehead demanded.

"Blood on the salt ground," she said, looking up, her eyes pools of shadow in the moonlight.

"Might of punctured an ox for something to drink," Wilson said.

"No, there are no hoofmarks," she said, her voice hushed.

"Whatever the case"—Mike nodded—"our friends aren't much more than a day ahead of us now. Noon heat apparently caught them halfway across, and they had to stop. Maybe someone smashed a thumb in the process of tightening a wheel rim."

Moon climbed onto her pony, and the ride continued. Soft, warm winds drifted across the featureless plain, bringing with it delicate odors of sage and a sweetness that smelled almost like honeysuckle.

The moon had disappeared beyond the rim of the Goshutes, and the eastern sky had begun its transformation to faint grayness when they found a second wagon, this one sitting forlornly with one wheel missing.

Slumped forward on the seat of the buckboard were two young men, hands bound with hemp rope. They had been shot, apparently at close range, through the heart.

"Bud Johnson," McLafferty said, his voice ringing hollow. "Sam Harrington. God damn it!"

Jacques had not really awakened and Moon drew his head against her shoulder to soothe him back to sleep, sucked in a quick breath.

"No," she whispered. "Elizabeth, Bessie. Do you think . . . ?"

"Dead—if they're lucky," Wilson said, kicking at the earth with the toe of one moccasin. "I'm right sorry this happened, gal. I know ye was fond of the youngsters. Something like this, makes you wonder if Old Man Gawd ain't asleep at his job."

Mike, Fiddlehead, and Moon looked at one another.

Dead. Dead if the two of them are lucky.

"We must bury these men," Moon whispered. "I will dig a hole."

Mike started to unstrap the half-shovel from one of the pack horses.

"Don't guess buryin' is going to help 'em any, sonny. I'm thinkin' we ought to keep movin'. Might save the females' lives, ye never can tell. Once the boatmen have had their pleasure, could be they would of jest left 'em behind."

"He's right, Moon," McLafferty said, returning to his gray. "Let's ride—keep close watch ahead. Play the cards as they're dealt out and perhaps bluff at the right moments."

The sun had just rimmed the eastward ranges when they found Bessie Johnson, wrists bound and gingham dress pulled up over her head. Her abdomen had been torn open.

"Vultures been at 'er," Fiddlehead called out. "Take Jacques on up ahead—he don't need bad dreams for the next two y'ars. Me an' Mr. Mike, we'll take care o' things."

Moon choked back a quick, half-gagging sob, detoured her spotted pony around the body, shielding the eyes of a still-sleeping Jacques even as the child started to come awake.

What of Elizabeth Harrington? Moon remembered the girl's delicate features, her slender form, her friendly, naive manner of speech, alone now, if she remained alive at all, among the vicious callous rivermen.

They were all on the verge of exhaustion when they reached the first sage-pocked rim that rose from the desert floor. Sandstone was interspersed with ancient mudflows in a series of terraces left from some primeval era when Salt Lake had been infinitely greater in extent, its shores lapping against the groundswell above them.

Wilson's mule balked, managed to get the bit between its teeth, set its hooves, and seemed on the verge of settling to the ground.

"Damn ye, they's carrots an' watermelons just ahead. Do I got to beat ye with the butt o' my Hawken? Let go that bit, ye flop-eared hawg."

"Don't hit it," Moon called out. "Is there really water ahead?"

Mike pulled the tattered map out of his jacket pocket, the paper worn and half-soaked with sweat. He tried to speak, and couldn't, having taken no liquid for the past several hours, though the temperature on the desert floor had risen to well over a hundred degrees by midmorning.

Fiddlehead slipped down from his mule, grabbed a nearly-empty canteen, and handed it to Mike. "Drink, damn ye! I come along for the pleasure o' watchin' ye gun down Laroque, not to do 'er myself."

Mike took a few sips and returned the container to Wilson. "I'm okay," he said. "Dry in the mouth, that's all. Across this rim there's supposed to be a spring of sorts—'marsh-hole,' it says here."

"Don't know as the mules is up to 'er," Wilson said. "Seem to be of a mind to pack 'er in, both o' them."

"We must lead the animals now," Moon said quickly. "They have brought us a long way, and now we must help them."

She, too, could hardly speak, and as she dismounted, she stumbled and fell, leaving Jacques still on horseback.

"Mother! What's wrong?" the child said after a

long moment, as if suddenly realizing what had happened.

McLafferty was at her side immediately, helped her to sit up. Wilson handed him the canteen, and he tilted it to her lips.

She swallowed once and then shook her head.

"I slipped, that's all. Help me up, Red Coyote. We must get to the spring. We cannot stay here."

Slowly, as in a dream, the two men and the woman and the boy trudged up the rise. Moon noted loose rock, freshly dislodged, and realized what had happened.

"Busted a wheel," Wilson said. "It ain't lying about anywhere, so they must of got it fixed somehow. Folks, keep your eyes peeled. Last thing we want to do is stumble into their campsite. Might prove fatal. . . ."

12 McLafferty stumbled to the crest and threw himself down, partly from exhaustion and partly from caution instilled by half a lifetime in the mountains. He blinked several times to clear his vision and then stared westward to the front of the Goshute Range, dry, ragged, gray-brown mountains perhaps as much as ten miles ahead. Between the rim upon which he lay and the mountains was an intervening basin, nearly treeless but at least speckled with sagebrush. And, yes, downslope just a few hundred yards was a single small grove of aspens, with marks of numerous wagon tracks heading straight toward the trees.

Where there were aspens, there was at least a chance of water. Beyond, out in the basin, though a winding cut of a drainage was clearly evident, likelihood of finding water in it this time of the year was not great.

Then he could actually smell water—water! And no doubt grass for the animals, if those passing ahead of them over the Hastings Cutoff had not reduced the damp area to mere stubble.

No sign of any human presence—no white dot

out in the sagebrush, indicating a cloth-topped buckboard or prairie schooner, and not a trace of smoke in the air. Only an undulating plain, gray-green in places with sage. Vultures or eagles high in the air, far out, black smears against blue afternoon sky, drifting with desert wind currents.

McLafferty stood up, waved to those struggling across the slope below him, though he did not call out.

New energy filled him as he started downslope, but he moved carefully, skirting away from the wagon ruts and approaching the grove from the far side.

Then he was in green shade, sunlight filtering through dancing leaves. "Quaking aspens." A wonderfully appropriate name for trees whose leaves seemed touched by thousands of invisible fingers as they trembled in the softly moving air. One almost expected to hear music, but instead heard only a soft hushing of breeze and a magic sensation of greenness.

Mike found what he sought—in the ooze below a claybank, a small channel had been dug out by others like himself. A two-foot-wide pool of clear water had formed, the water then spilling over a lip of sod and rock, trickling a few feet, and vanishing into an extensive area of marsh grass, which was irregularly pocked by water-filled hoofmarks of horses and mules and oxen.

He cupped water to his mouth with both hands and drank, then felt guilty. He rose, steadied himself, and trudged upslope toward the crest.

They were on their way down, horses whinnying, mules braying and coughing. A packhorse bolted past, almost coltlike in its enthusiasm, plunged into the marshy area, and began sucking at a water-filled hoofmark.

Firewood was scarce—previous bands of pilgrims having long since used whatever deadwood was about and having hewn down several smaller aspens as well.

Mike and Moon, working together, had brought in armfuls of sage, and Wilson had used a mule to drag down a pitch-filled juniper log from back over the rim. That evening, even after the heat of the salt desert, warmth from the campfire's dancing flames felt good, for the night air was distinctly chill.

Supper consisted of strips of jerky, boiled white beans, and flour cakes half-burned but doused with molasses, the latter a great treat for young Jacques. McLafferty drank heavily from a canteen of water as he ate, wiped his mouth, and poured a tin cup full of Wilson's wretched coffee mixture. Despite their physical exhaustion, Moon, somewhat revived by the brief period of rest, the meal, and the precious water, was impatient to continue their pursuit.

"We should sleep for only a few hours and then go on," she said as she sipped at her own coffee. "The moon will be bright the rest of the night, and we can cover many miles before morning."

"Cain't do 'er." Wilson frowned. "Them critters won't stand up to it."

"We've got to do it. Laroque and his men have Elizabeth Harrington with them. We can't let them . . ."

She broke off, a quick wave of nausea rising in her as she remembered the nightmarish glimpse of Bessie Johnson's body sprawled in dawn light out on the desert, the obscene violation of her young flesh.

Mike moved toward her as if to take her into his arms, then he stopped, put his hands into his pockets, and stood awkwardly for a moment before he squatted back down.

"Know how you feel, Moon. God damn it, I can't stand to think about that pretty little girl in with those rabid beasts either. But Fiddlehead's right. We've pushed the horses to their limit. They've got to have a night to rest and graze. If we keep going, they'll break down in the desert ahead of us. There's nothing we can do about it."

Moon turned away abruptly, trying to hide tears that suddenly burned her eyes.

Later that evening, as Fiddlehead and the boy slept, Moon and Mike tried to sketch out some plan of operation for the days ahead.

Their first objective, of course, was to free Elizabeth Harrington, a consideration that made the task of overcoming Laroque and his men that much more complicated. It was of absolute importance that Laroque should have no suspicion until the final, crucial moment of showdown.

"It will be best if we come upon them at night." Moon nodded. "I do not think he knows we're behind him—or he would not be heading west so rapidly. They would wait for us, try to ambush us somewhere."

"They may think we took the other route, and are planning to try to cut us off over on the Humboldt somewhere. The main thing is that we don't want to catch up to them unexpectedly, find them waiting up a draw somewhere ahead."

Moon was silent for a moment, staring at the ground, her forehead wrinkled. "Do you think she's still alive, Red Coyote?"

McLafferty shook his head. "Don't know. I don't even know whether I hope she is.... God! I thought I only wanted Laroque, but there's not a one of them that deserves to live, not after what we found out on the desert."

Moon nodded. "This man is like a crazy wolf, only a crazy wolf dies after a few days even if no one shoots it. When you fought him before, Michael, you should have plunged your knife into his heart. If you had done that, then my husband, who was your brother, would still be alive—yes, and all those others. But there was no way you could know what was going to happen."

"Fate, maybe. That's what the whites call it."

Moon puffed one last time on the stub of her cigar, frowned at the taste. She tossed the remains into the dwindling campfire.

"Coyote Man has many whims," she said after a long pause. "At least that's what Bright Shield would say. He means us no harm, but often we don't know why he causes things to happen. It's strange to be ... alive. We grow old if we are lucky, but by then we're not like what we used to be at all. There is happiness, but there is also much sorrow. And we just go on, always wondering where the buffalo are, or the deer, or if the wild cherries are ripe yet. Everything keeps changing, and after a time we don't know what it is that we feel. People who have been dear to us die, and yet we must continue to live until something calls to us out of the forest."

A long silence followed.

Then Mike started to rise.

"It's cold tonight," Moon said, not looking up. "Perhaps we should sleep next to each other—for warmth. One on either side of Jacques . . ."

McLafferty nodded, and the two of them walked slowly to where the boy was fast asleep. They did not speak as they lay down.

After a time Moon whispered, "Grandmother is caught in the branches of the trees. That's how it looks. It seems peaceful tonight, and yet there is no peace anywhere. Why didn't I leave Jacques with Bright Shield and Grass Flower? I have brought him to a place of great danger."

"When you get down to it," Mike replied, "the boy came because he wanted to."

"Yes, but how could he know what might happen?"

"None of us knows that, Moon Morning Star."

Shortly before dawn rain began to fall once again, hard, spattering drops at first and then gentling and becoming more continuous.

Moon awoke to find herself lying side by side with Mike McLafferty. Jacques lay on top of her, his head snuggled against her breasts, one hand moving softly against her ribs. Moon discreetly turned to one side, so that the child slipped in between her and McLafferty.

But she did not fall asleep again, instead lay staring into the darkness. In that cold hour she could not keep herself from seeing again the bodies of the two young men, of poor Bessie Johnson, an imagined vision of the pretty red-haired Elizabeth, helpless and alone among Laroque and his men. She shuddered, wished very much to wake

McLafferty and curl against his side, but fought the impulse down.

They ate hastily, cold food and no hot coffee. Massive thunderheads spotted the sky, and as the party rode ahead, toward the Goshute Mountains, they passed through patches of sunlight alternating with areas of dark shadow.

The animals were almost lively now, their energies having been restored by sufficient water and grass, and the humans as well felt invigorated, the need for haste strong in all of them, although they still had no clear idea of how they would proceed once they had discovered Laroque's men and their innocent captive.

Long before noon they had managed to cross the sage-covered basin, and were riding upslope now and approaching the mountains themselves. The wagon trail rounded an outthrust shelf of black-gray stone, and ahead they could see an abandoned wagon, on its side and tilted precariously partway down a talus slide.

McLafferty and Wilson withdrew their rifles from the scabbards and rode ahead, weapons resting lightly across their saddlehorns. Moon clutched the pepperbox pistol Mike had given her and hushed Jacques.

A spring trickled down from the bare mountainside above, crossing the wagon trail in an oozing mire. Close by, in the shade of a bent juniper, lay Larue Duncan, half-dead and with both legs broken, the result of his attempt to drive exhausted oxen up a steep incline. The wagon had slipped sideways and tumbled downslope a hundred feet, throwing the man out and crushing the bones just above the knees.

Duncan looked up at the two men, nodded. "You're Big Mike McLafferty," he said. "I was in the Far West Hotel when you faced down Jean Laroque—yep, and I was there in Fort Laramie when all the trouble got stirred up."

"One of Laroque's men, then?" McLafferty demanded. "Why'd he leave you behind?"

"Bust legs, both of 'em. As is, I wasn't no better than dead meat to them sonsabitches. Worst mistake I ever made was stringing along in the first place. Ain't got some tobacco, do you? Goddamned Frenchie even took that off of me. Left me here to die or get picked up by whoever come along next, which is you. Some whiskey, maybe?"

"Left ye alone for the vultures?" Wilson asked.

Duncan nodded, then glanced up as Moon and young Jacques approached. "Ain't that the Injun gal whose buck got planted back to Fort Laramie? Of course it is. I ain't likely to have forgotten. We figured you to be on up ahead somewhere. Jean's got a powerful urge to collect that money on you."

"Thought he might," McLafferty grunted, dismounting. He squatted down next to Duncan and handed him a tobacco pouch and a packet of papers.

Duncan coughed, gritted his teeth, and then, hands trembling, managed to roll a smoke. "Got some busted ribs," he said, fumbling into the pocket of his leather vest for a fire-striker. "Maybe a punctured lung into the bargain."

Moon had dismounted now, too, and stood over the man, her eyes hard. "Where is the girl? Elizabeth Harrington?" she demanded, slapping the cigarette out of his hand. "If you want something from us, you must tell us about her. Is she still alive?"

Duncan cowered back at the sharpness of her words, his hand going protectively to his chest as if he were afraid she would strike him.

"The redhead? Yeah, she's alive."

He fumbled on the ground to retrieve his cigarette, managed to light it, inhaled hungrily, and broke into a spasm of coughing. He closed his eyes, waited for the seizure to pass, then puffed again.

"Been having some trouble breathing, in fact. Yeah, that gal's up the hill, hiding," he continued. "Thanks, McLafferty."

"Up the hill?" Moon asked. "Then she escaped?"

"Yep. Guess ye found her brother and them back on the desert. Jean and the boys was screwin' her the past couple of days, until she started screaming and biting every time one of us come near. Then Laroque, I guess he busted up her face some, and she run off, come back down here. Wouldn't have blamed her if she'd put me under right away, might have done me a favor, in fact. Instead she give me water and started nursing me, just like I was one of her own. Only a kid, actually, hardly pokin' age. She took cover when we heard one of your mules yelling."

Duncan inhaled again, and once more he coughed, gritting his teeth and waiting for the pain to pass.

Moon dismounted, told Jacques to stay behind, and began to walk upslope toward a cluster of gnarled junipers. Within a minute or two, she returned holding Elizabeth by the hand. The girl's clothing was torn, her eyes blackened, and her face badly bruised. She glanced from one man to the other, recognition beginning to show on her face, and began to cry, dry, racking sobs of relief.

"How far ahead are your friends?" McLafferty asked Duncan as he momentarily studied the girl's features.

"Left me to rot yesterday morning," the riverman replied, puffing at his cigarette more carefully this time and then sucking for air. "Elizabeth here, she says they're on foot now. The oxen pretty much gave out as we were crossing the desert. Going up the hill yonder, one of them just dropped dead on the spot—I didn't see it, though. That was after I got rolled by the wagon. Two more was lame, and the other three didn't have it in them to haul the wagons any farther. Jean started yelling at everybody, which ain't unusual, and then shot the oxen. While the boys was cutting the varmints up for whatever meat was on their bones, the girl run off. I . . . can't get my breath. Been talking too much. Leave me rest a minute. Sure ye ain't got no whiskey?"

McLafferty rode on up the trail, reached a crest, and found the carcasses of the oxen, partly butchered. A dozen or more vultures were at work on one of the bodies, and a pair of big gray wolves looked up from another, unwilling to back away from their dinner.

Close by, two abandoned wagons stood in the middle of the trail.

Moon gently led Elizabeth Harrington to a small, rocky area where the little stream of water ran nearly clear. She dipped scraps of cloth and washed gently at the laceration on the girl's face, speaking soothing, meaningless words to her as if she were a very small child in need of comforting. Now that Elizabeth had begun to cry, it seemed as if she might never stop. Her breath came in ragged gulps as she tried to pull herself together, and then the racking, shuddering sobs would come upon her again, and she rocked helplessly, hands covering her face. Moon simply held her, crooned to her, let the tears flow. Jacques hovered close by offering such childish words of encouragement as he could think of, his small face wrinkled in sympathy.

Eventually the half-hysterical sobbing stopped, and the girl began to speak. She told very little of the long nightmare of her captivity, passing over it quickly and without detail as if she could not bear to dwell upon the experience. She spoke tonelessly of how she and her brother Sam, along with their friends the Johnsons, had had more difficulty near Salt Lake; another animal had gone down, and the soldiers had left them behind. They had acquired an ox from a Mormon settler and taken the Hastings Cutoff against his advice, for they wanted to keep clear of Laroque's gang, whom they believed would take the northern route.

At this point the girl began to laugh at the horrible irony of this decision, laughter that quickly turned into sobs again.

Moon sought to distract her with a question, not really wishing to hear the details of the murders of Elizabeth's brother and friends. "But you managed to escape from them. How did you do that?" she asked.

"Yes," Elizabeth said, shaking her head as if trying to comprehend the words, then steadying.

"The animals would go no farther. The men lost interest in me for a time, and I ran away, hid up in those boulders just this side of the crest until morning, and then came back here to see if Mr. Duncan was still alive. I wedged myself way down under the rocks, and Laroque couldn't find me. . . ."

"The mad wolf grows even more crazy," Moon said. "So now they are walking to this place called California. I think we'll catch up to them very soon, then."

McLafferty came up behind the girl and stood listening for some moments before he spoke. "He's leaving quite a trail of blood behind him," he said grimly.

At the unexpected sound of the masculine voice, Elizabeth flinched involuntarily, then caught herself and looked up at him as he continued.

"The way our luck's been running, Laroque will manage to join up with Ely Van Norden and his bluecoats—get an escort by the United States government all the way to the goldfields—with our scalps under his belt."

"Have to make 'er to the Humboldt first," Wilson said. "We got time to catch 'em before they get thar, but then, what? With them on foot, we could pick 'em off one at a time, by Gawd. That what ye two are thinkin'?"

Elizabeth Harrington's expression was strangely vacant as she listened to Moon, Mike, and Fiddlehead talk. The girl, as Moon realized, had her own reasons for wishing to see not only Laroque but most of the others dead as well. Why, then, had she bothered to help this man, Duncan? He'd been one of them, had gone along with the whole bloody business. Very likely, he was one of the ones who raped her.

Fiddlehead stared up the trail and shook his head. "I figger the Frenchie'll try to make it to the Humboldt, all right, but not with the thought o' meetin' up with Van Norden. No reason he ought to have confidence in the lieutenant ever comin' along. Nope, he figures to bushwhack the first wagon train as comes down off the Raft River Cutoff. Probably hunt an' take things easy until someone shows up. Meantime, him and the lads has got a long walk ahead of them. According to yore map, sonny, the trail still crosses the Toanos an' then south around the Ruby Mountains, after that north to Humboldt. That's a bit o' walking, as this child sees it."

"True," McLafferty agreed. "There may be pilgrims directly ahead of us, though. Laroque and his gang may not have as far to go as we're counting on before they find some wagons with healthy animals attached to them. One thing's certain—we can't afford to stay here. Moon, do you think we can put together a travois for Duncan? Don't want to leave him, but we simply can't wait."

But Larue Duncan had begun to spit up blood, and shortly thereafter he passed out. A few minutes later more blood began to dribble from his nostrils; then he coughed terribly, gagged, opened his eyes one last time, and expired.

Elizabeth had insisted on being allowed to dig a grave, but the rocky earth did not cooperate with her efforts. When Mike returned, she had managed no more than a shallow trench.

The body was placed within the small excavation, and Elizabeth closed her eyes and said a short prayer. Moon, Fiddlehead, and Mike heaped stones over the body, creating a creditable cairn, one sufficient to keep vultures, wolves, and coyotes away.

Moon allowed Elizabeth to ride Ghost, and she herself mounted one of the pack animals, bareback.

The party of five left behind the remains of Larue Duncan and proceeded toward the summit of the Goshute Range.

13 They passed down out of the mountains and onto the floor of another broad basin, where the vegetation, though still scant, was luxurious in contrast to the worst of their journey. A sluggish stream, hardly enough even to be denoted creek by mountain standards, dribbled its way across the basin floor, producing one or two marshy areas and sustaining cottonwoods along its length. Horses and mules were grateful for a midday stopover, dipping their noses into clear water and drinking deeply, then turning to the extensive grassy areas.

At least McLafferty now knew the size of the enemy contingent. Duncan had specified twenty-five men, not counting himself, and Elizabeth Harrington claimed she had counted twenty-seven.

What was clear was that Laroque's men were now staying precisely on the wagon route, their footmarks showing distinctly near the creek and on the sandy, sagebrush slopes that angled toward the Pequops Mountains straight ahead.

Elizabeth had not really been able to master the art of riding the spotted horse, that animal having so far totally ignored her commands and pleas.

Mike turned back and caught up to the recalcitrant animal, leaned over to take the reins from Elizabeth. "Maybe you'd better just give up on this bad-natured nag." He laughed. "You can climb up behind me. Grayboy, here, he can hold the two of us. Doesn't look to me like you weigh more than a gunnysack full o' nothin', nohow, as Fiddlehead yonder might say."

Even as he spoke, patting the saddle behind him, he saw that the words were a mistake. The girl seemed to shrink into herself, her expression confused as she stammered out hesitant excuses.

Damned fool, Mike cursed at himself. The kid's been through too much, can't bear the thought of touching another man, even something like riding double.

Moon had ridden up behind him, the pack mule snorting in protest at this foolish business of going first one way and then the other.

"Ghost is only jealous because I'm riding this mule." She smiled, leaning out and patting at the spotted horse's neck. "I will ride close beside Elizabeth and talk sense to this silly animal. We shouldn't let him get away with such tricks so easily."

With an expression of gratitude, the red-haired girl looked at Moon, even gave a little laugh, and the three rode abreast back to where Fiddlehead waited, Jacques seated behind him and laughing at the antics of his mother's horse.

McLafferty sensed that Elizabeth needed to talk— somehow to begin a continuum of words that would put distance between herself and the horror and degradation to which she had been subjected. She was young, with her entire life still ahead of her, but he was afraid that what had happened could in fact turn her away from life. He hoped she would respond to attempts to draw her out, to make the healing flow of words begin. Now she made only brief, soft-spoken replies, lapsing into long silences between. Her eyes were strangely vacant, looking into some distance of nightmare or perhaps visions of better times.

Benton had once told him of a pair of Sioux girls, sisters a year or so apart, who had visited one of the Mandan villages in the company of their father. A bit too much of McKenzie's rotgut whiskey had gotten loose, and Antoine Garreaux and his Arikaras proceeded to drink themselves half-blind, causing the Mandans to escort the unruly Rees out of the village. In the process, the Arikaras managed to grab hold of the girls and took them along, subjecting them to a gang rape, then turning them loose and proceeding downriver to their own village. The girls were not otherwise harmed, and by morning they had found their way back to the Mandan village, where they were taken in, only to discover that their father had gone searching for them. When the father returned, both his daughters were dead—dead at their own hands, having committed suicide rather than face dishonor among their own people.

Sometimes a thing doesn't hit you until after the danger's past—then it strikes you all at once, and you find out you simply can't live with it.

It was little Jacques who finally managed to lure Elizabeth into talking—asking her questions out of innocent curiosity, getting her to tell him simple stories of her girlhood in a place called Kentucky, a place the child decided was endlessly interesting and exotic.

Once started, Elizabeth rattled on about a beautiful quilt she had sewn and sold at a village fair, sold for a good price; a chicken she had once made a pet of; a tree house her brother Sammy had built when she was very small but would never allow her to share. Suddenly the mention of his name brought a quick flow of tears to her eyes.

"It's all right, Liz-beth. Maybe I will build a tree house someday if Red Coyote will show me how, and I will let you come inside. Can Liz-beth be my sister now, Mother?" the child asked, turning to Moon.

At these words Elizabeth broke down completely, sobbing helplessly as she rode.

Jacques looked confused, terribly distressed. "I'm sorry, Liz-beth," he said. "I didn't mean to make you cry."

"No . . . no, Jacques," she managed to say, her voice thick with weeping, "you didn't." She reached a hand blindly in the little boy's direction as if to touch him. "I would like . . . I wish . . . I would like to have you for my brother," she said. "I don't know what . . ."

She was unable to frame words to finish her thought, and Jacques watched her, his own eyes wide and beginning to glisten with tears.

"Could I ride with you, Liz-beth?" he asked suddenly.

"Oh! Would you?" she asked, then turned to Moon, eyes still wet but the storm of weeping beginning to diminish. "May he? I'd like that."

Moon nodded, and the transfer was accomplished, Elizabeth hugging Jacques on the saddle in front of her. She seemed to take great comfort in the child's presence, and now she began to open up, to respond to the adults' conversational questions as well.

McLafferty felt relief as he led her to talk more, the words coming almost in a flood now—how she had always been sweet on Bud Johnson and was bitterly disappointed when he suddenly took it into his head to marry Bessie Langtry; then how she met her own first beau at a church picnic; her abilities in school and how she hoped one day to attend an academy for young women and so perhaps herself become a schoolteacher; the deaths of her parents during a cholera epidemic; then she and her brother, working together, running the family farm themselves; after that the lure of new land in Oregon's Willamette Valley, a dream world Bud Johnson himself had painted in glowing colors, selling the farm, starting out . . .

McLafferty, momentarily caught up in this vision of land—a farm, no, a big ranch—kept thinking of ways in which what remained of Elizabeth's dream could still become a reality. He was looking beyond the showdown with Laroque now and assessing his own life in the process. Gambling or prospecting—were these really sufficient ends? Was there not a better way of living, a more stable and secure life—not in the settlements, but somewhere West, a place where a man could look out and see his own cattle grazing, maybe, and look the other way to see snow-capped mountains and forest-covered ridges? Well, from time to time, perhaps, he might ride into town and play a little at cards. There was something in the very idea of gambling that was utterly addictive for him. A man who was good at something, not just good but *damned* good, better than anyone, a man couldn't be asked just to up and leave that kind of thing behind him.

With trapping, it had been different—yes, because the fur trade had given out. But civilization wasn't the answer. Bridger, he had found a way of staying on in the mountains—by running a supply station, which is what the fort was. But Mike McLafferty had discovered a certain genius with cards, he had the right kind of mind for it. Along with that had come the necessity of being a dead shot with a pistol, something else he had a talent for.

"In Oregon," Elizabeth said at last, "no one will ever need to know what . . . happened, will they? But how will I get there? It all seems so hopeless now."

"Nothing hopeless about it. Moon and Fiddlehead and I will take you there—or maybe you can stay with us for a time, wherever it is we settle down. Me, I was on my way to California before I got sidetracked. Hell, maybe Oregon's a better shot at that. People get thrown together sometimes and . . . and what I'm saying is, we're your friends, Elizabeth. Right now we've all got to stick together. You and Jacques riding comfortable, little lady? A few days down the road and everything's going to look a lot better than it does today, I promise you that. Any time you want to rest, let me know."

McLafferty, you're making promises you may not be able to keep. No human can solve another's problems, and God himself can't undo what's happened to Elizabeth Harrington. But damn it, if you found a starving dog, you wouldn't just feed it a time or two and then tell it to be on its way.

Such an act implies an obligation, a kind of unspoken pact. The truth is, you're planning a solo attack against more than two dozen men, and you haven't the slightest idea how you're going to pull it off, or even if you've got the chance of a snowball in hell. What you've figured out so far: entrust Moon to Fiddlehead's care and then slip off alone. Whatever she's got in mind, you don't want her dead at the hands of the same man who murdered her husband. Fiddlehead will get her back to Leg-in-the-Water and the Cheyennes, and then maybe she can put her life back together again, her honor satisfied. Laroque's a dead man because that only requires one well-placed bullet, one touch of a trigger. But the chance of you getting away from twenty-five or so crazy dogs is somewhere between little and none, and you know it. That's as good a way to go as any, maybe, but it's all worth nothing if anything happens to Moon. Well, Fiddlehead will take care of things—unless you can somehow turn fire against fire, shoot and run and cut them down one after another. McLafferty, maybe it's the simple impossible challenge of the situation that's got hold of you, not allowing you to see things clearly. A fistful of garbage, and a big pile of chips on the table. So you raise and then light a cigar and stare across the table at your opponent, even though you're damned near certain he's got a full house or better and money to bet and doesn't give a damn whether he wins or not. . . .

Red Coyote, Moon noted, was skillfully leading the girl to talk, and she found herself merely listening, drifting at a steady rate across the great silent land as the stream of human words continued.

Gradually her own mount and Wilson's moved some distance ahead of the other two. Moon spoke now to the old trapper.

"When do you think we'll catch up to Jean Laroque?" she asked.

"Won't be all that long now, Moon. Tell ye what. They's some lakes to the other side of these mountains we're climbing, at least according to that tom-fool map o' Mike's. Wouldn't be surprised to find the whole gang sittin' on the shore an' wishin' they were back on the Big Muddy River, hustling cargo. Several lakes, in fact, little ones. Trail runs south, clear around the Rubies, then north to the Humboldt—Mary's River, we used to call 'er. Me an' Kit Carson, we trapped the headwaters one winter, an' the beavers was as big as cows, for a fact. Back in '03, it were."

"Those were *large* beavers, Uncle Fiddlehead," Moon laughed, mimicking young Jacques.

"That was before your Lewis and Clark went across to the Pacific Ocean. My father told me they didn't start out until 1804. Mike said the same thing."

"McLafferty?" Wilson chuckled. "Hell-fire, gal, who ye goin' to believe, a wet-behind-the-ears kid like him, or a honest-to-Gawd trappin' man like me? He's young. What does he know?"

Moon considered the matter and decided to change the subject. "Fiddlehead, do you believe Elizabeth is pretty? Her hair and eyes are the same color as Mike's. Perhaps I will not be alive in a few days. Do you think Red Coyote might. . . ? My son is already in love with her."

Wilson gathered the drift of the question. "No-whar as purty as you, Miss B'ar-Killer. If ye've started feelin' jealous, they ain't no need for it. Mike McLafferty's had you on his mind for a long while now—since before ye ever got married to White Bull. Told me about it when him an' me first started up from the settlements, an' that's the truth."

Moon smiled in spite of herself. "*Jealous?* No, that's not what I'm feeling. Did Red Coyote really tell you that? Why should I believe you? I don't think you have ever been to the headwaters of the Humboldt at all, and I don't think Salt Lake filled up the way you said it did. Now it would please me to listen to what you say, but how can I?"

Fiddlehead chuckled and sucked air through the spaces between his teeth. "What ye got to understand. They's such a thing as a tall tale, an' if a hawg can tell a good one, then it's by-Gawd true. If he cain't tell 'er the right way, then it ain't true. Thar's a certain skill to it, like huntin' buff'ler or trappin' beavers. On the other hand, they's a different kind o' true, an' that's what I jest told ye."

They crested the Pequops and moved downslope, westward, and into a shadowy ravine. Below, gray-purple, lay another broad basin. Shining above yet one more series of ridges and perhaps thirty miles beyond that rose the broad, snow-covered range called Ruby Mountains, a genuinely formidable wall impossible to traverse by wagon—Ruby Dome, Verdi Peak, and to the north of the chain, beyond a low saddle, Hole-in-the-Mountain Peak. The long white formation gleamed pink-violet, crests shimmering in late light, a huge red-orange ellipse of sun hanging there as if permanently suspended until it vanished when they moved ahead downslope.

Moon had been studying McLafferty's map, was able to read its printed notations without difficulty—something her father had taught her, a gift, he'd said, that she'd never lose. The big mountains, she now realized, were her greatest ally—if, indeed, they were able to cross through them on horseback. The emigrant trail ran far to the south, then back northward to Humboldt River, describing a wide V shape on the map. Somewhere on the far side of those Ruby Mountains, then, they would reach the wagon trail ahead of Laroque and his gang—unless the rivermen were foolish enough to attempt to cross the mountains on foot. If this were the case, then a showdown would no doubt occur somewhere on the back of the range—more than twenty on foot against three on horse and mule back. The fight was not Fiddlehead's Moon knew, but she also knew the old mountaineer had no intention of backing off or of playing some kind of secondary role.

And what of the possibility of disaster? That would leave her son in the care of Elizabeth, a stranger—two helpless ones alone in a wilderness.

There would be no disaster, Moon told herself. A need for revenge, for honor, had brought her all this way. She would not fail. It would be best, all around, if she herself were able to take Jean Laroque's life, no matter what happened to her in the process. Red Coyote would see to it that Jacques was protected, was given a home, possibly even a white man's education.

Grimly she envisioned Mike and Fiddlehead and

young Jacques standing beside a cairn of stones, her grave, and bidding her farewell. Perhaps Mike would then take Elizabeth for a wife—why not? The girl was one of his own kind. All in all, Moon didn't like her vision.

A change had come over her, she realized. She had loved White Bull, would always love him, would cherish the memories of their time together. But she was also feeling things toward Red Coyote she had never felt toward the one who was dead. Somehow, during the course of this dreamlike journey to avenge the death of one man she had loved, she had grown closer to another man—closer than she had imagined possible with any other human being. It was necessary for her to have this man, and she knew it.

Only there may not be any world after a few days, just darkness, perhaps a journey to a place only vaguely conceived of. It is difficult, difficult even to think of what may happen after Jean Laroque's blood spills out upon the gray-white earth of the desert.

They made camp beside a rivulet of clear water that splashed down from a series of rocky pinnacles above and then meandered serpentine, across a lush green meadow. In the upper branches of a crooked pine, a pair of eagles were nested. Fledglings were in the large basket-shaped nest, and the parent birds swooped past their campsite several times, screaming, before gaining darkness caused them to return to their lodge.

Fiddlehead went stalking off on foot, rifle in hand, and after a few minutes a shot echoed down the mountain, followed by a piercing whoop.

"The great hunter has killed us something for dinner," Mike said as he built up the fire. "Let's hope it isn't one of our own horses that wandered away from the meadow."

Wilson returned, half-stumbling through the growing darkness, a deer draped over his shoulders and blood dripping down his buckskin coat.

Moon butchered the animal as Elizabeth watched, repelled and reluctantly fascinated, just as she had always been on the farm at slaughter time.

"Children," Wilson said as the meat was roasting over the flames, "I've been thinkin'. Add it all up, this ain't such bad country. Deserts down below, forests up high, plenty o' varmints. Sonny, they's beaver upstream. Ain't that somethin'? Maybe all them y'ars we was lookin' in the wrong places. Ain't no Pieds Noirs out hyar, ye know. Diggers, maybe, but—"

"With poisoned arrows, "Mike said, winking at Moon. "Why back in '09, me an' King George of England, we hauled fifty packs o' plew out o' these hills, an' that's a fact."

Wilson shook his head and cut off a section of meat, chewed.

"Ye'll never get the hang o' it," he said, pronouncing the words with as much dignity as he could muster.

Elizabeth looked from Mike to Fiddlehead and then to Moon. She sensed good-natured humor, but neither man's words made any sense to her.

"May I sleep with Liz-beth tonight?" Jacques asked as Moon sliced off sections of juicy venison for him. "She says she won't mind."

* * *

Big Mike McLafferty and Moon Morning Star exchanged memories of White Bull, sitting across the campfire from each other after the others had retired. At length the moon rose, slightly deformed now and waning toward three-quarters, but its light was if anything brighter than it had been during their crossing of the Salt Lake Desert, dusting pinyon and juniper alike with a soft effusion of radiance.

The two had really not spoken of White Bull before—not more than general remarks about things they both knew well enough. Cheyenne tradition held that use of the name of one who had died actually hindered the spirit from making its journey across the broad band of stars at sky center, on to the Spirit World, a land similar in many ways to temporal existence, not a place of either punishment or reward, but a world in which death was said not to exist.

McLafferty honored this approach to death, convinced that the taboo against using a dead person's name at least helped to blunt grief's sharp edge.

But now it was Moon herself who mentioned her dead husband's name, asking Mike to explain to her how it happened that he and White Bull had sworn brotherhood.

Mike told his story but neglected to remark on the fact that she, Moon, had been the essential cause of their wrestling match.

Moon nodded.

"Wilson said that you wished to pay a bride price for me when that happened. Did he speak the truth?"

McLafferty sipped at his cup of coffee, gazed

off at configurations of stars in the westward sky.
"Would Fiddlehead lie?" he asked.

"I remember those days. I was just a girl then.
We only spoke a few times, you and I. Truly, I did
not know you wished to court me. I was lonely
after my father died, but I hadn't even thought of
marriage. You and White Bull were always together that year you lived among the Cheyennes.
You hunted together and ran your trap lines together, and sometimes White Bull helped you at
your trading post. If I had found someone else's
favor, what would you and White Bull have done
then?"

"We had already decided that one of us would
have you for a wife," Mike replied. "If there had
been another, we would have taken him on a long
ride somewhere and convinced him that he must
look elsewhere."

"So you two decided? Why, then, did neither
one of you let me know how you felt? It was only
after you rode away, Red Coyote, that my husband
began to visit Leg-in-the-Water's lodge where I
was living. One day White Bull brought fifteen fine
ponies to Leg-in-the-Water's lodge and tethered
them outside. He brought other things too: a fine
new pistol, and a dozen pairs of moccasins, and
vermilion and scarlet cloth, and a big cooking
pot—things that had come from your trading post.
Leg-in-the-Water examined the gifts, and that was
when I realized I was to be White Bull's wife. At
first I was angry, and I nearly decided to ride
away from the village. But where would I have
gone? I made White Bull wait three days before I
would agree to it."

"We stole those ponies from the herds of the

Many Lodges." Mike grinned. "White Bull and I and a gang of boys rode over to Big Horn River that summer. The Crows have numerous horses, so many they hardly keep watch over them at all. That was the only war party I ever went on. We left our own horses a mile or so away and sneaked in by starlight. The ponies made no noise, and we simply led them away—we could have stolen hundreds if we'd had a large group of warriors with us. White Bull left a Blackfoot moccasin in the meadow, and after that we drove our herd northward, toward Yellowstone River. It was a long ride and a good one—no one was killed and no one was wounded. I think Chief Yellow Belly and his Crows found the moccasin, because we later learned he'd led a great war party against the Piegan Blackfeet. So that was how my brother got the ponies he gave to Leg-in-the-Water."

"It is strange, Red Coyote. I never knew what was going on. Men are good at keeping their secrets from women, I think."

McLafferty grinned. "Women are good at keeping secrets also," he said.

They continued to talk for a time, and then McLafferty made a strange suggestion—that they climb up onto the mountain behind their campsite.

"The moonlight's so bright it's nearly like day, isn't it? What will we do when we reach the top of the mountain? Perhaps we should sleep instead. It is possible that we may catch up with Jean Laroque tomorrow—I think it may be tomorrow."

McLafferty nodded agreement. "You sleep, then. I'm wide awake, Moon. I think I'll prowl up the hill alone. Listen to the wind in the pines, maybe."

He rose, adjusted his hat, and strode off toward

the meadow's upper edge, circling about the horses and mules so as not to disturb them.

At the edge of a first stand of pinyons, he heard a whispered voice behind him.

"I am not sleepy either," Moon said.

Distance may have had something to do with it. They were a long way now from the medicine cave on the side of Laramie Peak. Possibly it was an awareness that time itself might have grown short, a proximity to danger that might claim either of their lives. Or perhaps it was moonlight on a mountainside and a soughing sound of wind among bristles of pinyon pines.

They found themselves face to face, their arms about each other, foreheads pressed together. He was clinging to her, his grip powerful so that she had momentary difficulty in breathing.

"Moon, I . . ."

Suddenly she did not know what to do, everything she had learned about men seemed to have deserted her. She opened her mouth to speak his name, and at that instant he pressed his lips to hers, *kissing*, the white man's kind of lovemaking, something Cheyenne women laughed about. Moon had never done it before, although once when she was twelve a drunken trapper in one of her father's camps had tried and been rewarded by a knee in the groin. She was not certain how to place her lips as McLafferty pressed his face to hers, both his big hands about her head now, his mouth working upon hers. Her heart was beginning to race, and she clung to him, clung desperately, felt weak inside, as though whatever strength she possessed were deserting her.

His urgency. Strength, male strength, male desire . . .

His tongue touched her lips, pressed insistently between them.

Then he drew away from her, still holding her as before but enforcing a distance she did not understand.

"I'm sorry," he said, the voice sounding far away and not at all like the words of Red Coyote. "Something came over me, and I . . ."

A long moment passed, and she said nothing, did not know what to say. Her thoughts were a jumble, all confusion. But was this not why she had followed him away into the moonlight? Was this not in fact why he had suggested climbing the mountain, whether he had known or not?

It was not *thinking* that caused her to act—nothing conscious at all. She closed her eyes and pressed her face forward, sought his mouth once again. Her lips were parted, she wanted him to touch her that way again.

She clung to him as he kissed her, would almost have been satisfied if they had remained that way, together, for half the night. His hands touched at her, stroking her hair, her arms, her back. Then he pulled away once more, and when he spoke, his voice sounded husky, as though he had been running.

"Moon, this is tearing me apart inside. I . . . I'm actually hurting . . . I want you so much. Don't hate me for it . . . I swear to Christ and Old Man Coyote himself, I'm only human. Gal, let's get back down off this crazy mountain before—"

"I don't want to go yet," she whispered, only half-recognizing the sound of her own voice. "I . . ."

He stared at her, and for an instant she half-supposed he had not understood her meaning.

"I want you to take me—here in the moonlight."

McLafferty pulled her to him, kissed her on the mouth, the cheeks, about the eyes, on the forehead, the throat.

"Take me now, take me, do something, I cannot stand this anymore. . . ."

He lifted her in his arms, and she felt almost like a child again. He laid her down gently and then his hands were upon her, struggling to remove her clothing. Cool air touched her breasts and moved over her bare legs; she felt bunchgrass and sand beneath her, then his mouth touching at her belly.

She moaned softly and reached down with both hands, felt the hardness of him, spread her legs, and guided him into her.

She did not feel like a child any longer.

14 Moon Morning Star was up well before dawn. Despite the lack of sleep, she felt fully rested and eager to continue pursuit of White Bull's murderer. She rekindled the campfire and set about warming over some remains of their previous night's meal, humming softly to herself.

Perhaps the lovemaking with Red Coyote was the cause of her renewed energy. She considered the matter for a time and then began to feel a terrible sense of guilt and sadness come over her. It didn't make sense—she wanted to cry and to laugh at the same moment. Even with all that had happened since the agonizing moment in the Cheyenne village, the arduous journey she had traveled, how could she have fallen so gracelessly into the embraces of another man, no matter what the circumstances?

Moon glanced at Elizabeth, still curled like a child in her blankets, bright hair tousled and one arm holding Jacques close against her. She felt a tightness in her chest, a swell of pity for the grief and horror that the girl, really just starting her life, would carry with her forever. Time would change the memories, soften the grief somewhat, but nothing before the great and final darkness could eradicate the pain. Perhaps the red-haired girl had the best claim of all upon the mad dog's life.

But she won't be the one to pull the trigger, Moon thought. She hugs Jacques as a little girl would hug a doll, for comfort against darkness.

Moon tossed a handful of crushed coffee beans into the blackened pot full of boiling water, hesitating a moment as the good aroma drifted up; then she shrugged and crumpled in some willow bark and sage leaves.

Fiddlehead emerged from his blankets and stepped to the fire, whiskers twitching as he sniffed at the brew.

"By the great hawg"—he chuckled—"ye've jest about got the hang of it. Now we jest drap in a mite o' chawin' tobaccy—"

"No tobacco in my coffee," Moon said, smiling greetings at the mountain man. "Look at the rest of these lazy ones, Fiddlehead. Maybe you and I should go off and find Laroque and let them sleep until noon. Here, I think the coffee is ready now. Give me your cup."

"Ain't ready till she's boiled fer a couple o' hours," Fiddlehead grumbled, but held out his tin cup anyway, watched her as she filled it, humming to herself.

"Ye're powerful chirpish this morning, Miz Moon," he said, squinting at her as he sipped cautiously at the steaming liquid. "Seems to me ye oughta be a tad tuckered, ye an' Mike both, climbin' around on the mountain half the night."

Moon made herself very busy, stirring at the

stewpot and pouring coffee for herself. She knew she was blushing and then couldn't keep her mouth from twisting up into a guilty smile. She rose abruptly, strode to where McLafferty was beginning to stir in his blankets, nudged at him with her toe.

"Up, Michael Red Coyote," she ordered. "Have you forgotten why we've come all this way? Fiddlehead and I are ready to leave now, but you may stay here with the little ones if you wish."

Mike sat up, wiped a hand across his face, and staggered toward the fire.

Moon repressed a shiver of remembered sensation as he smiled at her, his eyes lingering on hers for an extra moment.

His hands, his mouth, on me. Mustn't think this way. White Bull. . . .

She ladled out coffee and a plateful of beans and jerky for him, then moved to the other two, whom she had made an unconscious decision to lump together as "the children," choosing to ignore the fact that Elizabeth was only five years her junior, of an age when she, herself, had already been White Bull's wife for a year.

Elizabeth volunteered to clean the breakfast dishes, taking the tin plates and pots to the spring to rinse them, Jacques tagging along. Moon, meanwhile, was a maelstrom of activity, bustling about the camp, tying blanket rolls and fastening pack-saddles.

"Come, Red Coyote, the sun is halfway up the sky. Perhaps Fiddlehead and I will have to bring Laroque's scalp back to you. Come help me saddle the horses, Michael. Today we will kill the rabid dog. My dreams told me so last night."

Elizabeth, bringing the dishes back and kneeling to fit them into a packsaddle, looked up at Moon's fierce words, her face going white.

Moon saw and paused, going to the girl and crouching beside her, touching gently at a pale cheek. "Are you ill? Perhaps you should sit down for a moment."

"No," Elizabeth said, fumbling again at the straps on the packsaddle, "no, I'm fine."

"You're not, though," Moon insisted, staring intently into the pained blue eyes. "You suddenly went pale. You looked as though you'd seen a cannibal spirit. Tell me what is wrong."

"It frightens me, all this talk of blood and death. I have seen enough blood and death. All I want now is . . ." She broke with a convulsive suck of indrawn breath, tears suddenly spilling down her cheeks.

"I'm sorry, I did not think," Moon said, putting a hand on Elizabeth's shoulder. "You must not listen to me. I get carried away sometimes. Jacques never pays any attention to my talk, do you, Little Bull?"

Jacques shook his head, but watching Elizabeth cry, his own face contorted as if he might burst into noisy sobs himself at any moment.

"I understand," Elizabeth said, drawing in a long breath and wiping the wetness from her face. "Those men killed your husband. They killed my brother, also, and my friends, they did . . . other things to me. I suppose I should feel the way you do. But all I want is for the killing to stop. I want to find a quiet place, a safe, happy place, and just

stay there forever and never see any more death. I
. . . I'm not brave like you are. I'm afraid, afraid. I
don't want to see those men again."

"Don't cry, Liz-beth, please don't cry," Jacques
said, throwing himself violently into the red-haired
girl's arms. "I'll take care of you. I am a warrior,
and I won't let the bad men hurt you."

"Sometimes I think there are too many warriors
in the world," Elizabeth said, hiding her face against
the top of Jacques' head and hugging him tightly.
"Wouldn't it be good, Jacques, if there were no
warriors at all, and men only tended to their crops
and built their houses and lived in peace with
their neighbors, if there were no more guns and
knives and bows, but only plows and tools and
good books to read?"

Jacques listened to this passionate declaration,
glancing up at his mother with a puzzled expression as he considered Elizabeth's vision. "No," he
said after a time. "I don't think I would like that."

Moon, at a loss for words, touched the hair of
both heads, the bright red-gold one and the small
dark one, and turned back to the horses, leaving
the two to comfort each other.

"She all right?" Mike asked, pulling tight on his
cinch strap, punching Grayboy in the ribs to make
him deflate and pulling again.

"I don't know," Moon said. "She's been through
so much. I'm afraid I upset her. We shouldn't
speak about blood and death so often. She is too
young . . . too young to have seen so much."

Mike nodded wordlessly. Then, "Moon, last
night . . ."

"I knew what I was doing, Red Coyote. I wanted

you. Women are not the strong ones in matters of love, no matter what men think."

She spoke these words without raising her head, but now she looked up at him, her eyes suddenly shining, mysterious, her expression a strange mixture of tenderness and hostility.

"You are a good man, Michael McLafferty, but what we did—I don't think that was good. It seemed so at the time but it must not happen again. I promised my husband, I promised his mother and father that I would avenge his death. This is what we must be about. Perhaps later, perhaps when the blood debt is paid, I will be able to think about life again."

"Lady," Mike said slowly, staring at her, "I think the devil's got hold of your soul. But if that's so, then I guess he's got mine too. You know, the odds on us pulling this thing off aren't too good. As long as Laroque's on foot and we've got horses, there may be a chance—better than none, anyway. Still, it's no favor to White Bull if his son gets left to die out here."

"That will not happen, Red Coyote."

"The two of ye goin' to dither around there all day? Swear, I could o' saddled up a whole herd o' Crow ponies in the time it's took ye to slap blankets on them two degenerate nags. The Frenchie's up ahead waitin' fer ye, but he's bound to lose patience and move on by next week sometime."

They rode down from the Pequops and out onto the desert floor, heading for the jagged, snow-topped line of the Ruby Range. They were in dry country again, sagebrush and occasional stands of low, gnarled junipers, the land broken, with ridges and basins between, ground cut by sandy, steep-sided washes, dry this time of year but evidence of the occasional violence of storm, of water gathering and rushing in thick muddy torrents through ravines, carrying with it great quantities of the earth that had little in the way of vegetation to hold it in place.

Well before noon the sun had become merciless, heat waves shimmering out across the desert and drawing distant objects deceptively close at times. The Rubies glittered ahead of them, and yet as the small company plodded onward, the mountains seemed to recede so that they never drew nearer.

Elizabeth Harrington squinted into the glare, pulled herself upright on the Palouse's jolting back. After a small show of annoyance in which the spotted horse refused to move until the others had drawn some distance ahead, Ghost had behaved reasonably well this day, although it seemed to Elizabeth that the animal intentionally adopted a hard, stiff-legged trot that seemed to jar her spine clear up into her skull and caused her bones to ache intolerably.

She closed her eyes for a moment, a vision of Kentucky appearing vividly in red-tinted darkness. She saw green, gently rolling hills, cool groves of sycamore and oak, her own favorite place to sit and daydream for hours up in a big, old walnut tree across a little stream from the farmhouse. She smelled the cool, slightly musky fragrance of the broad leaves, imagined a twilight green among branches, soft bubbling sounds of the creek. And suppertime, her mother's voice drifting out through blue evening light, calling to her.

"Wake up, little one."

She opened her eyes to a relentless glare of light. They had topped a rise, and the Rubies rose ahead, faintly translucent and seeming so near she could reach out a hand and touch the snow, and yet distant as a dream of coolness and peace. Moon Morning Star rode beside her and watched her, smiling.

"You don't want to go to sleep and fall out of the saddle. You were daydreaming, weren't you? You looked as though it was a pleasant dream, anyway."

"I never really understood how wonderful it was," Elizabeth said, almost as if she still were in that other place. "I never knew until it was too late, and the whole world had fallen apart."

The two women were silent for a time, and Elizabeth again felt the ache in her bones from Ghost's jolting pace. Grasshoppers sang, leapt with long, whirring glides from the sagebrush as they passed, yellow and red underwings flashing. Little Jacques was riding some distance ahead, with the oddly named old mountain man, Fiddlehead Wilson. From time to time their words drifted back, and Elizabeth could hear the child ask a question or the drone of Fiddlehead's voice as he went on with some long story from an apparently interminable supply.

Such a strange way to live, Elizabeth thought, and yet Jacques seems happy, at home wherever he is. Could I ever be that way?

McLafferty rode near Fiddlehead and Jacques, he and Moon seeming intentionally to keep a considerable distance between themselves. Elizabeth wondered at this, for it was apparent even to her that they were deeply attracted to each other.

She looked at Moon, the half-breed woman having once again pulled slightly ahead, riding easily, her back straight and her movements harmonizing so naturally with those of the awkward packhorse that they almost seemed to be two parts of the same animal.

She is beautiful, Elizabeth thought, even living this way, sleeping on the ground, exposed every day to sun and wind, no hot water. A fierce, wild kind of beauty. And she isn't afraid of anything. I wonder if she really killed a grizzly bear, or did Jacques make that up? Mike's in love with her, I think. Of course he is. How could he not be? I can never be like Moon. I don't understand her, them. I wish . . .

It was a peculiar group, almost like a family, she thought, and they had taken her in without question, seeming to assume naturally that she'd be part of their family also. They were all kind to her, but they were violent, they accepted violence as a part of life. They planned, without any apparent compunction, to kill another human being, and even though that human being was Jean Laroque, the monster who murdered Sam and Bud and Bessie, who laughed when she told him she was a virgin and forced her to take him into her mouth, then pulled off her clothing, struck her when she began screaming, threw her down and rammed into her, at last turned her over to the others, as many as wanted her, and they brutalized her until she wished also to die . . . even then Elizabeth could not understand how Mike and Moon, kind to her, could so easily plan the man's death. Was it any different than what Laroque and Chardin had done out on the desert?

Thou shalt not kill. She had always accepted the commandment as absolute, but Moon did not, nor did Mike or Fiddlehead Wilson, did not seem to consider it at all. Even little Jacques wished to be thought of as a warrior. This aspect of her protectors frightened her. She couldn't put the contradictory elements together to make any sense. In her world, one kind of people were murderers, ones who were capable of violence, and they were outlaws, criminals. The others, civilized, Christian people, did not kill for revenge or for any reason. They relied upon a rule of law.

Which kind of people, then, were these she had fallen among? Or was there a third kind—those who recognized something like *law* but who chose to enforce it themselves? Yes. Here, in the terrible empty wilderness of desert and mountain, the idea almost made sense. . . . It was, she supposed, the way of the Indian peoples. Moon *was* Indian, more or less, and Mike and Fiddlehead had lived much of their lives among the savages—who, in fact, didn't seem *savage* at all. Laroque, Chardin, Jackson, Utti, and the others, though—filthy beasts without morals or mercy or respect for anything except their own lawless desires. . . . No, not beasts, Horses, cattle, the free-running antelope, they were innocent, beyond any awareness of good and evil. And in many ways, she surmised, the Indians were like them. How could anyone seriously suppose some being called Old Man Coyote, and not Jesus, was the protector of humanity?

Her head ached from incessant glare of reflected sun, and her body was a mass of pain, one part hardly differentiated from another, all hurting. She was very glad, then, after what seemed like an eternity, when McLafferty called a halt, and the group rested in the shade of an overhang in a small canyon, a thread of water still oozing among rocks and a tangle of willow brush and wild roses.

By the afternoon the heat was somewhat less fierce, a few thunderheads building over the mountains westward and the sun's rays slanting through a thin haze. The Ruby Mountains were, at last, appreciably closer than they had been in the morning, and before sunset the band reached the massif's foot. They continued southward a few miles toward a long, narrow lake they had earlier seen shimmering in the distance, a lake surrounded by a band of welcome green and in the shadow of the high peaks of the range.

Near the north shore they found remains of an encampment, one used by numerous parties of emigrants, and clearly showing signs of human presence only the night before. Moon rode up beside Mike, and together they leaned down and inspected the trampled ground, saw clear prints of heels in the earth, charred bones of deer or antelope, not all as yet having been carried away by coyotes, skunks, or badgers.

Moon dismounted, held a hand over the ashes of a campfire, felt warmth. "They were here this morning, then," she said.

"Looks like." McLafferty nodded, studying again the worn map he carried in his pocket. "Trail goes south, loops clear around this range. Too high to cross over with wagons, but we should be able to make it on horseback, come down ahead of them on the other side. What do you think, Fiddlehead?"

"Figger ye're right for once, Mr. Mike. Still lots o' snow up yonder, but we'll make 'er through."

The two men dismounted also, kicked at an empty whiskey bottle lying near the ashes, its paper label still intact.

Moon stepped to Mike and leaned over to look at the map he was holding. "The main route's to the north," she mused, "up along the Humboldt. If we could reach that . . ."

"What is it?" Elizabeth asked, her voice tense. "Is this where the rivermen camped last night, you think?"

Moon looked up and nodded, patting Ghost's nose absently as the Palouse nudged against her.

"Please, let's get out of here," the red-haired girl said, and Mike noted an edge of hysteria in her voice.

"Right you are, Sweet Betsy. Nothing to be gained by staying here. Tell you what—we'll head on down the lake a piece and set camp early. We could all use a little extra rest tonight."

"Sounds good to this hawg," Wilson agreed. "Reckon they's bound to be some fresh meat hereabouts—only water and forage to speak of in miles. I'll head off t'other side an' see what I can scare up. Here ye go, hoss," he added, lifting Jacques down. "Ye climb aboard there with yore ma."

Moon lingered at the campsite a few minutes longer, her eyes bright and her nostrils flared as she walked the area in circles, picked up bits of rubbish, used the toe of her moccasin to turn over others.

Like a dog, Elizabeth thought, a fierce hunting dog, or a wolf, maybe trying to catch scent of its prey. Laroque. She shuddered, her skin twitching at the thought of even being close to the spot where the men who held her captive had camped.

"I want to go. Please! I don't want to stay here," she cried out, her voice shrill, as if she might start screaming and not be able to stop, ever.

Moon glanced at her, seeming to emerge from some trance of her own, then nodded and swung onto the back of the pack horse, Mike lifting Jacques up behind her.

They camped in a grove of cottonwoods a mile farther down the shore of the lake. By the time they'd tended to the horses and built a fire Fiddlehead rode in with an antelope across his saddle. As a haunch roasted, they drank coffee and smelled an almost unbearable delicious odor of meat juices dripping and sizzling in the flames.

McLafferty pulled out cigars, handing one to Fiddlehead and another to Moon. Elizabeth watched in mild shock as the beautiful young half-breed woman lit the foul-looking black stogie, took a puff on it, and smiled.

The sun had passed behind the mountains several hours earlier, but daylight lingered in the sky. As they sat, smoking and talking companionably, thunderheads above the peaks flared tremendous red, and shadows out across the desert turned purple. The eastward ranges glowed an unreal, hazy lavender. From somewhere nearby a chorus of coyote music sprang up, quavering notes rising and falling with a seemingly intentional orchestral pattern of melody and harmony.

Elizabeth listened to the coyote songs, heard frogs beginning to call to one another and the faint lappings of lake water. A breeze stirred and the air seemed wonderfully fresh and alive.

"It's peaceful here," she said to no one in particular. "This would be a good place to live if it weren't so lonely."

"Might at that"—Mike nodded—"though I'd be more inclined toward someplace higher up in the Rubies, maybe. Meadows and the like. But it's pretty country, all the same. A man could get fond of the desert, as long as there are water and trees close around. Fiddlehead, you think there's a possibility of gold in these hills?"

"Might could be," Wilson replied, breaking off a twig of sage and chewing on it.

"A home," Moon mused. "You're thinking about a home again, Elizabeth."

"I don't know. It's just that I feel at peace here, maybe for the first time in a very long while."

"Yes, but I'm hungry," Jacques White Bull said. "How long do we have to wait?"

Fiddlehead leaned forward, poked his knife at the meat. "Nother two, three days," he said. "While we're settin' around, I might as well tell ye about the time me an' Benton found these here mountains an' why we decided to call 'em the Rubies. Was the winter of '08, I recall, an' a fiercer winter there never were. So danged cold we couldn't even talk to each other—the words jest froze in midair an' hung there, an' we'd have to build a fire to thaw 'em out so's we could find out what we said."

"Heard '09 was colder," Mike remarked. "Heard that year the fire stuck to the flint, and when you and Benton put the strikers back in your pockets, they'd thaw out and burn your backsides."

"Now, how would you know about the winter of '09, ye wet-behind-the-ears pup?"

"Just what I was told, is all."

"Wal, now, as I was saying"

Suddenly, from nowhere, the roar of a large-caliber rifle, followed by a blood-chilling shriek, and then a second shot.

Elizabeth screamed, crouched over, hugging Jacques to her as if to protect him with her body. Moon and McLafferty grabbed for rifle and pistol and leapt to their feet.

Only Fiddlehead remained seated, gazing out beyond the firelight and smiling faintly. "Speak o' the divvel," he said, and immediately after that a voice came out of the darkness.

"Halooo the camp! Ye lookin' fer company?"

The next moment a figure entered into the circle of light, tall, in greasy buckskins, and grinning from ear to ear.

Fiddlehead squinted, looked up. "Aloysius Benton, ye old hawg-sticker. I swear, me an' Mike hyar was jest talkin' about ye."

Mike laughed, holstered his revolver, and strode forward to shake hands with Benton; Moon walked behind him, still clasping a rifle. Benton pounded McLafferty on the back and then drew Moon into a bear hug.

"Looks like ye took on an extry hand since I seen ye last time, Michael. Right purty one, too. What kind o' lies has this ol' rotgut peddler been spreading about me, anyway?"

Elizabeth relaxed, and Jacques ran to greet Aloysius.

"Uncle Fiddlehead was telling us about the time when the words froze in midair, and you had to thaw them out with a fire, Mr. Benton," he said.

"Right ye' are. Winter o' '14, that was. Time when we discovered the lake o' fire an' the divvel hisself cuddled up next to 'er fer warmth."

Elizabeth looked at the two, shook her head. She was sure she would never understand any of these people, but in some ways they had become her own, and apparently her family now included this odd new member.

"That ain't it at all," Fiddlehead said indignantly. "I was talkin' about the *real* cold one, '09."

" '09? Naw, '09 was right mild year. Ye got extra chow? This child's brought his whole damned clan with him."

Benton turned, cupped his hands, and produced the cry of a wild tom turkey in the act of courting hens to his harem.

Within a few moments several additional figures appeared from out of the shadows—Big Dog Benton, Two-Tail Skunk, Pawnee Woman, and a yellow-haired white woman named Chastity Cosgrove, formerly of the Mormon persuasion.

15 Sunlight spilled across the huge trench of Ruby Valley, glittering from the surface of the long, narrow lake of meltwater that summer heat had drawn down from a dwindling snowpack on the backs of the mountains. Vultures, having perched for the night in a cottonwood grove, slowly fanned their big wings as they readied themselves for a day of spiraling through high desert skies in search of the leavings of mountain lion, wolf, and bear. Then, with a noise like that of a series of muffled pistol shots, they heaved themselves upward, gaining altitude and eventually drifting with wind currents.

Smoke rose from the McLafferty-Benton campsite, and strips of genuine pork bacon sizzled over open flames, oil dripping, sputtering, and flaring up.

Aloysius Benton, having had enough of Wilson's coffee the night before, insisted on brewing up his own variety—different from Wilson's only in that he did not add sage.

They had bacon, antelope steaks, and griddle cakes, the latter requiring the last of the jug of molasses that McLafferty had acquired at Bridger's post.

"That's Ruby Dome up above us," Mike said. "What do you think, gents? Ride south for a bit and then try to cross the mountains? It can't be as bad as it looks. Our option's to push like hell and come up on Laroque from behind. I'm for crossing the range."

"Startin' a war with a gang of dung-eatin' wharf loaders ain't exactly the best way of gettin' to the goldfields all in one piece, now is it?" Benton laughed, winking at Big Dog, Cozzie, and Two-Tail Skunk. "Tell ye the truth, though, this old wolverine's up for it. Jean Laroque's not real high on my list of favorite people, point of fact. Rainy weather, and I still limp a bit from that pistol ball he put into my leg over at Fort Union. Looks to me like Jean's gone complete crazy, like workin' along the Missouri sort of kept him in check, ye might say, and now he's of a mind not to kowtow to nobody. I tell ye, the riffraff that's heading west, ain't hardly one of them as ye'd want to pitch camp with. It's a strange thing—get a bunch together like that and out away from what ye might call restraints, an' they're subject to do jest about any damned thing. Van Norden an' his bluecoats don't make a hell of a good bunch of dog soldiers, not with half a continent to watch over. The smart thing, now, that's to find the looie an' his soldiers—an' for Elizabeth to tell him the whole bloody tale, file an official complaint. That way ye let the gov'ment boys take care of Swamp-water Jean. Of course, it do make sense for ye an' Moon to steer clear of the troops, considerin'."

"Where would you guess Van Norden is right

about now?" Mike asked. "You said you were with him over on Raft River."

"Thousand Springs, mebbe. Look on yore map thar, Michael. Wasn't far behind us—a day's ride, not more. Could be to the head of the Humboldt already, in fact. Make a sight better time on the regular Californy path. Man's crazy to go the Hastings route, an' that includes present company, though I guess ye had your reasons."

"Twenty-seven men?" Big Dog asked. "There are only five of us."

"Six," Moon said quickly. "I have not come all this way just to act like a woman who demands that her men avenge the death of her husband. I gave my word, and I'll keep it."

Fiddlehead glanced at Mike, then at Moon. "Sure enough," he agreed. "Six. Them's bad odds, 'Loysius, but we got the element o' surprise on our side. Laroque sleeps at night, just like a ordinary human critter. The river rats is south o' us now, makin' a big loop around the mountains. They be on foot an' not movin' too fast, otherwise we wouldn't of caught up with 'em so easy. Might not be more'n twenty miles down the valley, as I see it."

"Maybe six, maybe eight," Big Dog said. "Yellow Hair and Pawnee Woman both know how to shoot. They are very good at it. The leader of these men once shot Benton for no reason at all—since my father has never been known to make anyone angry at him. The rivermen are all guilty of murder and rape—the best thing we could do would be to capture the scum and turn them over to our women. Laroque is a man without honor. Not even the Blackfeet would act as he has done. We spend too much time talking. Let's go do what we must do."

Pawnee Woman, Big Dog Benton's *other* wife and the least loquacious of Aloysius Benton's entourage, paid little attention to the talk of the men. Instead, she studied the expressions, first of Moon and then of Elizabeth Harrington, and attempted to understand precisely what the relationship between these two was to be. The red-haired girl was silent, her face stark white, and she looked at the ground as if she were unwilling to listen to the men's talk of killing. But the other, Moon Morning Star—her eyes glittered more fiercely than those of any of the men.

Finally Pawnee woman spoke directly to Moon. "You suffered at the hands of this La-roque first, but now the men wish to have a great warpath. The revenge-taking is yours, not theirs. You must do as you think best."

"Women are not allowed to speak during a council," Two-Tail Skunk grumbled. "That is because they would always wish us to shout insults at our enemies and nothing more."

Fiddlehead laughed. "Don't think that's exactly what Moon has on 'er mind. Skinnin' alive's more like it. Ye remember what kind o' meat it was she brought in, 'Loysius? Wal, let's find us an easy trail up through these leetle hills hyar. It's time to be gettin' on, jest like yore overgrown kid says."

They moved south a few miles along the wagon trail and then turned their animals toward the precipitous wall of snow-draped mountains westward, climbed through a series of jagged arroyos where horses and mules experienced difficulty with their footing.

At length it was necessary to lead the animals along, but even that expedient did not solve their problem.

"It's one step forward an' two back," Fiddlehead sang out. "This rate, an' we'll be back at Bridger's Fort by morning."

Jacques, insisting he could climb as well as anyone, trudged along behind Moon and ahead of Elizabeth, not once asking for rest. At length he stumbled as they traversed a scree, and Elizabeth immediately reached down and lifted the child into her arms.

Moon turned, shook her head. "Give him to me, Elizabeth. He's too heavy for you to carry."

McLafferty, working Grayboy and the cross-eyed mule on the slope below, glanced up, perceived the difficulty.

"I need someone to ride on my shoulders," he called out.

"I want Red Coyote to carry me, then," Jacques insisted. "Women aren't strong enough."

"Traitor," Moon hissed, smiling. "All right, if Mike really needs a rider, go ahead."

The boy, his energy suddenly renewed, scrambled his way back to Mike, who hoisted him up.

"Flatland ahead," Two-Tail Skunk called from a pine-dotted rim above. "Now it will be easy. Big Dog, tell them to hurry!"

The going grew easier, at least.

They moved ahead, riding their horses and mules once more, ever upward but now through mixed growth, chaparral, piñons, firs. Along a small, cascading stream, dogwoods were blooming, the big white flowers hanging almost like fruit among the branches.

Above that were snowfields, not continuous but scattered about here and there below outcroppings of broken limestone. A few flowers were blooming, small clusters of white and yellow and red, and glacier lilies dotted the slopes.

"Look back," Mike said to Moon. "Isn't that something? This is big country, big. . . ."

"It's all big country." Moon laughed. "We've never been anyplace where it wasn't big."

"Haven't been this high up before, either. With a view like this, we could almost settle that dispute you and Fiddlehead were having."

"What dispute, Red Coyote?"

"About whether the world's flat or not. You said if you could see enough of it all at once . . ."

Moon stared into Mike's eyes—strange, dancing points of light in them, a different kind of excitement than she had ever seen before.

"Even from here," she replied, recalling the discussion, "it doesn't look either round or flat."

"Sure as hell isn't flat, anyway. These mountains may not be as high as Cloud Peak or the Grand Teton, but they're not giving away much. Ruby Dome, over there, she's a fair enough mountain. On a good day from up here, we could see damned near to Salt Lake."

"How could we see farther than right now?" Moon demanded. "The sky is completely clear."

"Got a point there." Mike nodded, grinning. "But wouldn't this be a fine place to live, if there were a way of doing it? I'll bet Old Man Coyote sits up here at night and thinks about how he created it all."

They crossed the back of the mountains, then through a high basin area whose rims were dotted with stands of bristlecone and limber pine, the old trees twisted and bent into strange configurations. Red willow and what appeared to be a variety of huckleberry grew along a clear, cold, shining stream that drained away northward, a likely branch of the Humboldt, as Mike figured.

Then they were on their way down, the big knob of Ruby Dome rising above them, down through thickly forested terrain that diminished as they descended into a series of broad green mountain meadows across whose width several clear rivulets ran, meandering in serpentine motion and joining at the low end.

Mike drew Grayboy up beside Moon and pointed back over his shoulder. "If we were looking for land instead of a murderer," he said, "this would be a fine place. Summer pasture for cattle, at least—maybe a big ranch house down below somewhere, at the foot of the range. Are you up for homesteading, Moon? Since Leg-in-the-Water and Bright Shield *gave* you to me, I think I'll exercise a husband's prerogative and—"

"A husband's what?"

"You admit I'm your husband, then?"

"I didn't say that, you did. Red Coyote, did Benton give you a bottle of whiskey while I wasn't watching? I have come all this way with you for only one reason."

"I haven't forgotten what we're about." Mike bit at his lip, stared at the woman, then shook his head and forced a grin. "The long trail's almost at an end. Another day or two, and those vultures we saw this morning could be picking all our bones. But right now, you have to admit it, this place shines. Okay, I'll get hold of myself. But damn it, this would be good land to own—now, wouldn't it?"

Moon shook her head. "I have lived among the Cheyennes too long," she said. "How does anyone own such a place? Yes, it is beautiful—like an island of green in the middle of a desert, floating, the way those islands seemed to be in Great Salt Lake."

"You'll do it, then?"

"Do what, Red Coyote? Give me that whiskey so I can dump it out. Men always get crazy when they drink."

"No whiskey, not a drop. Maybe after we plant Laroque, then you and I will have a nip or two. You up for it, or not?"

"Drinking?"

"No. Building us a damned ranch—right here in the Rubies."

"I thought you wished to go find gold in California."

"Hell with the gold. Answer now!"

Moon smiled and then caught herself on the verge of pursing her lips as if to kiss him. Shook her head again. "Maybe," she said.

McLafferty stared at Moon, then winked. He drew his Colt-Walker and proceeded to fire three shots into the air.

The other riders in the troupe, up ahead, turned and looked back to see what was going on.

"The Pieds Noirs are attacking," Mike shouted,

then kicked his heels to the gray's sides, galloped off, singing as he went:

The poor coyote stole my meat,
Then I had nought but bread to eat,
It was not long till that gave out,
Then how I cursed the Hastings route!

"Mr. Mike, ye gone loco, or what?" Fiddlehead Wilson yelled.

"Red Coyote acts funny sometimes." Jacques laughed.

Moon stroked her son's hair. Strange, she thought, strange. Tomorrow we may have gone into the long darkness, Red Coyote and I both, and yet he is like a child today, he makes jokes and acts as if the world is just beginning. Perhaps it is for us, or perhaps it is ending. And yet I feel it too—we cannot control what will happen, and so our minds choose to play. I do not feel that I will die, and yet . . .

Sunset flared across the sky, thin bars of stratus glowing orange-red above the Sulphur Springs Range. Here, near the base of the Rubies, were broad areas of grassland, hardy shortgrasses that looked as though they might provide proper forage for cattle. Cottonwoods rooted along the banks of several small streams that flowed down from the mountains, while higher up were groves of quaking aspen extending to the margins of a forest of piñons.

Three nearly naked Indians studied them from a safe distance, pointing and otherwise gesticulating, and then vanished, on foot, shadowlike, into a chaos of boulders and piñon pines.

"Shuckers," Benton said, his Hawken across his old pinto mare's saddle. "They damned near done in Joe Walker an' Meek when they headed over to California in '33—Bonneville's brigade, ye know. Don't have horses, an' they don't have guns. Jest as well, too. Dip their arrows in rattlesnake poison, for all the good that does. *Te-moas*, they calls themselves—at least I think that's the bunch around here. Myself, I never been this far west before. I want to see the Pacific Ocean before the Big Coyote comes to pay me a call. A damned griz jest about did it for me last winter, busted me up pretty bad, too. Anyway, it got me to thinkin' about things I hadn't got around to as yet. So when me an' Big Dog got our business tended to over at Bridger's place, I talked the young folks into headin' west with me. Anyhow, they need me to look out for 'em. That Two-Tail Skunk, he's subject to fall into any hole that's near him."

McLafferty studied the grizzled face of the man who had befriended him when he was a greenhorn boy of fifteen, years earlier.

Half a lifetime ago, from my perspective. Benton hasn't changed much—seems as timeless as the mountains themselves. Hell, he's still got the same damned horse as when I first met him, and it wasn't a colt then.

Moon Morning Star rode up to where the two men were talking, Elizabeth jogging along behind on Ghost, the girl's blue eyes shining.

"All right," Moon said. "We will come back here, if that is what you wish, Red Coyote. Can you really build us a house, or are the gun and the deck of cards the only tools you know how to work with?"

"The lady wants to bust sod?" Benton asked. "What in hell for?"

"It's your turn to answer," Moon persisted.

"A house, is it?" McLafferty laughed. "Moon, you've sure got big ideas for a half-breed female. But maybe Aloysius will bring us back here for the burying. What do you say, Benton?"

"Shame to spoil it with the likes of Jean Laroque. Just leave 'im out to dry if you ask me. Ain't even a wolverine'll touch him."

"If you wish me to have your children, Mike McLafferty, then you'll have to build me a proper home. I didn't always live in a Cheyenne lodge. My father built us a nice log house in Michigan Territory, though I was too young to remember very well."

"Then you did have a home once," Elizabeth said. "And now you'll have one again. Oh, Moon, how wonderful."

"Well, like I said, I don't remember much, only that my mother kept everything in just the right place."

"Yes, that's how it is."

"Maybe." Mike grinned. "Isn't the sunset beautiful? The air's different here on the desert—morning and evening, the light seems to shine right through things. Aloysius, how long do you think it'll take us to get to California?"

"You son of a bitch," Moon said. "You asked me in the first place, or don't you remember? To hell with you!'

"Matter of fact," Mike said quickly, "I'm a pretty fair carpenter when it comes to working with logs. How big do you want the kitchen?"

"To hell with you, McLafferty. Maybe I'll scalp you—take *your* hair back to Bright Shield."

That night, Moon and Mike slept together with Jacques between them. They talked little, even after the child was fast asleep; Mike slipped his hand over to rest upon Moon's and she did not withdraw from the touch, was in fact grateful for its warmth. She found it impossible to fall asleep. She thought of the battle to come, but oddly that troubled her less than other matters Mike had brought into the open. She did not feel ready yet to talk about a man-woman partnership—not while the meeting with Laroque loomed almost immediately upon them.

Moon reflected upon her life with White Bull, a life more or less free of any problems except those of survival, a life in which both danger and constant moving about were essential elements. And Red Coyote? This was a man who stood with one foot in wildness and the other in an unfulfilled need to settle down, a desire for some sort of predictable existence. Did she feel that need as well? Was her life with the Cheyennes now closed to her forever because she had gone in pursuit of Laroque? Would she even wish to return?

With McLafferty there was the possibility of a new life. Yet perhaps true and enduring commitment was simply not part of his nature. He had already left one wife behind, a proper woman and a proper home. Was he likely to leave her as well, maybe return to St. Louis? Had there been other Indian women among the Crows, possibly, or the Assiniboins? What, after all, did she know about Michael John McLafferty?

She knew that she was in love with him, in love in a way that she had never even experienced with White Bull.

Love. It was a kind of madness, a blindness to all practical considerations.

Maybe the strange and exasperating complex of sensations she was feeling was purely and simply the result of her own loss, a deep longing for what had been ruthlessly taken from her with White Bull's death.

Love? Moon could not come to terms with what she felt—only that it seemed good when McLafferty was near. There was rest in his strong arms and there was craziness of sexual desire in his embrace. The mere smell of him triggered off something inside her, something that she apparently had very little control over, as did the sound of his voice. So it was with the animals: a male bird cried in the night, and in the morning a particular female sought him out.

She could not explain what she was feeling—only that she knew she was feeling something somehow far more powerful than any defense her conscious mind could construct. Furthermore, she realized now, she had mysteriously begun to give in to it that morning outside the fort, when McLafferty recognized Ghost and came riding over, looking for his friend White Bull.

"Red Coyote," she whispered, "are you still awake?"

A mumbled reply, and Mike turned over on his side.

"How would we live?" she asked.

A long moment of silence followed.

"Raise cows and kids, I guess. Go to sleep, you

little hellcat. We got serious business ahead of us tomorrow."

Moon closed her eyes, smiling.

A gray cloud cover drifted across the desert during the night, and by morning a thin, cold, mistlike rain was blowing in. Fiddlehead was up early, oiling his Hawken when the others awoke. A fire was already blazing, and Wilson's soot-blackened, blue-speckled coffeepot was pouring out fumes.

Pawnee Woman and Chastity Cosgrove boiled strips of venison and camas roots gathered the previous evening, much to the displeasure of Jacques, who had not yet quite accepted the fact that his molasses was all gone.

The small band had just finished breakfast when Benton cupped one hand to his ear.

"Them's pistol shots," he said. "I think that's what they be."

"Thunder," Fiddlehead replied, stubbornly concentrating on his coffee. "Ye others hear anything?"

Big Dog shook his head and glanced at Two-Tail Skunk.

"Don't hear nothing," Skunk said.

"Pistol shots," Benton insisted. "Michael, let's you an' me mosey on down to the crick. Cain't be but a mile or two away."

Aloysius Benton and Mike McLafferty were back within an hour, and with them was a short, gray-bearded individual wearing a black stovepipe hat. The green eyes beneath a mat of bushy black eyebrows were blazing with indignation.

"Folks," McLafferty said, "this is Mr. Phineas

Brown. He and his fellow Californians have just been set upon by Laroque, Chardin, and the rest of our friends."

Brown gestured with both hands. "The Satan-possessed heathens took our wagons and oxen and our weapons as well, all but a couple of pistols they didn't find. Didn't harm us physically—didn't have to. The whole crew of them had guns pointed at us when we woke up. I knew we should have brought dogs! As it was, we were taken advantage of as easily as children. We've had nothing but good luck since leaving Independence, and now this! Left us with nothing. Pocket watches, money, supplies all gone. They had in mind to take our boots away as well, but I persuaded them the result would be no less than mass murder itself. Then they began shooting at our feet, and we were obliged to run for cover. Mr. McLafferty says you people have been trailing these men. Well, they're too much for you, I can see that. Too many of them, and all armed. I don't know what my fellow pilgrims and I are going to do, but any assistance you might render would be greatly appreciated."

"Wal," Benton said, tugging at his own beard, "the dockhands ain't far ahead. Two, three miles up the trail is all. Mike figgers he caught a glimpse of 'em as we was riding down into the flat. I guess we can catch up whenever we want to. What Phineas hyar says, them oxen ain't much piss an' vinegar left in 'em. Beats walking, but that's about all. So mebbe we ought to get our wits together."

"Stripped us blind," Brown muttered, "our guns and the whole ballywhang. I'll kill the God-cursed son of Satan with my own hands, if I get the chance."

Moon nodded at Mike. "We will overtake them after dark," she said, her voice cold with determination. "We've come a long way for what happens next, Red Coyote."

16 Big Mike McLafferty leading, Hawken loaded and primed, Colt-Walker .44 resting comfortably at his side; the band of ten now moved down to the main wagon trail, to Phineas Brown's weaponless emigrants. Brown, the nominal leader of the group, was welcomed back with bad-natured enthusiasm.

Brown called the men together, introduced his newfound friends, and suggested a plan for retrieving the stolen wagons, animals, weapons, and cash with Mike McLafferty in command. The Argonauts, however, outraged though they were in having their outfits stripped from them, were far from willing to get themselves involved in any gun battle. As Mike and then Wilson spoke of how the stolen equipment and animals might be reclaimed, even Phineas Brown's enthusiasm for a showdown appeared to wane. Nonetheless, stiffening his back, the little New Englander insisted that he wished to go along.

A quantity of food was left with the emigrants, as well as one pistol and some ammunition, and McLafferty turned Grayboy northward.

The small attack force rode toward the Humboldt, into the face of the cold, misty rain, scheming and planning and keeping a keen eye on the trail ahead of them.

By midafternoon they had still not managed a sighting of Laroque and his crew of renegades, and Benton called a halt.

"Time to take a blow," he said. "Look, we got blue sky yonder. Fiddlehead, your prediction was off by a couple hours. Maybe we'll get our moonlight after all. Well, me an' Big Dog'll do some scouting for ye. Michael, how far you figger it is to the Humboldt junction? What's that official map got to say?"

McLafferty studied the worn and folded sheet of paper, squinted at the ridges to the west and the peaks of Verdi and Ruby Dome to the east. "Ten miles, Aloysius. Don't think it's more than that. We're close. I calculate they'll make camp just south of the river, probably where the two streams come together."

"That's what a sane man would do, more likely than not. About wharf rats, ye cain't be sure."

"Not if they's other Californians on t'other side," Fiddlehead countered. "If they's one thing Jean Laroque won't pass up, it's a chance to do some hell-raising. Be it a small party with some females along, ye can bet him an' Chardin are going to make the best of 'er. A few brush lodges with Shuckers in them, it'll be the same story."

"Then how would we be able to cross the river at night?" Phineas Brown demanded. "Just shooting across the water isn't going to do any good."

"Like I said." Benton nodded. "Me an' my overgrown kid hyar, we're going to go take a look-see.

Have some chow and see if ye can talk old Fiddlehead into makin' ye some coffee. Phineas, ye'll
enjoy it, I promise. Michael, move 'em out in
about an hour. We'll meet you along the trail
somewheres. Moon, you make certain Two-Tail
Skunk don't skulp nobody while I'm gone."

Only a few trailing clouds remained, and the
sun was dropping toward the horizon when Benton and Big Dog met their cohorts, the group now
within a mile or so of the main California Trail.
Laroque and his men were camped on a point of
land just at the confluence, precisely where McLafferty had predicted they'd be. No one else was at
the junction, and the rivermen had apparently
decided to wait until morning to take their new
wagons across, though the Humboldt presented no
genuine obstacle, the stream being little more than
a large creek winding through the desert and destined, as the map indicated, to die in a sink some
three hundred miles westward, virtually within hail-
ing distance of the Sierra Nevada and California
itself.

"Here's the plan, then," McLafferty said. "First,
we pull up into position, and that means on foot.
It's essential that Laroque and the boys are not
aware of our presence until the moment of the
attack. If we can manage to get to within a couple
of hundred feet of them and not be detected,
then there's a very good chance that most will end
up jumping into the river to save their hides. If
they catch wind of us too soon, then we've got a
gun battle on our hands and that's a problem,
considering."

"What about the women and the child?" Phineas

Brown demanded. "Do you propose they stay here, or what?"

McLafferty glanced at Moon—saw that she had not the slightest intention of being left out.

"The women have to be kept at a safe distance," Brown said, removing his stovepipe hat and examining the lining. "If what we're about to attempt turns into a disaster, they must be in a place where they'll not be discovered. Moon, I understand the intensity of your feelings—your husband fell victim to the leader of these men. That being the case, I realize nothing any of us can say is likely to dissuade you from participating. But the teenager and the child must remain with Miss Cosgrove and the Indian woman."

Elizabeth swallowed, then put her hands on her hips, looking white-lipped but defiant. "I won't stay behind," she said. "I can't shoot, but I can load. I'm going with Moon and Mike and Fiddlehead."

"Jacques needs you, Elizabeth, in case . . ." Moon said gently. "I hoped you would stay with him."

"I need to do this, Moon. I can't let you go without me. I wouldn't be able to live with myself if I hid away and let you risk your lives."

"Liz-beth comes with me." Fiddlehead nodded. "Hell fire, it'll be safe enough. Ain't like any of us was goin' to get hurt, after all. The leetle gal can load for me, whichever rifle I ain't usin' at the moment."

"You sure that's a good idea?" McLafferty asked. "I—"

"Sonny, how many times I have to point it out— ye're still wet behind the ears. If Liz-beth's with this old dawg, she'll stay safe an' sound. Benton there'll tell ye."

"Pawnee Woman loads for me," Benton agreed, "an' Cozzie loads for Big Dog. Whole thing ought to come off slicker'n your basic greased pig."

"Well, *someone* should stay with the child," Brown objected. "You're not going to tell me you plan to take a four-year-old into battle?"

"I want to go. I am a warrior," Jacques pleaded.

"Next battle, partner," Mike said. "This one you're sitting out."

"Yellow Hair will stay with the small warrior," Big Dog declared. "Pawnee Woman will load for my father and me both. Little Warrior, I expect you to keep my woman safe."

Cozzie looked at her husband, started to speak, then glanced at Jacques, nodded silently.

"Damnation!" Fiddlehead chuckled. "I by-Gawd kind of feel sorry for them rats, now that we've run 'em to ground. Way I see it, they ain't got no chance at all."

Big Dog Benton glanced at his father and shrugged. "Skunk and I must put on our warpaint. McLafferty, when you get all this figured out, you tell us what to do." He gestured to his two wives, and with that, he and Skunk strode away, the women following.

"Tell me one more time, Michael, jest what is it you an' Moon hyar plan on doing to old Jean when ye get him?" Benton asked.

"Skin the son of a bitch alive." Moon Morning Star smiled, reaching behind her head and beginning to undo the long trailing braid of her hair.

* * *

Moon moved silently away from the group, climbed upon a small ledge on a sandstone formation, sat with her back against the grainy rock still damp from the rainstorm but warming in late sunlight. The sun was now a crimson ellipsoid resting on the jagged ranges to the west. A thin, fanlike cloud formation above flared blood-red as she watched, slowly darkening to maroon.

Blood in the sky, everything the color of blood. The sun is gone, now. Perhaps we will not see it again.

The sky gradually darkened, the last tinge of crimson leaving the clouds, and in the silver of early twilight the evening star emerged glowing with pure, blue-white intensity,

The evening star that is the morning star, the star of my husband's people. I am half-French, half-Iroquois in my blood, but tonight, for you, my husband who is gone, I am all Cheyenne. After that, the world will have changed once again, and perhaps I will not be part of it, or only that part which lies in darkness and returns in grass thrusting up from the darkness. If so, then perhaps we will be together in another place, perhaps not. I don't know.

Coyotes sang again, their trembling music clear and ringing under the stars. Moon drew out a small pot from the pouch that she carried slung over her chest, dipped her fingers into it and carefully smeared the black paint made from tallow and charcoal across her cheekbones and forehead. She drew a pattern of broad stripes, then another streak from lower lip down across her chin and under. It was the pattern she had seen White Bull wear into battle once; it was the black of victory, defying tradition and telling his enemies, in effect, that he had already won.

Tonight I act in White Bull's stead and for his honor. Thus, I wear White Bull's face. Tomorrow, if I am alive, I will wear another face, and I will be another man's woman. I think that you will understand, my husband who is gone, for I will have kept my promise to you. You are in one world and I am in another, and in this world my heart has chosen its mate.

For an instant, then, the world seemed to change, as if a mask things wore had slipped for the time, and another had taken its place. Ghost, and White Bull riding him at a gallop, the long streamers on his warbonnet trailing across a star-crowded sky, lance high and bronzed shoulders gleaming in invisible sunlight. Then the point of his lance dropped, thrust forward, and Moon knew, although she couldn't see the face of the enemy, that the man was dead.

Then White Bull was walking toward her, smiling; as he neared, his face changed, became the face of a coyote, Old Man Coyote, grinning and beckoning to her as a voice spoke out of the darkness, a voice that came from everywhere and nowhere, a voice like the singing of coyotes and like thunder over the mountains and like the rippling of a stream, all these things at once, and much more.

One Above dreams, and the dream keeps changing. For a little time you are here, and then you are gone. The dream has changed for you, Moon Morning Star. After this night you will no longer be Morning Star. That is the way One Above's dream proceeds, and the way it should be, although none of us understands it. Ride well to-night, and it could be that you will remain upon the earth for yet a time.

Coyotes still sang, but the music moved away from her now. The sky was dark and thickly scattered with stars. An evening wind blew, and a little distance away she could see the campfire and the forms of the others moving about. There was that, and nothing more. The mask was drawn back upon the face of things just as it had always been.

Moon climbed down from the ledge and walked toward the fire to join the others, Mike stepping away from the group to meet her as she approached. She wanted very much to embrace him, to allow herself to be folded in his arms, but she did not; instead, she held up her hand in formal greeting, as one warrior would to another.

McLafferty looked puzzled for a moment, and then, as they moved into brighter light near the fire, he saw her face, stared intently for a moment.

"Tonight I am White Bull, Michael McLafferty. Tomorrow, if we are still on the earth, I will be Moon, not Morning Star any longer, not White Bull's wife."

Three fires were burning on the point of land at the confluence of the South Fork and the main stream of the Humboldt. Thin bands of stratus were running the desert sky, and residual moisture in the night air hung in wisps of trailing vapor above an area of still water just upstream from the crossing. Few stars were visible, and a westerly breeze drifted upstream, filling the night with an odor of sage and mesquite.

Big Dog had slipped to within perhaps thirty feet of the nearest of the campfires, keeping up-wind of where the oxen rested, still in their traces and chewing their cuds. From where he lay beneath a big greasewood bush, Big Dog could easily observe the group, as well as hear their voices rising in minor argument.

Big Dog recognized a few of the men who had caused the disturbance in Washakie's village at Bridger's Fort. Laroque was squatting close by the middle fire, a jug of liquor in hand. The tall, rangy man called Cottonmouth was stretched out a few feet away, head propped against a bedroll. Others among the faces: Sam Kurtz, Alphonse Tournier, Smoky Joe Utti, Delaware De Guerre, and Pig-Sticker Jackson.

"Damn shame we couldn't of held on to the little redhead," Smokey Joe said, walking over to his booshway and reaching for the liquor jug.

"*Mais, non,* what have you done for your keep today?" Laroque demanded, taking another swig. "Always I have to carry you, eh?"

"Give me the damned jug," Smokey Joe said, his words but not the tone of his voice a demand.

"Go catch a pronghorn an' stump-break 'er," Jackson suggested. "You were the one was supposed to be hangin' on to her ass. Ain't got no one to blame but yourself, Monsieur Utti. Since you lost 'er, mebbe it's yore turn in the barrel, by Christ!"

"Pull your pecker out of them breeches, an' I'll cut the poor little thing off. " Smokey Joe laughed.

Laroque handed him the jug and after one pull insisted on having it back.

The rivermen's rifles, Big Dog noted, were

stacked against a cottonwood. Beyond that, each man was wearing a holstered pistol. Two ponies were tethered in a grassy area beyond the wagons and oxen.

He'd seen enough. He turned about and slithered on knees and elbows back through the brush cover toward a low, sage-covered rim where the others were waiting, already in position, perhaps fifty yards from the rivermen's camp.

"Give 'em time to get sleepy," Benton urged. "In matters like this hyar, confusion's the main ingredient. What moon we got's jest pokin' the rim now. Actually, them thin clouds ain't hurtin' a thing. Kinda spread the light around, they do."

"Wagh! It's jest like I said." Fiddlehead grinned.

McLafferty spun the cylinder of his Colt-Walker twice and then, for the fifth or sixth time, checked the spare cylinder that he kept, loaded, in his coat pocket.

"Another ten minutes or so," he whispered, "and Moon and I are going down."

"Sure that's a good idee, Michael? Us hawgs didn't come along just to watch the show, ye understand."

"Insurance, Aloysius. When a card-man *has* to win, he keeps at least one ace up his sleeve."

"Wondered how ye did 'er."

"Never had to win before. It changes the whole nature of the game. Fiddlehead, you've got to keep the girl back out of trouble. Elizabeth, do you hear me? Stay behind Fiddlehead, and keep low."

"Don't see no cause why ye two should be havin' all the fun," Wilson grumbled. "Me or 'Loysius, either one could probably handle the entire she-bang all by ourselves. Hell fire, what difference if old coyotes like us get put under? I'm thinkin' it's more important fer ye lovebirds to keep yore hides in one piece. Leetle Jacques has got a right to grow up, at least, and someone's got to tend to marryin' off Liz-beth when the time comes. I bet 'Loysius agrees with me."

"That I do," Benton said. "Big Dog, Skunk, an' I'll go down, if anyone's obliged to do 'er."

"Mutiny among the ranks." McLafferty chuckled. "What you gents say makes sense, but only *logical* sense. Moon and I . . ."

"Have come a long way for this thing," Moon finished the sentence. "But my claim comes first, there is no other way."

"Iron-headed squaw," Fiddlehead muttered. "Have it yore own way, then, but gawddamn it, *be careful*. This lame bull's jest startin' to get fond o' the both of ye."

"Red Coyote," Moon whispered, "we're wasting time. Let's go."

"Don't do nothin' stupid until after them hawgs is all quiet, now," Benton said again. "Michael, if I never taught ye anything else, it was to use yore head."

"I hear you, Mother," Big Mike replied, momentarily grasping the older man's shoulder. "It'll all be over in just a few minutes, and then the bunch of us can get back to whatever it was we were doing before insanity came to visit. I have it on good authority that there's so much gold in California a man has to hire a mule train just to haul the stuff into an assay office every day."

"Twice a day, most likely," Wilson muttered as

Moon and Mike slipped away, downslope, into a tangle of silver-shadowed chaparral.

A few moments later Benton heard gravel sliding from the bank below.

"That kid always did have heavy feet," he whispered to Fiddlehead. "Yer powder dry, old-timer?"

"Ye be older'n I am," Wilson replied. "Keep an eye peeled, if ye can still see that far."

Jean Laroque, uneasy but not quite able to put his finger on the cause, rose from his blankets and stepped to one of the dwindling campfires, put a couple of short sections of dry-rot willow onto the bed of coals, and then heard something like pebbles sliding down a bank, rattling. Was someone out there? The damned emigrants, perhaps? If the odd little man in the black hat and his friends had hot footed it all day, then there was an outside chance it might be them—one or two, perhaps, with enough gumption to attempt something.

Enfant de garce, he thought, I will use them for target practice. Why did I let that leetle runt talk me into leaving them their *chaussures? Eh bien*, now they will die with them on.

Laroque stared into the moonlit shadows a moment longer and then removed his pistol from its holster. He checked the cylinder, raised his weapon, and fired once into the general vicinity of the noise.

"Jean, why are you shooting?" Alphonse Tournier called out. He rose from his bedroll, came stumbling over to where Laroque was standing next to the now blazing campfire. "Eh, Jean, let your old friend have some more of the whisky, *non?*"

"Go back to bed and rub your toadstool for a while, *mon ami*. I hear rats out there, that is all."

As Laroque finished speaking, pistol shots spurted from the rim above the clearing. Tournier grasped at his throat, blood pumping out between his fingers, and twisted wordlessly sideways into the flames.

Men erupted from their blankets as Laroque, bellowing, leapt away from the fire and sought cover.

More gunfire came from out of the hazy darkness, red-blue points of light from the sagebrush rim above the encampment. The rivermen, some scrambling for protection away from the firelight and others dashing to the cottonwood to fetch their rifles, shouted curses at one another. Several were hit and dropped at the first volley. One man tripped over another and sprawled spread-eagled on the damp earth, then was struck in the back of the head as he attempted to rise.

The heavy echo of buffalo rifles sounded from above, and Delaware De Guerre doubled over, screaming and clutching at his abdomen, attempting futilely to prevent his intestines from spilling out.

Oxen snorted and bellowed, rising from sleep and thrashing about. One team pulled free from its tethers and lunged ahead, dragging the wagon into the Humboldt River. The oxen tugged ahead, oblivious to the stream's current, pawing water and mud until they had made the crossing and were up the bank on the far shore.

Gunfire flew from both directions now—Laroque's men took what cover they could find and began to shoot toward small bursts of light from above. One of the horses pulled loose from its rope and galloped across the clearing, a forehoof striking one of the campfires and strewing hot coals about.

"There's a goddamn army up thar," Pig-Sticker Jackson shouted. "It's every man for himself, boys!" With these words Jackson made a dash for the river, but a Hawken roared and he flopped face-down, caught in midstride.

"Any man runs, *sacre Dieu*, I'll blow him away before he's taken five steps," Cottonmouth Chardin yelled. "Do not shoot until you have something to shoot at."

For a minute or more there was no gunfire from either side, only soft gurgling sounds from the westward-flowing river and the groaning of the one remaining team of oxen as the animals attempted to pull loose from a heavy line that had been secured to a cottonwood.

"Hold yore fire, lads," Benton's voice boomed out. "It's Jean Laroque we want, not the rest of ye. This hyar's Aloysius Benton talkin'. Jean, it appears we got some business with ye."

Further silence.

"Benton? *Enfant de garce*, this is Jean Laroque. Have you gone crazy? Friend of me, who is with you? Already you have killed several of my men. What is this business you speak of?"

"Jest business, is all. Tell the boys to put their pop-guns away."

"What in hell you doing, you damned old fool? Come down here, *s'il vous plaît*, we will talk about this thing. Show yourself, Benton. . . . This, it is *entre nous*, eh? McLafferty with you? Me, I been looking for him—he is worth money."

At that moment Moon Morning Star, pistol in

hand, stood up at the edge of the irregular circle of firelight and walked forward.

"Forget about Benton and McLafferty," she said, her voice emotionless, "I'm the one who's after you."

Laroque stared at the woman's painted face as she walked slowly and deliberately toward him.

Then he remembered.

17 "I am Moon Morning Star," she said, raising her pistol, "widow to White Bull, the Cheyenne war chief you killed in the village next to Fort Laramie. I want you to know who I am before you die, Jean Laroque."

The Frenchman burst out laughing.

"*Vraiment, ce n'est pas possible!* The squaw, she comes to meet the one who pursues her? Benton remembers a bullet I put into his leg, yet he will not face me.... Put down the gun, *chérie*. Even though you have smeared your cheeks, I think you would rather make love, *non?* Where's McLafferty?"

"You killed White Bull—now you must think upon what is about to happen. You must look at your death." Moon drew a deep breath, looking steadily into the Frenchman's eyes.

Mike McLafferty was horrified when Moon suddenly stood up and began walking toward Laroque. She had moved too quickly and too unexpectedly for him to grab her and pull her back. He cursed under his breath as he realized the impossibility of getting to her without precipitating a volley of gunfire from the rivermen; then he slipped away through the brush at an angle to emerge as close as he could to where Jean Laroque was standing, pistol in hand but not yet raised for firing.

"Cottonmouth," Laroque called out. "*Mon frère,* do you see what we have here? This Indian woman wishes to be given presents in exchange for her husband. What do we have that we can give her, *peut-être?*"

"There is only one thing I wish from you," Moon replied, her hand trembling as she held the pistol before her.

A shot whistled from where a group of rivermen had taken protective cover behind the remaining wagon.

Moon spun, staggered, and fell, but not before she managed to fire her weapon.

Laroque lunged to one side, but the woman's bullet struck him in the groin. He let out a gasp, stumbled, dropped to hands and knees.

He felt pain, but realized he could still move. He crawled toward the spot where his pistol had fallen, and reached for the gun. A sensation of blackness swirled about his eyes, and he fought it back. He screamed, made a final desperate effort to grasp the weapon, then held it.

McLafferty observed from a strange sense of distance, as though he were dreaming and knew he was dreaming, yet couldn't awaken.

He shouted incoherent syllables and leapt into the firelit area, immediately emptying his pistol at a knot of rivermen as they emerged from behind the wagon's shadowy form. Shots cut into the sod at his feet, and another sent his Mexican hat flying.

Gunfire erupted from the rim above, and McLafferty was vaguely aware of the loud *hoo-ki-hi!* Benton had sent echoing across the river, a war cry of the Crow Nation.

Mike grabbed one man by the throat and hurled him to the ground, then leapt upon him and delivered a blow with the barrel of his Colt-Walker.

He rose and saw Laroque, pistol in hand, struggling on hands and knees. No time for thought—he yelled out Laroque's name and leapt toward the Frenchman, fell, slid, and grabbed for his enemy's gun hand.

The pistol was jarred loose, bounced, and spun about on the trampled earth.

A heavy blow struck across neck and back, and Mike twisted away, senses reeling.

Ye ain't hurt none. Get up, hoss, or someone's goin' to blow yore brains out, sure as green buff'ler shit.

Mike stumbled to his feet, one hand already fumbling desperately for the loaded cylinder inside his coat pocket.

Cottonmouth Chardin stood a few feet from him, weapon raised.

He's grinning, the son of a bitch is grinning at you. . . .

But Chardin's face disappeared, suddenly altered into a mask of blood, and the gun dropped from his hand.

Concussion. A Hawken cap-and-ball rifle at close range.

"Michael, ye knothead, how many times do I have to tell ye. . . ?"

"Where's Moon, Aloysius? Is she . . . ?"

"Get that damned pistol loaded or ye'll be sending up daisies!"

Mike snapped the cylinder into place as he glimpsed Fiddlehead Wilson clubbing one of the river rats to death.

Big Dog, Pawnee Woman, and Two-Tail Skunk, once the battle was fully under way, moved upstream through a tangle of sage and proceeded down a small draw to the Humboldt River.

They waded into the stream, keeping to shallow water above the wagon ford, and worked their way toward the encampment, weapons and ammunition held above their heads.

"We are missing all the fun," Skunk complained. "Big Dog, I don't like your battle plan. When we went on a warpath with Yellow Belly or Pine Leaf, we always went right after our enemies. Last year when Pine Leaf killed Heavy Otter, that was the way battles ought to be fought. Now we are going swimming while the others are firing their weapons"

"Keep your voice down, Two-Tail. Pawnee Woman, stick your knife into him so that he will be silent. Hurry! Both of you, hurry!"

"Big Dog, look," Pawnee woman whispered. "Men are crossing the river up ahead—seven or eight, I can't tell."

"They run away," Skunk said. "Should we let them go or kill them?"

"We can get them later if we need to. Keep moving."

"What if Laroque is among them? McLafferty will not be pleased with us."

"Keep moving, damn it! We're almost to the ford. Wagon's right above us on the bank. Pawnee

Woman, take my rifle. You stay behind us. Skunk and I are going on up."

As the men moved into shallower water, Two-Tail Skunk caught his foot on a driftwood log embedded in mud. He tried to regain his balance but slipped sideways, going under. He rose, blew water out of his mouth, and shook his head. "God damn! Pistol's all wet. Give me that rifle."

"Keep your voice down Skunk. Use your bow. We'll drive them out into the clearing. They won't come this way—not into darkness and gunfire both."

McLafferty heard shots from beyond the cottonwoods next to the river, and suddenly those of Laroque's men who had taken cover there came rushing forward into the clearing, less as a counterattack than in utter confusion.

Mike didn't question what was happening. He dropped to one knee and began to fire, taking deadly aim.

One man fell—then a second. A third, knife in hand, veered toward Fiddlehead as the old man was frantically jamming another charge into his buffalo rifle. Mike turned and fired, the shot low but still effective.

"Owe ye one, sonny," Wilson sang out as he brought the butt of his rifle down onto the fallen man's throat.

Big Dog Benton and Two-Tail Skunk emerged from behind the wagon, Big Dog's pistol blazing as Two-Tail Skunk let loose one arrow after another, the feathered shafts striking home.

From both sides a withering hail of lead cut into the few remaining Missouri rivermen. Even Phineas

Brown proved himself adept with pistol and rifle. Within moments it appeared to be all over. Gunsmoke, gleaming in thin moonlight, drifted on a soft west wind, trailing out of the firelit area and into darkness. Frogs began to croak, tentatively at first, and then with greater enthusiasm, while across the river an ox was bellowing.

The little New Englander, weapon still at the ready, stepped out into the encampment and admired the mélange of bodies strewn about. Behind Brown came Elizabeth Harrington, an expression of sheer horror masking her delicate features as she gazed upon the confrontation's aftermath.

McLafferty was kneeling beside Moon, her body half in his arms, her head against his chest.

"Benton! Get over here, goddamn it! She's alive—she's just—"

"My arm," Moon whispered. "The bullet went through the flesh of my arm. I must have knocked myself silly when I fell, hit my head on something . . . a stone, I don't know. Where is Laroque? He's dead, then?"

There was blood down the side of her face, still oozing from a gash on the temple. More blood dripped from her fingertips, and there was a red mat on the deerskin blouse, just below her shoulder.

The others gathered near Mike and Moon, Fiddlehead Wilson pushing through and kneeling beside McLafferty.

"I saw ye go down, B'ar-Killer, an' this child thought ye was finished. By the big red balls o' Satan hisself, I think ye're goin' to make it. Hell, Moon, ye're jest scratched, so to speak. Ain't nothin' to worry about, though ye probably don't feel so good right now. Meat don't spoil in the mountains, as Bridger says, an' she's even more true in the desert."

"Moon, stay still. Damn it anyway, woman, you're hurt. Let's get you patched up as well as we can."

"Help me, Red Coyote. I'm all right. I want to see Laroque's body. I shot him, didn't I?"

"Nailed him clean," Benton said. "He's yonder, sprawled out."

Moon stood up, still wobbly, and clutched with her good hand at Mike's shoulder. "I'm getting blood all over you," she said, then began to laugh, laugh hysterically, as the aftermath of shock came over her.

"If you insist on moving, then put your weight on me," Mike said. "Moon, damn it, you little hellcat—"

"Watch out!" Elizabeth screamed. "A gun—he's got a gun!"

Big Dog Benton recognized the face of Sam Kurtz—blood all over the front of his leathers and dribbling from his bearded mouth, yet still quite alive, on one knee and aiming a pistol toward the group who stood close around Moon and Mike.

"God damn all of you," Kurtz grunted, small crimson bubbles forming on his lips. "God damn your souls to hell."

Big Dog started toward Kurtz, his own body in direct line of fire, fully expecting to absorb the blast of the pistol. But no impact came.

Elizabeth, much closer to where Kurtz was kneeling, had flung herself toward him, screaming a long, agonized wail as she did so.

The dying Kurtz tried to turn, then fell forward, gasping, yet was able to hang on to his weapon. "Little Red," he wheezed as he pointed the gun at Elizabeth, "you crazy-ass bitch!"

The girl threw herself down upon the man just as the pistol went off.

When Big Dog reached the two, the girl was pounding with both fists doubled at Kurtz's face, the riverman attempting feebly to direct the gun at her once more.

Big Dog kicked the weapon away, pulled Elizabeth to one side, and thrust a knife into Kurtz's throat.

Benton's son lifted the sobbing girl, held her to his chest. He too, he realized, was trembling.

"You saved my life," he said softly. "That was a very brave thing to do. You're lucky to be alive, Little One."

Jean Laroque's body was not among the dead.

"Several escaped across the river," Two-Tail Skunk said. "We saw them but let them go. Yet Laroque, he could not have been with them. Moon shot him."

"Crawled away, by Gawd, while we was havin' fun," Fiddlehead snorted, wrinkling his nose and revealing a gap-toothed grimace. "Benton, mebbe ye an' me are gettin' old. Time was when we'd of concentrated better on what we was doin'."

"Not a good time to find him now." Benton shrugged. "If he's still live, he's got a gun. Ye can bet he wouldn't have jest crawled off to die, though he probably bled to death anyhow. I figger it'll keep till morning. He sure as hell ain't goin' to get far, seein' exactly whar he was hit. Doubled over like Moon hyar caught him in the fly o' his breeches, he was."

"A rattlesnake can still strike even if it's blown in two," McLafferty said. "But I . . . we can't let him get away, not after hunting and being hunted all the way from Fort Laramie. If he *is* still alive, then White Bull's honor has not been avenged. No, I'm going after the bastard, dark or not. There's moonlight enough. I'll find him wherever he's hidden."

"I'll go with you, Red Coyote," Moon said, pressing her wounded arm with her good hand. "It is my right."

"Benton, can you keep control of her? Phineas, see if you can find that whiskey jug Laroque was drinking from. Clean out her wounds."

"I'll handle the matter for ye." Fiddlehead nodded. "Me an' Liz-beth, we'll take care o' Moon. Jest don't go gettin' shot, ye damned fool idjit."

McLafferty and his two Indian companions proceeded with extreme caution, working their way systematically downstream along the Humboldt, half-feeling and half-seeing by light from the westward arcing moon.

Boulders submerged beneath the river's dark surface looked like bodies; driftwood logs left high on the banks by spring floods appeared to be men crouching in wait. A frog leaping outward from a muddy bank was nearly enough to warrant a shot and more than sufficient to cause pulses to quicken.

"The one who is pursued, he has the advantage in this game," Two-Tail Skunk said. "We must move about, while he needs only to remain still and wait for us to stumble upon him. Then, *poof*, three shots from his pistol and we will be floating down this little river, not him. I think we should wait until morning light, Mike McLafferty."

"My friend speaks the truth," Big Dog Benton agreed. "I think we have come more than a mile now. How did Laroque go this far, hurt as seriously as he was? Perhaps he is lying dead back in one of the thickets we have already passed by."

"Or maybe he didn't come this way at all," Skunk suggested. "Maybe he crawled upstream—or crossed the river onto the other side. We have not found blood on the grass. Even if it was there, how could we see it? I do not like this fighting at night. It is not possible to kill an enemy properly if you cannot see him. I think we should rest. It will be morning soon, and then we will find Jean Laroque— either him or his body. Me, I think he has bled to death."

"Much wisdom," McLafferty said. "How can I argue the point? But damn it, I couldn't just stay here and twiddle my thumbs, either. A thousand miles or more, just to lose the bastard when we all thought he was lying there facedown, dead as a doornail?"

"White men have strange expressions," Big Dog mumbled.

"Do you think he could have made it across the river—maybe floated with the current? More likely than not, that would just start the bleeding again."

"Maybe he wasn't bleeding at all," Skunk said. "Perhaps Moon's shot hit his belt buckle."

"He was leaking, all right. Her bullet hit him right in the crotch; it was all over him. I had him dead to rights, but then I got clubbed across the back. After that, there was just too much going on for me to look for him, too busy watching out for my own hair, I guess. No cure for it—it happened, that's all. He's a canny son of a bitch, always was, with more tricks than the biggest whorehouse in St. Louis."

"Sometimes they don't even speak English," Big Dog said to Two-Tail Skunk.

"That is why we have to help them look for dead men in the middle of the night," Skunk replied.

"What's that over there—where the rapids tail out?" Big Dog asked, his voice hardly more than a whisper.

McLafferty studied the shadowy form in the midst of the river.

"Might be him at that—twisted around a rock. Keep me covered. If the thing moves, fire away at it."

McLafferty waded into the river, struggling to retain his footing against the current, swift at this point, and at the same time stumbling ahead over fist-sized rocks in the bed, stones that dislodged under pressure of his steps, slipping away with the current. It turned out to be a twisted section of juniper, limbs broken off, held in place by the force of water against the rock.

McLafferty waded back to shore.

"You going to leave him there?" Two-Tail Skunk asked.

"Red divvel," Mike growled. "You knew it was a chunk of wood all the time."

Skunk grinned and patted Mike on the back. "Why didn't you take his scalp?" he asked.

They crossed the river after a time and proceeded up the north bank, bypassing the now-quiet encampment where the battle had taken place only a few hours earlier. Benton and Wilson had moved everyone back to the protection of the low rim, inasmuch as no one had any heart for trying to sleep, with nearly twenty corpses lying about.

"Hellooo the camp," Mike called out. "This hyar's the gambler!"

"Gambler my Aunt Fanny!" Benton's voice came echoing back. "Ye hawgs found anything?"

"Many shadows," Two-Tail Skunk yelled. "My moccasins are wearing out."

At length, perhaps a mile above the encampment at the forks they stopped to rest.

"Just happen to have one cigar left," McLafferty offered. "You gents like to join me in a smoke?" He bit off the end, lit the stogie, and passed it to Big Dog.

"Not very strong," the Crow said, puffing three times and blowing smoke out through his nose, then passing the cigar to Two-Tail Skunk.

Skunk sucked at the rolled-up tobacco, shook his head, and coughed loudly. "Poison," he said. "You two smoke. I don't want any more."

"Not supposed to swallow." Mike chuckled, reaching out.

"I didn't. White man's poison, that's what."

The first thin gray light of morning came, and they still had not found either Jean Laroque or his remains. Weary now, moving slowly and not speaking often, they entered the fatal encampment.

"Some of them look as though they were sleeping," Big Dog remarked. "Everything is peaceful now."

"Lots of scalps here," Big Dog said, gesturing at the bodies. "Yet no one has taken any. It is strange."

A fire burned on the rim, and McLafferty smelled coffee or what the two old mountain men construed as coffee.

Fiddlehead Wilson came jogging down from the rocks, his Hawken in hand. "Wal? Did ye find 'im?"

"No luck," McLafferty replied.

"Mebbe ye looked in the wrong place, then."

"Seems likely."

"Ye ever notice, Mr. Mike, how a thing's always in the last place ye look for it? Gawd's honest truth, now ain't that so?"

Big Dog shook his head. He was looking around for a likely place to sleep—had almost forgotten about his two wives, the women no doubt lying side by side up on the rim, waiting for his return.

"Ye searched downriver an' then upriver, am I right?" Fiddlehead asked.

"Exactly " Mike nodded.

"That's how come ye was lookin' in the wrong places. Hell fire, sonny, he crawled off over to the South Branch. I figger he's half-dead or mebbe all the way dead, over close by them willows yonder. Swear to Gawd, ye'd lose yore underwear every time they's a high wind, if it weren't for me."

"Big Dog, you and Skunk go on up, have some coffee if Fiddlehead hasn't drunk it all. We'll go over and take a look. Wilson won't be happy otherwise."

The two Indians nodded, turned, walked toward the thin line of smoke that curved and drifted upriver, dispersing in gray predawn air.

*　　*　　*

Jean Laroque sat with his back against a thick-boled willow, pistol in hand, almost precisely where Fiddlehead had predicted he'd be.

"*Enfant de bâtard*, that is you, McLafferty, *non?* Come this way, I have a present for you. I have stayed awake all night, but now I am getting sleepy. What did the squaw give you to make you track me down? Why does it take you so long? The soldiers, I think they will arrest you and the bitch also, hang both of you. I am guilty of nothing, but you have committed murders. You did not wish to face Jean Laroque alone, *non*, you send out the woman to be killed in your place, *peut-être*. You are the coward, just as I always believe."

Laroque turned slowly, grinning like an insane person, and laughed. Then, almost casually, he fired three times in the general direction of Wilson and McLafferty, who dived for cover.

"Are you dead?" Laroque called. "I cannot see very well."

"Put the pistol down, Jean. Throw it over this way," Mike answered. "I'll do what I can for your wounds, and then we'll let the law handle things. It should have been you and me, face to face, just like you say. That Cheyenne you put under—he was White Bull, my blood brother. I could kill you right now, but you're all busted up. The law can handle matters. I'll be happy enough to watch you hang, I guess."

"Sonny," Fiddlehead whispered, "damn yore soul, don't ye go standin' up, now."

Wilson grabbed Mike around the back, wrestled him down.

A fourth shot whistled through the leaves, then a fifth.

"You not taking Jean Laroque anywhere."

Five shots. He's saved the sixth for himself . . .

McLafferty pulled loose from Fiddlehead's grasp and sprang forward.

Laroque had already raised the pistol to his own temple. "The squaw, she suck you good, just like she did me?" Laroque called out as he pulled the trigger.

The hammer snapped, but there was no explosion.

"Goddamn, *inutile!*"

Then McLafferty kicked the weapon from his hand.

Mike and Fiddlehead carried Laroque, half-conscious now, past the death camp and on to the rim. Most of the group had awakened and were eating a breakfast.

Two-Tail Skunk had already ridden south to inform the other Argonauts that the *"military venture,"* as Phineas Brown called what transpired the night before, had been a *"grand success."* Wagons, oxen, supplies, valuables, and even the two saddle horses all had been reclaimed, and, miraculously, without loss of life.

Fiddlehead and McLafferty struggled up the rocky rise, Laroque's heavy form slung between them. They laid him down, and Mike rolled a blanket and placed it under the wounded man's head.

Laroque blinked his eyes, suddenly alert once again, and stared from one person to another.

"*Sacre Dieu*, where is the half-breed bitch? *Moi*, I was looking forward to meeting her again. She is dead, *non?*"

"Where's Moon?" McLafferty demanded, a sudden tightness of premonition in his throat.

"Sleepin'." Benton shrugged. "She lost some blood out thar last night, an' we figgered it best to—"

"No I'm not," Moon said, rising with some difficulty from her pallet. "Red Coyote, you found him? I hoped he was already dead, that it was over."

She made her way to McLafferty's side, put her good arm over his shoulder for support. The other, Mike noted, had been bandaged and put into a creditable sling—Wilson's work, almost certainly.

"*Mais, oui,* I hoped you were dead. Well, wash the war paint off your face, you not bad-looking *femme. Eh, bien,* now what happens?"

Moon reached into the folds of her dress and withdrew a pistol. Before anyone had time to object, she placed the barrel to Jean Laroque's forehead and pulled the trigger.

She continued to stare at the dead man, pistol still raised, until Mike put both arms around her. Then she collapsed against him as if all the strength had suddenly drained from her limbs.

"Now it is over," she said, her voice toneless.

"Yes, it's over" Mike nodded. "I'll take care of him. Come lie down."

"No, Red Coyote. First help me walk to the river. I want to wash my face. White Bull's woman is dead. Now I am only Moon."

18 Lt. Ely Van Norden held up a gauntleted hand and reined in his bay, the troops behind coming to a ragged halt as they approached the junction of the South and East Forks of the Humboldt.

"Trip's raised hell with discipline, Sergeant," he grumbled. "See what you can do about getting the men in some semblance of a formation."

Sgt. Wells, a short, blocky individual with dark hair showing threads of gray, although his large mustache was still coal-black, turned to bark orders at the troops, while Van Norden moved up onto a rise and lifted a field glass to his eye. Vultures circled perhaps two miles ahead, a great black swarm of birds swinging wide loops against the westering sun. Some were drifting down and then rising again over where he figured the rivers forked.

Yes, some activity on the ground. He rode higher up the spine of sage-dotted sandstone, looked again. All he could make out was a pair of wagons, human figures moving about. He rode back down, spoke to Wells again.

"Party ahead at the Forks," he said. "Could be Laroque and his gang of troublemakers, in which case it would make sense to approach with caution. You've heard the stories."

"Person hears lots of stories on the trail, sir," Wells said, stroking his drooping mustache. "Still, if half what we've heard about that bunch is true, I'd say they've gone blood-mad."

Van Norden dabbed a handkerchief at the perspiration on his forehead, considered, then spoke, waving his right hand in a forward motion. "Well, let's see what we've got, Sergeant. Move 'em out."

Benton lifted another heavy stone into place on the cairn he was building, then straightened up, rubbing at the small of his back with both hands.

"By Gawd, Fiddlehead, this ain't the kind o' work a couple o' old Rocky Mountain goats like us is supposed to be doin'. Danged voyageurs ain't worth it."

"My feelin' all along." Fiddlehead nodded, pulling a pouch out of a pocket, a pipe out of another, and beginning to tamp his willow bark and tobacco mixture into the bowl. "My vote was fer leavin' the worthless bastards out for the buzzards. Birds has got to eat, too."

"They were white men, whatever else they were," Phineas Brown said from where he rested on another heap of stone. "It's the only decent thing to do."

Big Dog glanced over at the little wagonmaster and scowled. He then went back to his own work, his bare back gleaming with sweat, muscles rippling easily as he lifted and carried heavy chunks of stone and placed them onto a growing mound. Chastity Cosgrove and Pawnee Woman worked together at another cairn nearby, and most of the Argonauts were likewise engaged in the labor of covering the earthly remains of the Laroque-Chardin party.

Wilson lit his pipe and passed it to the elder Benton, who stretched and gazed eastward along the Humboldt, its shiny narrow ribbon of water disappearing beyond a jumble of low ridges.

"Comp'ny comin'," he muttered. "Most likely the blueboys showin' up a day late, per usual."

"Yep," Fiddlehead agreed, pulling himself up and looking in the direction of Benton's gaze. "I see the dust, all right. Mebbe we should be thinkin' on what version of the Gawd's truth to pass along."

"Brown, ye figger ye could get a few more o' yer puddin'-belly flatlanders to hauling rocks 'stead o' scratchin' their arses? Know it's too much to ask o' you personal, but maybe them two over there who's heavin' pebbles at the vultures might stir theirselves. Be good if we had 'em all more or less covered when the looie an' his sojer boys show up. Partly yore fat in this fire too, ye know."

By the time Van Norden and his troops pulled in, nothing visible remained of the battle scene except eighteen stone cairns. Big Dog and his two wives were scraping sand over dark patches of blood. Aloysius Benton and Fiddlehead Wilson were perched on one mound, passing a pipe back and forth. And Brown and his pilgrims lounged about in various poses, some leaning on shovels and others lying down in the shade of their wagons.

The lieutenant halted his men, and then he and his sergeant rode on ahead, fording the river. He drew up and stared at the strange scene.

"Afternoon, Lieutenant. Figgered you an' the boys'd be showin' up sometime. Climb on down and set a spell. Nothin' much to be done here."

"You're Wilson, aren't you? I remember you from Fort Laramie."

"Thought ye might," Fiddlehead said, his expression deadpan.

"Yes. Some matter of a fugitive Cheyenne woman. We'll discuss it later. What in God's name has happened here, Wilson?"

"We found 'em this mornin'." Wilson shrugged.

"Jean Laroque an' his gang," Benton added. "Heard they was the ones burnt out a bunch o' Mormons an' killed some emigrants back on the Hastings Cutoff."

"You *found* them this way?"

"Well, no, they wasn't covered up. We done that," Wilson said, "me an' Benton hyar an' his son, there, the big 'un, us an' Mr. Brown's party."

"Big Dog and Two-Tail Skunk and Pawnee Woman and myself hauled rocks, but Mr. Benton and Mr. Wilson oversaw things very effectively," Chastity Cosgrove put in, wiping at her face with her sleeve.

"They were the same men who robbed my wagon train just two nights past, Lieutenant. Phineas Brown here, sir, and I must say that while I don't like to see such a fate overtake any human creature, still, if anyone can be said to deserve his end—"

"Just *found* them?" Van Norden repeated. "What would you say happened to them, Mr. Wilson?"

"Best we could figger out, Mike McLafferty an' his female sidekick—you recollect that half-breed woman, I guess?"

"Quite well," Van Norden said dryly. "I'm carrying a government warrant for their arrest. There's a sizable reward on their heads. Get on with your story, Wilson."

"If ye'd stop interruptin' me all the danged time, I would. As I was sayin', me an' Loysius figgered McLafferty an' the half breed squaw potshotted the whole gang of 'em from that rim over thar."

"Yep," Benton nodded. "That's whar we found the two of 'em, up on top an' dead as a pair o' matched doornails."

"McLafferty and the woman are dead too? Mind showing me which pile's which?"

Wilson took off his bearskin cap, scratched at his straggly white hair.

"You recollect which pile we planted 'em under, 'Loysius?"

"Nope. How 'bout you, Mr. Brown? You recall where the woman an' the big red head be?"

"Can't say that I do, Mr. Benton."

Van Norden stared hard into the three men's faces, glanced over the rest of the group. "No point digging up the dead, I guess," he said finally, reaching into a breast pocket and withdrawing a pair of folded papers. "Not much point in hanging on to these warrants, either."

With a quick action he ripped the pages across, then tore them into small pieces and tossed them away from him, the fragments fluttering wide in a slight wind and landing here and there among the stone cairns.

"Sir," said the mustachioed sergeant, "I think—"

"Can't arrest dead people, Sergeant. However it happened, it's one less thing for me to worry about."

"But sir—"

"Let's move 'em out, Sergeant Wells. We've got

a lot of trail to ride between here and the gold-fields, a lot of damn-fool emigrants to look out for. I can't concern myself with a gang of dead troublemakers. McLafferty's done me a couple of favors. I'll cover the matter in my written report to the commandant in Sacramento."

Van Norden touched his gloved hand to the brim of his cap in the direction of Wilson and Benton, turned his mount, and slapped the reins across the animal's neck. Wells followed, and the two men recrossed the Humboldt. The sergeant shouted out a command, and the troops moved off downstream.

Once out of sight of the Forks, Sergeant Wells drew his horse up beside Van Norden's bay. "Sir, I really think you should have questioned those men further. It's uncharacteristic of you to be so casual. There were eighteen dead men back there, more if they covered up two at a time. How could McLafferty and the Cheyenne woman have killed everyone in Laroque's party? Impossible, that's what I think. Then, who did kill them? Those two old mountain men and the others, they had to be in on it."

"Some things, Wells, I guess we'll never know," Van Norden said, his mouth closing in a firm line so that the sergeant knew the issue was settled.

Morning light slanted red on snowfields high up on Ruby Dome, the grass and bright clusters of wildflowers glittering with drops of water. Four people—a man and a woman riding double on a big gray, and a young girl and a child on a speck-led Palouse, trailing a packhorse and a mule—emerged into the meadow from a pine-covered ridge. All showed signs of exhaustion, circles of fatigue traced beneath their eyes. A dark-haired boy slumped in front of the girl, asleep, and the woman, one arm bound against her side with a swath of dirty cloth marked by bloodstains, leaned heavily on the man, eyes half-closed.

"Here's where we stop," Big Mike McLafferty said, reining in Grayboy at the foot of the meadow, Moon stirring against him and looking around.

"Are we home, Red Coyote?" she murmured drowsily. "My arm. Why does it keep hurting? So tired."

"Can you hang on there for a minute, Moon? Yeah, I guess we're home for the time being, anyhow. Don't figure anyone's going to come up here looking for us. The troops aren't going to trouble themselves too much over that gang, that's my guess."

They had ridden most of the night after resting through the afternoon following the battle, taking cover a few miles south of the Forks, then moving across and up into the Rubies sometime around midnight.

Mike dismounted, then helped Moon down, half-lifting her from the saddle. Elizabeth also dismounted, tending to Jacques as Mike unsaddled the horses, and spread out blankets under the shade of a big pinyon.

McLafferty built a small fire, made coffee, and cooked the last of the antelope meat, rousing Moon and persuading her to eat and drink.

"You've got to get something in you, Little Warrior," he said. "You lost a lot of blood back there."

She sipped coffee, chewed on a portion of meat, and leaned back against Mike's saddle. Elizabeth and Jacques were already sleeping soundly, both having dropped off while Mike was preparing the meat. Hot drink and food seemed to revive Moon somewhat, and she stared up at Mike, her eyes bright.

"You look terrible, Michael McLafferty," she said. "Your face is very dirty and there are little red spikes all over your chin."

"You don't look so great yourself, Miss Moon Morning Star. I've seen better in a third-rate cathouse in St. Louis."

"Not Morning Star. I told you that. Moon McLafferty now."

"McLafferty? Hell, you figure you got me all branded and hog-tied? So we killed a few voyageurs. That's nothing to get serious about."

But her eyes had closed. She had fallen asleep as he spoke, and he pulled a blanket over her, lay down on the side away from her wounded arm, curling his big hand around her good one.

Well, you've gone and got yourself a family, Michael McLafferty. Not exactly what you had in mind when you left St. Lou, was it? Old Man Coyote works things out in damned strange ways. White Bull's woman—no, not anymore, Moon McLafferty, she says. All right, then, my woman, my child, yes, and it looks like Elizabeth too. That one surprised me—probably surprised herself as well. She's got a bit of the devil in her, after all. Going to have to watch out for her—her and the Little Bull both. That kid's going to be outsmarting everybody by the time he's twelve. Already can lie about as good as Fiddlehead and Aloysius.

Never built a damned house before, not from scratch. Only about two months to get some shelter up. Winter comes early up here. You've got yourself into it good this time, Big Mike.

"What the hell," he muttered. "Live and learn, as my father probably said the day after they buried him."

"What are you saying, Red Coyote?" Moon asked drowsily.

"All the treasures of the Orient I would heap at your feet to make you mine, Princess Moon, but now I own you, I will keep you barefoot and pregnant and handcuffed to the bed."

"You talk foolishness, white man. Go to sleep."

Jacques White Bull was awake and bright-eyed by noon.

Elizabeth rose and gave him some jerky to eat, admonished him to play quietly and not to wander far away, then sat for a time looking out across the meadow. Bees hummed among the wildflowers, butterflies drifted above the grass, and a flock of small birds darted about. Then a big one floated high up, hawk or vulture or eagle, she could not tell; when the shadow of wings sliced across the tufted grass, the small birds all took flight, hurrying toward the safety of trees.

Peace, Elizabeth thought. No, only the illusion of peace. The small birds eat butterflies, hide from the bigger birds who would eat them. Peace is only what we think, but that's enough, that's all we have.

Jacques played in the thick grass, laughing as he ran after dragonflies, their wings glittering like jewels.

Elizabeth watched the child, smiled, and felt unaccountably content.

We could live right here, build a house up there, below the spring. . . . That's up to Mike and Moon. Maybe they won't want me to stay. No, I think they will. A family . . .

She dozed again.

It was nearly sunset when Mike and Moon awoke to a fire burning brightly and the smell of coffee and fresh venison steaks sizzling above the flames.

" 'Bout time ye come to, ye lazy dawgs," Fiddlehead Wilson said, squatting near the fire and cutting a plug of tobacco into shreds against a flat rock. Opposite him Aloysius Benton whistled softly through his teeth as he greased his Hawken with animal tallow. Nearby the remains of a skinned deer carcass hung from a tree limb.

"Yep." Benton nodded. "We was beginning to think them reports about you bein' dead was true."

Mike sat up, rubbed at his eyes with the heel of his hand, then grinned.

"Aloysius, Fiddlehead, you old possum-pounders." He laughed, slapping the mountain men on the shoulders. "Ain't seen ye in a dawg's age. I was jest talkin' 'bout ye, telling' the gals here 'bout the time back in '15, or maybe it were '16, when you an' me was surrounded by the Blackfeet up to Colter's Hell. . . ."

"Weren't talkin' about nobody, ye fuzz-faced tenderfoot," Wilson growled. "Ye was chewin' yer piller, is what ye were doin'."

Moon sat up slowly, her face twisting with pain. Mike held out his hand to her, but she shook her head, pushed herself slowly to her feet.

"Set yerself down hyar, Miz Moon. Ye're still

lookin' a trifle peaked," Benton said, stepping to support her with a hand under her good elbow.

"How the hell did you feel the last time ye took a .44 slug in yer hide?" Fiddlehead snorted, pouring out a cupful of coffee and handing it to McLafferty.

"I can walk by myself," Moon insisted. "It's only a little stiff from sleeping. But thank you, Aloysius," she added. "I am very glad to see both of you. Where's the rest of your family?"

"On their way to Californy, prob'ly 'bout halfway to the Humboldt Sink by now. They sent along their best regards to ye, said they'd stop by on their way back if they can find ye here. Reckon me an' the Fiddlehead, we'll catch up to 'em over on the Truckee somewheres if the goldanged Shuckers don't get us first."

"Smells to me like that grub is about cooked," McLafferty said, grabbing at a steak with his knife.

"Ain't never gonna get you civilized, sonny," Wilson said. "I keep tellin' 'im ye gotta *cook* it fore ye eat it. Cain't kill the worms an' whatnot if she ain't as black inside as out. Look at that, it's still bawlin', ye danged heathen."

Big Mike laughed, skewered another piece of the meat for Moon.

Elizabeth returned with a bunch of watercress gathered from the little stream that trickled across the meadow, Jacques trailing closely at her heels, his small bow clutched in his hand.

The sun dropped behind the rim of the Diamond Mountains to the west, and the talk gradually tapered off as the group ate hungrily. Moon discovered to her chagrin that she couldn't cut her meat with only one hand, and so resorted to holding the steak and tearing off mouthfuls with her teeth, Mike laughing at her and calling her "Fair Savage." Under Elizabeth's persuasion, Jacques was enticed to eat a few bites of watercress, although no amount of gentle bullying on her part could convince Fiddlehead that the green stuff was not "pure pizen."

"Human critters, well as wolves an' bears an' cantamounts, eats them what eats that kind o' trash, least that's my rule, an' I ain't lookin' to get et."

As darkness grew complete, a soft *whuff* sounded just at the edge of the circle of firelight, then another from a different side.

Elizabeth started, looked toward the noise, saw a pair of glowing reddish-yellow eyes. "Dear Lord," she said, "what's that?"

The others glanced around, saw more eyes, almost a complete ring of shining just beyond the light. Benton grinned, tossed several chunks of meat to the crowd.

"Old Man Coyote's little brothers." Mike chuckled. "Most likely this is their mouse-hunting ground. You notice all the little holes? They'd like for us to leave."

"Sorry, coyotes," Jacques said. "We're not leaving, but you can have some of our dinner."

He followed Benton's example, throwing meat to the waiting circle, laughed to hear soft scuffling sounds and see a pair of eyes disappear momentarily as the meat was gulped. As an experiment, he tossed a handful of watercress as well. "They don't like it either," he announced.

" 'Course not," Fiddlehead grumbled. "Smartest critters on earth, coyotes is."

"Other than people, you mean," Elizabeth added.

"Never said that at all."

"You see any coyotes feedin' us?" Benton laughed.

After a time the song dogs withdrew, their quavering calls ringing across the meadow and diminishing into distance. Dinner over, Elizabeth put Jacques to bed under the trees, and sang herself as well as the boy to sleep.

Mike passed cigars to Benton, Fiddlehead, and Moon, and the four conspirators lit up.

"Going to have to walk back to Bridger's Fort for more of these, I guess. Lady's got the habit real bad now."

"You talk nonsense, Red Coyote," Moon said calmly. "I don't know what I want with you anyway."

"If you didn't have that busted wing, I'd show you what you want." He grinned.

Moon ignored him, and he turned to Fiddlehead and Benton.

"So why aren't you two old reprobates on your way to California right now, along with Big Dog and company?"

Benton shrugged, picking at his front teeth with the tip of his knife. "Mostly jest stopped by to tell ye Van Norden ain't likely to trouble you no more. Official, looks like the two of ye is dead."

"Glad to hear it, I guess," Mike said. "Funny, I don't *feel* dead."

"Yep, deader'n hell, an' yore bones planted back there at the Forks. The looie even tore up them papers he had for yore arrest, bein' as ye was expired an' all."

"How about that?" Mike laughed. "Don't suppose it was anything you two said—like reporting our deaths, for instance. Well, Van Norden's not a bad sort. He's one of the few military people I've ever met who could tell how the stick was floating."

"Once it's pointed out to 'im, anyhow," Fiddlehead grunted.

"Certainly wouldn't have said anything intentional to fox 'im." Benton grinned. "What be yore plans now, Michael? Still figurin' to squat someplace hereabouts, or what?"

"Me and Mrs. McLafferty here and the young'uns are kind of figurin' to plant right hyar," Mike said, winking at Moon as he affected the patois of the fur trade.

"Mrs. McLafferty, eh?" Benton grinned. "Some preacher back at the Forks hitched the two o' ye while ye was reloadin'?"

"Don't recollect, Aloysius. What the lady here told me, that's all, and I'm not the one to refute a lady's word."

"I said no such thing," Moon scowled.

"Sure you did. Just this morning."

"That doesn't count. I was out of my head with pain."

"Don't figger ye' can unhitch that easy once ye done hawg-tied yerself," Fiddlehead drawled, winking at Moon.

"You men always stick together."

"Sure you don't want to winter here with us, the two of you?" Mike asked. "I could use an extra pair of hands to get us a shack built before the snow flies."

"Naw, thank ye kindly," Benton said. "Like I told ye, this child's got a strong hankerin' to see the Big Water. Besides, somebody's got to keep an eye on that overgrown kid o' mine."

"An' I gotta make sure this half-blind ol' hawg don't stumble in a badger hole an' break his leg catchin' up to Big Dog an' the rest o' them."

"We'll be sorry to see you go," Moon said. "I guess you want to look at the Big Water, too, Fiddlehead. I would like to go there someday. Maybe you can see far enough across the ocean to tell if the world is round or flat."

"Naw, I know the answer to that one. I figger the Pacific's about the same as Salt Lake, only more of 'er."

"No," Moon said, "my father told me there are fish the size of twenty buffalo in the ocean, and trees on the hills there three times as tall as the tallest cedar on Laramie Peak."

"See hyar, Michael," Benton suggested, "why don't ye an' yore family come on out to the gold-fields with us?"

"Maybe next year we'll see you there," Mike said. "The little woman's got a nesting instinct bad right about now, and you both know how it is to change Moon's mind once she's fixed on something."

"Red Coyote said he would throw himself off the top of Ruby Dome if I didn't promise to settle here with him." Moon laughed.

"Not so, not even close.'

"Maybe it's Elizabeth who won't let us leave this spot, then." Moon nodded. "But I still want to see the big fish and the big trees someday. Will you take me there, Michael McLafferty?"

"Only if you're very, very good."

'I *am* very, very good. Maybe tomorrow I will show you," Moon said, her eyes gleaming in the firelight. "But now I am going to lie down next to the children. Good night, Fiddlehead, Aloysius. I wish we could convince you to stay for a while."

Fiddlehead shrugged, scratched at his cheek. "Could be ye'll see me before Ol' Man Winter sets in. I still think ye're loco to perch up here 'stead o' down to Ruby Valley, though. Come January, ye'll have cause to remember this hawg's words o' wisdom."

"There you go." McLafferty grinned and then sucked at his cheek. "Mr. Wilson, you're abandoning lambs to the slaughter if you leave us now."

Moon, her face still looking a bit drawn, went to her buffalo robe under the trees, lay down, and fell asleep as the voices of the men droned on by the fire. Some time later she half-woke as Mike settled himself beside her, and she stirred, moved closer to him, her hand inching down to rest on his crotch.

McLafferty sucked in a startled gasp. "You do that, you're asking for trouble, busted wing or no," he whispered.

"Go to sleep, Red Coyote. Maybe tomorrow. Men have no self-discipline."

Benton and Wilson were gone when they awoke in the morning, early sun glittering among the pine needles. Fiddlehead had left another of his cryptic notes:

Goodby fer now. May be Ile
see ye before ye think. The
walls goes on the sides an
the roof on top, Mike.

                                    F.W.

Epilogue

It was evening, the sun red-orange and slightly flattened as it touched the ragged ranges to the west, and the shadows stretched long across the mountain meadow beneath the high knob of Ruby Dome. Big Mike McLafferty continued to work despite failing light, hacking limbs off a slender lodgepole and fastening it in place with the others. He was stripped to the waist, and Moon smiled, watching the play of muscles under the freckled skin with its curls of reddish hair on chest and back. She sat leaning against a large chunk of stone nearby, her arm freshly bandaged and in a sling made of checkered cloth, one of Mike's old shirts having been used for the purpose.

"I think you are well-named, Red Coyote," she said. "Not only do you have the same kind of mind as the little song dogs, you are furry like they are. I don't know if I want to lie down with you after all. I think it will tickle too much."

"Shameless hussy." McLafferty grinned. "You want those kids to hear what's on your mind?"

Moon glanced down to the stream where Elizabeth was gathering more bunches of watercress, Jacques helping her by crouching and pouncing into the water, shrieking with laughter as he tried to catch small frogs that leapt from the banks and hung just below the surface, eyes bubbling above. Closer at hand a fire burned brightly, a chunk of venison skewered above the flames, and a stewpot full of beans and a battered coffeepot steaming on either side.

"They can't hear. How could you know what I'm thinking?"

"Women have one-track minds. You didn't object to my fur the last time."

"Maybe I just didn't tell you. That is a very funny-looking house you're building us, Michael McLafferty."

Mike stepped back, squinted at the lean-to he was constructing of poles and saddle blankets, the whole barely big enough to shelter four people against a rainstorm.

"This is a white man's house," he said. "You just don't remember too well. If you don't have anything better to do than criticize, why don't you get me a cup of that coffee? It's too dark to work any more tonight, anyway."

Elizabeth and Jacques White Bull trooped back to the fire, the girl's dress soaked from Jacques' splashings, but her cheeks pink and her blue eyes sparkling. She set about getting dinner ready, talking excitedly as she cut meat, then ladled out beans onto tin plates.

"This is a fine place," she said. "I've been walking all over. Up on the far rim, just below the spring, is the best place for a house, Michael. We can get a cabin up before winter, can't we? And then, next spring, we'll start on the real house. It's got to have an upstairs, at least an attic, and a porch on three sides. Oh, and at least one bay window with a window seat on the south side where we can sit and read in the winter."

Mike and Moon looked at each other and burst out laughing.

"What's a porch?" Jacques said, and then, without waiting for an answer, "I want a porch, too."

"You've got some tall plans for me young lady." Mike laughed. "You sure you don't want to go back to Kentucky? You must have some people there somewhere. And what about Oregon? I thought you had your sights set on Oregon country."

Elizabeth looked stricken. "Of course. I'm sorry. I was going on like I was part of your family, but I know I'm not. I was taking too much for granted. I have an aunt in Kentucky, my mother's sister, but I haven't seen her since I was five. I'll write her."

"Isn't Liz-beth going to stay with us?" Jacques asked. "I thought you wanted to be my sister, Liz-beth."

"Of course she's staying with us," Moon said. "We are your family, Elizabeth Harrington, if you want us to be. But it will be lonely here. What will you do for a beau?"

"I think she can find one when the time comes," Mike said, winking at the girl. "They'll be trooping in all the way from Bridger's Fort to the gold-fields when they get wind of this redheaded stunner. I'll need a shotgun and a good supply of rock salt."

"I can make Liz-beth a bow if she wants one,"

Jacques offered. "And I will teach you how to hunt. I've shot, oh, lots of things. Mike knows."

Elizabeth gave Jacques a quick hug, then handed him a plateful of food and looked from Mike to Moon, her eyes brimming and threatening to spill over with tears. She stepped across the fire and hugged Moon and gave Mike a quick, shy kiss on the cheek.

"How 'bout some grub fer this child too, thar, sister?" Mike drawled in imitation of Fiddlehead Wilson. "I'm near froze fer meat, I tell ye."

Elizabeth, still beaming, fixed a plate for Mike, but Jacques looked down, his lower lip beginning to pout.

"When's Uncle Fiddlehead coming back?" he demanded. "I miss him.

"No man knoweth the comings and goings of Fiddlehead Wilson," Mike said solemnly.

"But I want him here," Jacques insisted. "He didn't even say good-bye."

"It would only have made us sadder," Elizabeth said. "Are you going to eat your salad so that you can be as big and strong as Mike someday?"

"Nope. Me an' Fiddlehead don't eat that green stuff."

Outside the fire circle, a low *whuff* sounded again, the glowing eyes appearing in their places.

"Going to have a regular ritual here, I guess," Mike said. "Look, Jacques. You'd better toss them some meat before they get mad and eat us."

Jacques threw food out to the song dogs, but he still looked disconsolate. Everyone, in fact, became a little subdued, a sense of sadness at day's end, or perhaps something more.

"Oh, hell," Mike said finally. "I guess I miss the

old coot too. I wouldn't even mind putting up with his ungodly lies all winter. Not much we can do about it, though. Fiddlehead does what he wants to do."

Great washes of stars appeared, and to the east, above the high saddle between peaks, there was a glow from the rising half-moon. The campfire burned low, tracings of orange and blue running across red embers. Inside the lean-to Elizabeth and Jacques lay curled together, like puppies beneath a blanket.

Mike McLafferty and Moon glanced at each other in the dim light, a trace of a smile on the woman's softly curved mouth. Without a word, both rose, Mike stooping to gather up the rolled buffalo robe they'd been leaning against. Hand in hand they walked quietly away from the camp to the meadow's upper end, the moon rising above the rim as they walked.

Behind a screen of willow brush, Mike stopped, began to lay out the robe, but Moon shook her head, her eyes glittering silver.

"I think I will make a great deal of noise tonight," she said. "You'll probably hurt my bad arm and I will cry out."

Mike grinned, picked up the blanket, smacked the rounded curve of her buttock as she turned away.

"You do that again, and it will be you who cries out," she said, and then her hand darted and clutched his groin, squeezed. She laughed low in her throat.

Mike growled, dropped the blanket. "Now you've

done it," he said, pulling her against him. "Noise or no noise, this is as far as we go, lady."

"Let me see what you have here." She laughed. "Maybe it's not large enough to play with."

"You'll think large," he groaned, drawing her down with him to the robe, and then her mouth was on his, tongue probing as one hand squeezed almost painfully at his erect member.

Then she had moved, mouth replacing hand as he lay back and gasped. His fingers tore at her clothes, and she sat back, helping him to work the dress with its one slit sleeve down over the sling. Naked, she rose above him, his hands fastening on the soft roundness of her breasts, almost silver in moonlight, the nipples dark and erect. He ran his hands down the length of her narrow waist, touched at the warm, moist center of her as she crouched above him, his fingers working, manipulating until she moaned, the muscles of her hips tightening.

She was crouched above him, staring into his face and smiling a challenge. "You don't mind?" she whispered.

She slid down onto him slowly, both moaning, and then her haunches were moving rhythmically, her head back, throat taut, loose black hair trailing down across her breasts. She made whimpering sounds, moved faster, convulsing, and he arched up to thrust into her again, pounding, both breaths coming raggedly, building, their bodies slippery with perspiration, minds in abeyance. They were only bodies, moonlight glinting off flesh, gleaming in slitted eyes, sensation mounting to the point where it seemed almost unbearable.

Moon cried out, a high, keening wail, her whole

body shuddering, tensing, arching back, eyes closed. Mike groaned, thrust, gripping her hips, pulling her down hard on him, and then felt release like white fire playing through his nerves, the world slipping away into utter, peaceful darkness.

They slept, holding each other tightly, Mike instinctively avoiding her wounded arm, his fingers touching her abdomen. The half-moon rode high among the stars, and crickets sang in the meadow below where they slept.

When McLafferty awoke, the sky was beginning to turn gray with the coming dawn, and Moon leaned above him on her good arm, staring into his face. He grinned, drew her down against him.

"So, Mrs. McLafferty," he said, "now I own you, fair and square."

"You're wrong, Red Coyote. I own you, not the other way around. It always was that way."

"That a fact? Maybe I'll have to teach you another lesson, like last night."

"You may teach me many lessons, Michael. I am a very good student. But the fact remains—"

"Nope, nope." Mike chortled. "You said it yourself. Moon McLafferty. From now on you're hitched. Maybe I'll import a whole passel of young Ute girls to keep me company when you're great with child, as the saying goes."

"Like hell! One wing or two, I can still use a knife. Yes, these would be good hanging from my lodgepole once my slave has finished my lodge," she said, her hand darting to his groin.

Mike closed his eyes, felt desire rise again as she squeezed, her breast bobbing against his mouth.

"I think I love you, Mrs. McLafferty."

"Maybe I love you too, Red Coyote," she said,

nuzzling against him, "although for the life of me, I can't think why."

Just after the first of September, summer heat vanished on the high desert fronting the Ruby Range, and mornings found frost on yellowed tufts of sweet grass alongside the stream that bubbled its way past McLafferty Ranch. Willow leaves went yellow, and a day or so later the same arcane chemistry of light and temperature began to work on stands of quaking aspen that grew along many of the ravines lacing the sides of the high rounded limestone massif of Ruby Dome.

A gray owl that haunted the ridge above the tightly chinked log house changed its nightly cries, adopting a deeper and seemingly more melancholy tone; ever-present bluejays that remained at a distance during the long process of raising the cabin now gave up their outraged choruses and drew closer, sometimes perching in a big pinyon growing close beside the house.

A pair of ravens found them as well; they floated by both morning and evening, curious and indolent, taking note of each new addition: the woodshed, the outhouse, a lean-to stable for the horses, a drying rack, the beginnings of a toolshed where, Mike promised himself, he would one day enjoy the almost sinful pleasure of having every kind of implement the owner of a prosperous ranch might need.

Putting up a house, he explained to the low-gliding ravens one afternoon, with benefit of no more than a hand ax, bow saw, hammer, and a large screwdriver that doubled as a chisel, had not been the easiest of all possible chores. The big black birds seemed tentatively sympathetic, drifted back for another look-see, then caught a wind current and went flapping away westward.

After the first autumn rainstorm had pelted the McLafferty homestead, finding several avenues of ingress through the split cedar shakes Mike and Moon and Elizabeth had virtually woven into place on the roof, Mike announced that he would have to make a trip to one of the Mormon settlements to buy a wagon, a pair of draft horses, and a load of supplies to see them through the winter to come.

Moon had misgivings about McLafferty's proposed adventure, but she saw the necessity and relented good-naturedly, remarking only that if he were not back in three weeks, she was coming to find him, her Hawken rifle loaded and primed, its triggers set.

McLafferty completed his venture to Salt Lake in record time, a week going and a week and a half returning. Not even the Hastings Cutoff this time of the year provided any great difficulty, and the trail was now devoid of emigrants and would remain so until the early months of summer.

The Rubies, high and bare when he left, were a stunning white on his return, for the two days of heavy rain that had fallen while he was in Salt Lake City had left a considerable new snowpack on the range. Aspens, a harmony of twittering gold before, were now thin gray skeletons against the dusky greens of piñon and juniper along the lower ridges. High up among the limestone crags, he surmised, the twisted bristlecones were already locked in their six-months of winter.

Mike passed by Humboldt Forks, stopping to survey the mounds of heaped stones, and urged the draft horses on south.

Ten miles short of home, Mike realized a few snowflakes had begun to fall. The temperature, well below freezing that morning, had begun to rise, even though the sky had become increasingly overcast.

"Winter's upon us, horses," he sang out. "But by heavens, we're ready for her now. Getting close, just past those cottonwoods up ahead. Enough of this damned wandering about!"

Jacques came running out as Mike approached the log cabin, and Elizabeth was only a few steps behind.

"Where's Moon?" he bellowed. "A man comes home, by God, he wants to see his woman!"

"Inside." Elizabeth laughed. "There's a surprise for you, Mike. No—two surprises."

McLafferty dismounted the buckboard, gave Elizabeth a quick hug, and lifted Jacques onto his shoulders. He stared up into an increasing snowfall and then strode toward the house.

A good fire was burning in the clay-and-rock fireplace he and Moon had constructed, and Moon was sitting on the hearth. It dawned on Mike that she was fashioning a wrapping blanket, the sort the Cheyennes used to bundle newly arrived infants.

She rose, smiled, and threw herself into McLafferty's arms.

"Wal, kiss 'er, ye dunghead idjit. Then we got to

get out an' split firewood. This hyar house has got more air leaks than a Nez Percé fish net. If ye want me to live with ye, civilized and proper, then by Satan's bones—"

"Moon," Mike said, looking askance at both her and Wilson, "who is this person?"

"Our new foreman," Moon replied as she grasped McLafferty's beard with both hands and kissed him.

"Figgered ye might need some help here." Wilson grinned. "Hell, I ain't never been a godfather before."

By the year 2000, 2 out of 3 Americans could be illiterate.

It's true.

Today, 75 million adults...about one American in three, can't read adequately. And by the year 2000, U.S. News & World Report envisions an America with a literacy rate of only 30%.

Before that America comes to be, you can stop it...by joining the fight against illiteracy today.

Call the Coalition for Literacy at toll-free **1-800-228-8813** and volunteer.

Volunteer Against Illiteracy. The only degree you need is a degree of caring.